# A GRAVE HALLOWEEN

## IN Lost Haven

ISBN       978-0-9983933-9-1 Paperback
           978-0-9983933-8-4 eBook

## Dedication

**For you, beloved reader.**

# THE LOST HAVEN
# COZY MYSTERIES

## THE LAST RESORT IN LOST HAVEN

## A GRAVE HALLOWEEN IN LOST HAVEN

# A GRAVE
# HALLOWEEN
# IN
# LOST HAVEN

## BOOK TWO
### OF
## THE LOST HAVEN
## COZY MYSTERIES

# CHAPTER 1

The decapitated head gazed flatly out at the late-October world, seeing nothing and completely ignoring the flies crawling over its stiffening flesh and peeking out of its gaping mouth.

The tongue lolled, exhausted from being so very dead.

The milky eyes did not see Jenna Hooper, Belma Winkle, and Lawrence Donald staring back at them with a mixture of disgust, pride, and simmering envy.

The ears could not hear what they said through the plate glass display window.

For they-just like every other part of the head, were not only deceased—they were also made of chocolate.

"It looks so real," Jenna said. "I'm horrified."

Belma blushed. "Oh, sweetie. Thank you so much. Do you think it's too soon? You know, after the whole..."

She mimed conking herself on the head, a reference to the June bludgeoning murders of Ingrid Gallagher and Harrison Kavanaugh.

Jenna said, "I think it's fine. Everyone knows what Halloween means around here."

"It's incredibly offensive," Lawrence said. "Not because of the dead people, who cares about that? It's offensive to me as a food artist. I can totally see the spatula marks right there, just above the slice through the neck."

"Those are where the killer slipped and made extra cuts," Belma said. "Dummy."

Jenna noticed something else about the severed head, but decided not to mention it.

Lawrence, squinting and tilting his head this way and that for perspective, decided otherwise. "Is it supposed to look like me?"

"What?" Belma said. "Of course not. Jeez Lawrence, not everything is about you."

She nudged Jenna, gave a tiny nod and mouthed, "It's totally him."

Jenna clamped down on a grin and pulled her thick sweater tighter against the morning chill.

She loved October in Lost Haven.

The fiery leaves, showing off so very briefly before drifting to the ground to form huge piles for the children—and some adults—to dive into.

The local restaurants switching their menus from light summer fare to the denser, endlessly and unfairly more delicious comfort foods like the smashed sweet potatoes with butter, cinnamon and honey at the Lakeside Grille, the shockingly heavy frosted pumpkin donuts from Baker's Cousin, and the root beer and clove-glazed ham at Sidesaddle.

And of course, another highlight was the terrifying and intensely competitive haunted attractions that opened their creaking doors every year in the hopes of making everyone in town wet their pants. They even had tally boards at the ticket booths, proclaiming nightly and seasonal totals. No names were associated with the marks, of course, but everyone knew if their wet pants were up on that board. It would be completely unacceptable if it weren't so ridiculously fun.

But Jenna's favorite part of the Halloween season in Lost Haven was the transformation of Main Street and the entire downtown area from a quaint, artsy town on the coast of Lake Michigan into a haunted village strewn with cobwebs, cornstalks, and leering Jack-o-Lanterns. You couldn't turn around without bumping into a bristly spider or stumbling into the clutches of a grinning skeleton.

It was delightful.

The Main Street shops engaged in a (mostly) friendly contest of who could create the best Halloween window display, and so far Belma's severed Not-Lawrence head was setting the bar very high.

Belma turned from adoring her work and scowled at the real Lawrence. "Is yours ready yet?"

"No, my dear. Quality takes time. But good for you—it's nice to have speed when talent is lacking."

"Can you give us any hints about it?" Jenna asked.

Lawrence contemplated for a moment. "It will probably be the most amazing thing you've seen in your entire life."

"I like the confidence," Jenna said. "But you haven't seen mine yet either."

Lawrence and Belma glanced at the new Welcome Shoppe, which after three months of construction (when two had been promised) was nearly, almost, just about done.

"Let me guess," Lawrence said. "It's a pile of sawdust covering up wads of used masking tape."

Belma shook her head. "No, it's an empty paint can with Styrofoam construction worker cups inside, all of them half-full of cold coffee. How old are they? It's a mystery."

"Enough," Jenna said. "You've torn me out of my Halloween bliss and brought me back to reality, where I have to go make sure the finish carpentry and caulking is actually being done. Ideally, done right, but at this point I'll settle for done."

"Finish carpentry?" Belma said.

Lawrence frowned. "Caulking?"

"You don't want to know," Jenna said. "My new Welcome Shoppe is being haunted by a handyman. He won't go away. I need an exorcist."

"Have you tried showing him your new book collection?" Belma asked.

"You know what?" Jenna said. "Lawrence, that *is* your head in the window."

Belma gaped. "Jenna!"

"I knew it!" Lawrence crowed. "This is a disgrace. You got my eyebrows all wrong, and the earlobes are a total dumpster fire. Go get your spatulas, let me show you how it's done."

"That's *exactly* what your stupid earlobes look like, and I used actual dumpster fire photos to sculpt them."

Jenna left them to holler and snarl at each other and headed toward her eerily silent Welcome Shoppe.

No hammers pounded.

No brooms swept.

No screw guns turned.

It was time for an exorcism.

———

J enna took a brief moment to stand outside and admire the progress on her new shop. It was a quick, necessary cheer-up before entering into the stress and drama of actually *finishing* the dang thing.

It was two stories, the facade made almost entirely of glass to bring in the sunshine, show everyone outside how inviting and cozy it was inside, and let those inside enjoy the view of Lilac Park. Well, Lilac Park when it wasn't being systematically turned over to exhume the residents of the Sanctuary Cemetery, but that process did have a certain Halloween allure.

In the summer, the reading nook on the second floor mezzanine would even provide glimpses of the Lost Haven Marina with its towering sails and obnoxious yachts mingling in the sparkling water.

But the main attraction for nearly everyone who wandered in was at the back of the first floor: a winding staircase that led down into the past, into Sanctuary. At the bottom of those stairs, patrons could see the original Welcome Shoppe being painstakingly reclaimed from the dune sand by the Lost Haven Restoration Society.

The plan was to eventually dig out all of the Sanctuary businesses and allow customers to move through the Main Street shops above and below, climbing up and down to see how much things had changed—and how much they had not.

The restoration progress was constantly being halted to bring in structural engineers to stand around looking at beams, walls, and trusses, knocking on studs and making notes in their tablets. This was irritating to the owners and customers alike, but acceptable. No one wanted Sanctuary's Main Street to collapse and bring Lost Haven down with it.

Well, perhaps Bart Kavanaugh and Sherri Lander

did, but they were both in prison for murder, so it didn't matter much.

Jenna gazed at her new shop: the wall of glass, the plush couches beckoning from the mezzanine, the driftwood archways accenting the high ceiling.

She still couldn't quite believe it was hers.

After the whole Lost Haven Resort mess and murders, the town had a sizable budget and contracted crews and machinery sitting unused. And with the discovery of buried Sanctuary and the tourism potential it unearthed, the town council and Lost Haven Credit Union began passing out money and loans like the free samples in the Welcome Shoppe.

The new building went up shockingly fast, a blur of construction workers, concrete mixers, and the occasional crane truck, then one day it was there, 95% done and close enough to open for business with apologies for the mess.

The monthly loan payments still made Jenna cringe, but this had been her best summer at the shop by far, and the fall and winter seasons would bring in entirely new batches of tourists. She'd even been debating on whether or not to replace her old coffee pot with an espresso machine off the reading nook.

It was expensive...

*Do it! You and everyone who comes in will love it.*

McTavish might raise an eyebrow at her invasion into café territory...

*He raises an eyebrow at everything nowadays. But let's run it past him anyway.*

The thought of the new machine hissing and sending fresh coffee smells through the shop made her slightly giddy.

Then she walked through the wide, double glass doors and remembered why she'd needed the cheer-up.

The reason her shop was still at 95% done.

Stinking Jimbo Gelderson.

———

Jenna smiled as she entered, just like she did every time. The heavy, elegant doors were *hers*. The shiny new hardware on them was *hers*. The "Pardon Our Dust!" sign just inside the entrance was also, unfortunately, *hers*.

The smile faltered when she realized the sign had dust on it. Not construction dust. It was the normal, everyday, sitting-in-one-spot-too-long dust. People had been pardoning her dust for far too long.

"Jimbo!" she called.

"Yah!" His response came from down the spiral staircase.

Jenna walked the length of the shop, trying to stay upset despite her lovely new hardwood floor and the long display case along the left wall that also served as the check-out counter. She passed the new shelves on her right, huddled in the middle of the floor under a milky plastic tarp. They would eventually be spread out and augmented with end caps and display tables, but not until the work was finally done.

So, in fifteen years?

She peered over the railing and found Jimbo turning a small screwdriver on the post at the bottom of the stairs. His white fluffy hair matched his spotless t-shirt and painter's jeans. How he never got them dirty was a complete mystery—though it was possibly because he never did any actual work.

Jenna said, "What are you doing down there?"

"Railing was a might bit loose." He finished with the screwdriver and looked up at her, blinking like an owl behind his heavy glasses. "Don't want anyone taking a spill down here, do we? Them Chicago folks are just looking for a reason to sue."

Jenna's jaw tightened. "Okay, thank you for fixing that."

It was perhaps the most infuriating part about working with the man. He would do a million tiny things—oiling hinges and picking at water spots on the display glass—that were certainly helpful but amounted to zero progress at the end of the day. He was getting paid by the project rather than the hour, so thankfully he wasn't wasting her money.

Just her time.

All of it.

"Jimbo, did you get the baseboards and trim for the mezzanine windows in?"

"Oh, goodness no." He trudged up the steps, turning in a tight circle as he rose. "Gotta let the wood sit a bit more, get used to her new home before I put any nails through her. Wood's gotta breathe, Jenna."

She imagined choking him with a piece of wood. The irony would be so delightful.

"We were almost ready to go," Jimbo said, "then the big rains hit the past few days and the humidity got us back to square one."

Jenna frowned.

*Rain affected baseboards? Then what's the point of having them inside?*

She let it go.

*He either knows exactly what he's doing, or he's loony. Either way, he won't budge.*

"How about the new toilet?" she asked. "That doesn't need to breathe, right? I mean, why would it want to?"

"Ha! Nope, ol' Johnny don't need to breathe."

"So that can go in today. Even now."

"Well..."

Jenna gripped the railing and prayed the bolts would hold. If they came loose and Jimbo lost another day with his bucket of wrenches, she might just burn the whole place down again.

"Gotta finish the grout first," he said, "then put

*those* baseboards in before the throne takes its rightful place."

"So, the grout then. Today."

"Well…"

—

Jenna spent the day welcoming customers and tourists, showing them where to find the driftwood picture frames among the crowded shelves, and refilling the fall treat samples and tiny wax paper apple cider cups.

She featured four of the local cider mills, and each had their own secret recipe of apple blends and cider extraction techniques. The competition was almost as fierce as the Main Street Halloween displays, but both of those were amateur hour compared to the Lost Haven haunted house rivalry.

The three most popular haunts had a morbid presence in the Welcome Shoppe, each vying for the cash and screams of locals and tourists. There was a vintage, bloodstained electric chair from No Sanctuary; a fake steel hatch on the floor with motorized zombie fingers reaching through from Ghost Ship; and a real coffin with a not-real corpse inside leaning against the wall from the Lost Haven Morgue.

Jenna was giving the hatch a light cleaning and having a hard time determining what was actual dirt and what was painted on when Jay Cabo came in. Even with the new double doors in place, he filled the entrance at 6-foot-5 and 240 pounds. The extra-large green smoothie cup looked like a shot glass in his hand.

He stood inside the doors, frowning at the entire collection of haunted items. "I still don't get it."

"You don't have to get it," Jenna said. "You just have to go with us."

"Paying to have people scare you." He shook his head. "You know, people used to pay me to *not* get scared."

"Bodyguards never get scared?"

Cabo thought about it for a moment. "Scared is the wrong word. Vigilantly concerned."

"That is a terrible band name. And you're still coming tonight."

"It's that big of a deal?"

"Uh, yeah. Jay Cabo, this is your first Halloween in Lost Haven, so questions like that are permitted. But there are some things you'll need to know before you set foot in any of these haunted houses."

"Jenna, I don't *need* to know about all the gossip, who's cheating on who, and the small-town rivalries. I'll just go, have a terrible time, and we'll call it a night."

Jenna ignored him and presented the electric chair.

"First, we have No Sanctuary. An intriguing name now that there actually *is* a Sanctuary, but I digress."

"You digress a lot."

"Don't distract me. Come sit in the bloody electric chair."

Cabo frowned again.

"Seriously," Jenna said. "It'll be worth it."

He sighed and crept toward the heavy wooden chair, watching it from the corner of his eye even though he was walking straight toward it.

"What are you doing?" Jenna asked.

"What is *it* going to do? That's what I want to know."

"Oh my...Jay Cabo, you're a scaredy-cat!"

"Wrong. I told you—I've been trained to be wary. I'm being wary."

"You're being a big baby. Here, watch."

She dropped into the electric chair and kicked her feet up, doing a little dance to show how harmless it was.

All while counting in her head: *One...two... three...*

She pulled herself out before she got to *four.*

"See? Your turn."

"So if nothing happens, why should I do it too?"

"Because it's fun."

"You know what I do for fun? Squats and overhead presses."

"Yeah, that's a whole other thing we need to talk about. Right now we're discussing how to properly navigate the complex social structure of Lost Haven's haunted attractions. Without wetting your pants, ideally."

He seemed unconvinced.

"Wait here," Jenna said. "I think we're missing the proper motivation."

She went behind the counter and rummaged through the stockpile of stuff that would eventually become her Halloween window display. She found what she needed and peeked over the counter: Cabo was still staring at the chair, his back to her.

Perfect.

She got within two feet of him before firing up the electric chainsaw, which was shockingly loud within the closed space. Cabo jumped a good foot into the air, sloshing green smoothie onto the hardwood. He bolted forward and tried to tuck his huge frame behind the electric chair. His eyes took up his entire face.

Jenna killed the chainsaw. "Well done!"

"What are you doing?!"

"Giving you proper motivation. In a haunted house scenario, when given the choice to freeze and face the chainsaw or go forward, you always go forward. Which you did. Congratulations!"

Cabo stood and leaned against the electric chair. "My heart...I think I pulled my neck. And I spilled my smoothie!"

"Totally worth it. Here, have a seat. I'm sorry I scared you."

Cabo sat in the electric chair. "Not scared. Startled. There's a difference. Being startled is a reflex, a survival response to a threat. It's there to keep us alive."

*One...two...*

Jenna nodded. "Of course. We evolved to have fight or flight when facing electric chainsaws."

*Three...*

"You know what I mean."

On *four*, a low hum filled the room and Cabo shot out of the chair—again spilling green smoothie—and slapped his free hand over his backside. He spun around, wild-eyed and flushed.

"That thing just buzzed my butt!"

Jenna hopped up and down, clapping. "Isn't this fun?"

"No!"

"Wait, watch."

Cabo took a step backward and glared at the offensive piece of furniture.

Another hum emitted from it, this one much quieter, and then a piece of paper slid out of a crack in the end of the right armrest. It dangled there like a tongue sticking out, mocking Cabo's ready stance.

Jenna plucked the paper out and read, "'No Sanctuary: Lost Haven's Most Terrifying Haunted Attraction. This death certificate is good for one free victim admission with the purchase of one victim admission. Enter if you dare, and have a shockingly good time!' See? I told you it would be worth it."

Cabo was not as enthusiastic.

"It's a buy-one-get-one-free coupon," Jenna said. "For tonight."

"Yeah, I get it," Cabo said. "Totally not worth it."

Jenna's brow wrinkled. "Hold on. This says 'Limit one per victim.'"

"So?"

"Belma comes in here at least five times a day to sit in the chair."

They both studied the chair for a moment, and then collectively decided to never discuss its relationship with Belma again.

"I'll make you a deal," Cabo said. "Don't startle me anymore, and I'll go tonight. I'll even listen to the silly drama with these places."

"Deal. But there's nothing silly about embezzlement, a secret brothel, and everyone involved apparently destined to burn in hellfire."

Cabo's eyebrow twitched. "You don't say?"

Then Jimbo's owl-y face popped out from behind the shelves and yelled, "Did I hear a chainsaw up here?"

Jenna agreed to pay for Cabo's replacement smoothie.

# CHAPTER 2

Jenna, Belma, and Lawrence burst into the Lost Haven Bodyworks clinging to each other and cackling like lunatics.

Cabo was placing the last rolled-up yoga mats into a rack. He watched the three alleged adults stumble across the floor and nearly crash into the new Pilates machine before veering dangerously close to the water cooler and skidding to a halt. They broke apart and collapsed onto the wooden cubes used for box jumps.

"Should I ask?" Cabo said.

Belma tried to catch her breath. "We're practicing our flying wedge. Classic haunted house defense strategy. If we're all huddled together, we can't be killed."

"Or you all get killed at the same time," Cabo offered.

Lawrence waved him off. "You clearly have no experience in this. The point of the flying wedge is to be the person in the middle, where it's safe. The struggle for middle wedge is constant and intricate. It's like a microcosm of society."

"I use my boobs and butt," Belma said.

Jenna nodded. "I know who is ticklish where."

Lawrence shrugged. "I cover myself in baby oil. Slick!"

Cabo looked at each of them and decided to change the subject. "It is literally one minute after eight. You people closed early to do this?"

"Heck yeah," Jenna said. She slapped one of the Halloween in Lost Haven maps down on the box next to her. "This is our plan of attack. First, we go to the Sanctuary Café, fuel up, and abduct McTavish to come with us if possible. Then we go around Lilac Park, trying not to fall into any of the open graves, and hit Ghost Ship. If we survive, we follow the shore south and east to No Sanctuary. It's doubtful we're still alive after that, but if we are, we come back to Main Street. We refuel at the café and drive to the Lost Haven Morgue where we shall forever rest in pieces."

"Let's do it," Belma said.

Lawrence asked, "Why are we still sitting here?"

"Eh," Cabo said.

Jenna stood. "We thought that's what you would say. That's why we have agreed to grant you middle wedge status for the night."

"Guys…" Cabo said.

The three of them approached him, chanting, "Middle wedge! Middle wedge!"

"I haven't showered this afternoon," Cabo warned. It had no effect.

"Middle wedge! Middle wedge!"

They huddled around him and began, in a mass of linked arms and hunched shoulders, to shuffle toward the door. Cabo—who could have halted the entire group just by planting his feet—couldn't help grinning. He went along with it.

"Middle wedge! Middle wedge!"

Lawrence whispered, "If you wet your pants, you get moved to the tail gunner position."

"What's that?" Cabo whispered back.

"Just keep your pants dry, buddy, and you'll never have to find out."

"But—"

"Middle wedge! Middle wedge!"

Halloween in Lost Haven carried them out the door into the night, completely unaware of what waited for them across Main Street.

———

They paused outside the Bodyworks long enough for Cabo to lock the doors and activate the security system, then shuffled along Main Street to the north end of the block. A small crowd was sitting at the tables in front of the Sanctuary Café, but they were all Lost Haven locals—they recognized the middle wedge and respected it.

The four of them grabbed an empty table in the corner near a patio heater with a fine view of the mini excavator parked across the lane in Lilac Park. The heavy rains from the past few days had halted the exhumation work, and the pleasant aroma of damp earth and wet leaves drifted on the inland breeze from Lake Michigan.

McTavish glided out of the café with a white towel over one shoulder, the tiny Mr. Wolfie trotting along-side. McTavish's expert eye surveyed the other tables, found no coffees, teas, or other cups or plates in need of attention, and turned to Jenna and the crew.

He spotted the Halloween in Lost Haven map and grimaced.

"You caved," he said to Cabo. Disappointment seemed to bring out his Scottish brogue even more.

"Their strategy is flawless," Cabo said. "But just so we're clear, I have middle wedge."

McTavish blinked. "Shall I call a doctor, or bring a cake?"

"It's a good thing. I think. But no cake. I'll celebrate with a green smoothie."

Everyone else at the table groaned. Cabo's green smoothies were a secret concoction with ingredients known only to him and McTavish, and the two of them constantly tinkered and tweaked the formula trying to find the elusive results Cabo desired.

In the meantime, the discarded formulas had created several unfortunate side effects. There was green smoothie 3.3, which turned Cabo's skin a light shade of lime for two days. The Hulk jokes were endless and unavoidable.

4.2 made his face and feet go numb. That week of Bodyworks yoga would forever be known as "Yergah Clershes."

And of course, the infamous 6.0. No one spoke of this atrocity, but the echoes of Cabo's explosive flatulence still haunted Main Street and the nightmares of those who witnessed it in person.

"The rest of us will be having espresso," Jenna announced. "We want our nerves jangling and our adrenaline dangerously spiked."

"And no full bladders," Lawrence added.

McTavish nodded. "As always, the grace and elegance of this group leaves me speechless. I'll be off before it overwhelms me."

"Can you cut out of here and come with us tonight?" Jenna asked.

"Oh, lassie, I'll not be tempting the true wraiths by seeking entertainment with the false ones. The McTavish line thoroughly respects the realm of the dead—it's what keeps us out of it for as long as possible."

He turned and was gone.

Jenna watched him go and couldn't help replaying the entire conversation for awkwardness or resentment. She and Cabo had been semi-responsible for putting his former employers in prison—okay, *entirely* responsible—and she felt guilty about it every time she saw him.

Plus, it happened right after his long-time employer was murdered.

It didn't help that one of the convicts was also Mr. Wolfie's owner, so the dog probably despised her as well.

McTavish seemed happy, and he still lived in Horizon House to oversee the massive estate's upkeep for the historical tours that came through, but Jenna carried the feeling that she owed him something.

An apology?

*For what, identifying two murderers?*

Money?

*Seems crass. And very Kavanaugh, which will just make it worse.*

"Jenna!"

She snapped back to the table. "Hmm?"

"Cabo is asking about the secret brothel," Lawrence said. "We figure you should fill him in, since you're a prostitute."

"Lawrence!"

"I mean, the town historian. Sorry."

Jenna settled into her seat, loving the autumn chill

that slipped past the heaters and made everyone want to gather just a bit closer to each other.

Where to begin?

———

Jenna said, "The Lost Haven Morgue haunted house used to be a meat processing facility."

"That's a nice way of saying it," Belma snorted. "It was a slaughterhouse."

Cabo grimaced.

"Who's telling this story," Jenna said, "me or you?"

"You, if you tell it right."

Jenna continued. "They built it around nineteen fifty when the plot was about halfway between downtown and the farms raising stock to the east, but as the town grew and got closer to the facility, residents started to complain about the smell."

"I bet," Cabo said.

"So they moved everything to a bigger facility near Holland and shut this one down. This was in the early eighties, so refrigeration and transportation were much better. The building was abandoned for ten years or so, until Martin Ritter asked the township if he could lease it for the month of October. Nobody was beating down the door to buy the place, so they said sure, why not?"

Lawrence chuckled. "If they only knew."

"So Martin opened the doors to his first haunted house in nineteen ninety-three," Jenna said.

"Was it scary?" Cabo asked.

"I was three years old, so I can't say for sure."

"It was scary," Belma confirmed. "It was all sort of cobbled together and looked very unsafe, so you were never sure if something was supposed to just *look* like it could collapse on you and burst into flames, or if it actually would. And the actors—you couldn't tell if they worked there or were some random lunatics who'd been living in the slaughterhouse and you were trespassing in their hovel."

"That sounds terrible," Cabo said.

Belma nodded. "It was a blast."

"What did you think?" Cabo asked Lawrence.

"I was only eight, but even at that age I looked more youthful than Jenna."

"Hey," Jenna said. "Anyway, if you asked Martin Ritter, he'd tell you it was the scariest haunted house in Michigan, if not the United States, possibly Earth and beyond. And a lot of people seemed to agree with him because they went back year after year, and folks started traveling from Grand Rapids, Kalamazoo— some even from Detroit—because word had spread. Eventually Martin had enough profits to buy the slaughterhouse and work on the haunt year-round."

"Martin Ritter..." Cabo said. "I haven't seen him come in to check out Bodyworks. Or even heard the name before now."

"There's a very good reason for that," Jenna said.

—

**M**cTavish brought the drinks and passed them around, along with a bowl of bite-sized pumpkin cookies from Lawrence's Elegant Confections.

"Traitor," Belma said.

McTavish leaned toward her. "Mi'lady, you give me a discount on those chocolate bats flying out your door and I'll be more than happy to fill my bowls with them."

"Instead of the cookies?" Belma asked, her interest piqued by an opportunity to supplant Lawrence.

"In addition to," McTavish corrected.

"Never mind."

McTavish straightened. "These wonderful, spite-free biscuits are especially delicious when dipped in your piping hot espressos, brewed from fresh beans ground by my own hands mere moments ago. I cannot speak for their deliciousness when dipped in Mr. Cabo's green…substance…but I feel it's safe to assume you would regret it immediately. Enjoy!"

All eyes slid to Cabo as he took his first sip of the smoothie. It was the color of an aging avocado shell with pieces of something that looked like banana strings floating within. He took a huge gulp, swished it around, swallowed, and smacked his lips.

"Yum."

"That can't be true," Lawrence said.

Jenna asked, "Which version is this? 7.3?"

"8.1," Cabo said. "We had a full version bump with the addition of sardines. They've been a game-changer."

"Well, that's enough horror for me," Belma said. "I'm good until next year."

Cabo halted just before another gulp. "No, come on, finish the story about what's-his-name. Ritter."

"Martin Ritter," Jenna said.

Cabo nodded vigorously, his mouth full of 8.1.

Jenna sipped her espresso and took a moment to savor the heat and the strong, bitter bite that ended with a tiny shiver as the first jolt hit.

"So this is why you've never heard Martin Ritter's name mentioned in Lost Haven..."

———

Jenna said, "Last year, the Lost Haven Morgue had its best Halloween season ever. People came from Detroit, Chicago, even took the ferry over from Milwaukee to get scared by Martin and his professional actors."

"Martin's Maniacs," Belma added, "all the people who perform in the Lost Haven Civic Theater, plus some high-energy amateurs who passed the auditions."

"He had auditions?" Cabo asked.

Jenna said, "Here's the thing: Martin was very traditional when it came to scaring. He felt the best way to scare people was with other people—not animatronics. That was a big point of contention between him and No Sanctuary, but that's a whole different story."

"So, what, he brought in professional haunted house actors? If there is such a thing."

"Oh, there is," Jenna said. "Martin's theory was he'd spend all this time and money creating the perfect ambience for scaring—the light, sound, texture, even smells—and just when you're ready to run screaming into the night, someone pops out of the shadows and you're all, 'Oh, hi Brad,' because you see Brad all the time at the grocery store, buying soup."

"Soup," Cabo mused.

"The point is, it ruins the mood. You know Brad isn't going to murder you with the blood-spattered hatchet he's waving around. He's just going to hit you with some ham and bean breath, maybe ask if you've tried the new hearty beef brisket."

Lawrence shuddered.

"So Martin was running a pretty big operation," Cabo said.

"Massive," Jenna said. "He even had brief negotiations with Harrison Kavanaugh to build a permanent haunted attraction inside the Lost Haven Resort, back when it was first being planned."

"How brief?"

Jenna turned to Lawrence. "What would you say? Ten minutes?"

"Less. I think Kavanaugh's exact words were, 'Get this lunatic zombie away from me before I kill him for real.'"

Cabo frowned. "Zombie?"

"Oh, yeah," Jenna said. "Martin gave his pitch presentation in full makeup. He never broke character, even when Kavanaugh's lawyers dragged him out."

"You have to admire the dedication," Belma said. "But..."

"But?" Cabo said.

"But then he stole everything," Jenna finished. "One year ago, on Halloween night, right after the best night of the best season the Lost Haven Morgue ever had, Martin Ritter took all the cash from the entire month and disappeared."

Cabo's eyebrows went up. "How much are we talking?"

"Just under a million dollars."

Cabo almost sprayed green smoothie on everyone at the table, barely averting complete disaster and a potential quarantine of the café for biohazard decontamination.

"A *million* dollars?"

"Poof," Lawrence said. "Gone. And then things got *really* weird."

"They're already weird enough. But go ahead, I gotta know now."

"So Martin's lead actress, Dina Polk, was—"

"Wait!" Jenna pointed a finger at Cabo. "I know what you're doing. You're stalling. You think if we sit here jabbering long enough, it will be too late to actually go to the haunted houses."

Cabo cursed into his cup.

"Busted," Jenna said. She raised her tiny espresso mug, "To a wonderfully terrifying night."

"Cheers and fears," Belma toasted.

Lawrence lifted one of his pumpkin cookies. "I wish you all a swift and painless death. Except for Belma."

They finished their espressos and watched with growing horror as the sludge at the bottom of Cabo's green smoothie slid into his mouth.

He slapped the empty cup onto the table. "Let's see how this one goes."

"Ominous," Lawrence said.

Jenna stood and zipped her light jacket over her sweater. As soon as they left the aura of the patio heaters the night's chill would begin to creep in.

She announced: "Because you tried to lure us into missing our haunted fun, Jay Cabo, we now must take a short cut."

"But it's in the marina," Cabo said. "We go down

Main, take a right on Second. We're pretty much there. I don't see…oh, no…"

"Oh yes."

Jenna pointed across Main Street at Lilac Park, where strips of yellow barrier tape rippled in the wind and the shapes of large machines loomed around the open pits of excavated grave sites.

"We must walk upon the hallowed ground of the Sanctuary Cemetery to begin our night of nightmares."

Belma clapped.

Lawrence pulled a thick hood over his head, preparing for the delightful worst.

Cabo grimaced and jabbed a thumb toward Jenna. "Is she going to talk like this all night?"

"All month," Belma said.

"Harken!" Jenna proclaimed. "The darkness hides many a terror, and—"

Lawrence stood. "Okay sweetie, we get it. Let's go before my espresso wears off."

"But I have a whole speech prepared."

"Good for you. That's incredibly sad, but good for you."

———

The heavy scent of damp earth grew stronger as they stepped into Lilac Park. The excavation crew, which consisted of Dr. Angela Taft, the medical examiner from the Lost Haven Lakeshore Hospital, Bob Wedell from Wedell's Hardware with his new ground-penetrating radar device, and any volunteer with a shovel, had left some of the stone paths open but taped off pretty much the entire northern half of the park.

The result was an inadvertently creepy haunted trail winding among the leafless lilacs, dark ponds with a skim of mist, and the occasional gaping hole that used to contain a wooden coffin from the Sanctuary Cemetery. The holes were extremely deep, through topsoil and sand down to the original hill that used to be the cemetery, then another six feet to free the buried coffins.

Jenna led the way past a backhoe loader that, backlit by the streetlights from First, looked like a dinosaur skeleton. Or a giant scorpion.

"Isn't this the best?" she said. "Look, who do you think was buried there? A Kavanaugh? A Mink? And how did they die?"

Cabo sidled behind her and between Lawrence and Belma. "What's this thing called again? Middle wedge? We should practice."

"Another one!" Jenna said, pointing to a seemingly bottomless hole on the left. The coffins were all going to the medical examiner's office for processing, which included photographs, DNA sampling, and a full autopsy to determine age, cause of death, and, possibly, with all the other collected information, identity.

"I have a question," Cabo said, averting his eyes from the open grave. "I assume the teenagers around here like to sneak into this park to get frisky."

"Uh, yeah," Lawrence said. "And not just teenagers."

Belma giggled. "We used to call it 'Lay-back Park'."

That dangled in the October air like a spider web full of egg sacs until Cabo said, "Jenna?"

"No comment."

"Pfft," Lawrence scoffed. "You don't have to worry about getting caught by the cops when you're *with* the cops."

Jenna, who had dated Lost Haven deputy Garrett Bower for nearly ten years before catching him cheating, wondered if it was illegal to push someone into an open grave.

*Probably, but what if it's Lawrence? Is there an exception for that? A jury of peers would certainly understand.*

Cabo said, "My question is, are you freaked out now that you know you were on top of a cemetery?"

"Well," Belma said, "if the park was too full of kids making out, we'd just go to the Lost Haven Cemetery and find a spot. So...no."

"I hope people come and get freaky on my grave," Lawrence said. "Maybe I can get some mood music in my headstone. No! A headstone shaped like a headboard!"

"Forget I asked," Cabo said.

They were near the middle of the park, approaching the statue of Marinus Mink, patriarch of the Mink family. The Minks were one of the four founding families of Sanctuary, and the statue portrayed Marinus gazing toward Lake Michigan cradling a child in his left arm and wielding an ax with his right. Jenna knew it represented how the man had help save dozens of people trapped on boats during the marina fire of 1889, but on this night the statue perfectly suited its invented legend of Marinus the Boogeyman.

The excavation crew had apparently found a Sanctuary grave nearby—a hole had been started near the base of the statue, right in front of Marinus. It was partially filled in with mud and leaves from the recent rains, and someone had the good sense to tie the statue off to some metal stakes to keep it from tipping into the hole should the ground around it give way.

Belma said, "I heard they might have to move the statue to get to all the graves."

"Oh, no," Jenna groaned.

Cabo asked, "Not good?"

"The Minks. They all live in Chicago now, or Vale, or wherever else they need to go to feel important. But they still have homes here, and come back once a year to pay tribute to Marinus and make sure none of us townies forget how great they are. If we have to move the statue, even temporarily, they'll throw a fit."

"So don't tell them," Cabo said.

Lawrence put a hand on his shoulder. "Jay Cabo, you haven't lived here long, but it's been long enough to know gossip flies faster than Belma's blind dates."

"Oh, they fly alright," Belma winked.

Lawrence gagged. "My point is, if no one tells the Minks, and they hear it unofficially, it's a whole different kind of mess. Like if I told you, I don't know…McTavish is out of protein powder."

"Don't joke about that," Cabo said.

"See? You'd want to hear it from him. It just adds more drama coming from me."

"Listen carefully," Cabo said. "Is the protein supply okay?"

Jenna laughed. "I think I found the theme for my Halloween display next year."

The light breeze from the lakeshore swelled into a brief, strong wind, sending leaves rattling along the path and blowing the dry ones out of the shallow hole near the statue.

Something caught Jenna's eye—an object flapping in the wind but not being carried away by it. She glanced into the hole and thought it might be light rippling off the shallow, muddy puddle at the bottom, but she wasn't sure. Whatever it was had been on the side of the hole, further up…there!

The other three kept walking for a few steps, and then noticed she had stopped.

"Going for a swim?" Cabo asked.

Jenna didn't answer. She got her phone out, swiped and tapped the flashlight on, and illuminated the grave.

"Is that a tree root?"

Cabo stepped next to her. "Maybe. It looks like landscaping cloth."

Whatever it was, it poked out of the packed soil directly in front of Marinus, about four feet below ground level. It looked like the dirt around it had fallen away in the rain.

"The crew has to be careful about gas and power lines running through here," Belma said. "And who knows what the Sanctuary people had strung up. Remember, that used to be above ground."

Jenna crouched and pushed the light closer. She could see a rough texture, a slight ridge that ran horizontally with the root, or power line…but why would a root or power line flap in the wind?

She leaned in just as another gust picked up. The buried object fluttered again, shaking bits of dry mud off.

Jenna stood and took two large steps back.

Lawrence took four. "What is it? Gas? Arcing electricity? I'm highly conductive."

"It's cloth," Jenna said. "I see bits of thread

hanging along the ridge there, the seam. I think it's a dress."

"A dress?" Cabo said.

Jenna used her flashlight to check the dark trees and shrubbery around them.

"Guys, I think it's a body."

# CHAPTER 3

Jenna stood with Cabo, Belma and Lawrence just outside the new yellow tape in Lilac Park. This strip had been run by Deputy Garrett Bowers, and though it was the exact same color as the exhumation crew's construction tape, the POLICE LINE — DO NOT CROSS printed on it carried much more authority.

To emphasize this point, Garrett stood on the other side with his arms crossed.

"Can you tell who it is?" Belma asked him.

Garrett's eyebrow twitched. "By looking at a few inches of fabric? Sure. It's the Queen of England."

"She's still alive," Jenna said.

"Maybe."

"In England."

"So you say…"

"What happens next?" Cabo asked.

Garrett hooked his thumbs over his gun belt and puffed his chest a bit, a woeful attempt to level up to Cabo's size. "Detective Olson from the state police will be here in the morning. My guess is he'll call in the forensics crew and they'll get to work with their little shovels and brushes."

Jenna said, "And there's no chance it's someone from Sanctuary Cemetery? A body that got shifted in the sandy soil and worked its way higher?"

"Thanks for that nightmare," Lawrence muttered.

Garrett pulled out his foot-long flashlight and poked it over his shoulder, flooding the hole with intense blue-white light.

Without turning around, he said, "You see that button?"

"No, Garrett, I can't see anything from here."

"It's on the seam of the dress, or whatever that cloth is. You can just barely see it peeking out from the mud. It says 'Old Navy'. I know that store's been around a while—it even has 'Old' in the name—but I don't think anyone who lived in Sanctuary got their clothes by driving to the mall."

He clicked the light off and re-holstered it.

Case closed.

"Well," Cabo said, "I don't know about you guys, but I think it would be pretty tacky to go enjoy ourselves getting scared by fake dead bodies when we just discovered a real one."

Jenna had to nod. "Well played Jay Cabo. Now we'll look like monsters if we still want to go to Ghost Ship."

"I mean, if you're comfortable disrespecting the miracle of human life…"

"Okay, enough." She turned to Garrett. "Will you be okay here by yourself?"

"Of course, Jenna." He glanced back at the open grave and the barren lilacs, their dry branches clicking in the wind like bony fingers. "And I have backup on the way."

"McTavish is open until midnight. I'll ask him to send some coffee over to keep you guys warm."

"Great, thanks. And don't find any more bodies on your way there, please."

They turned and headed back toward Main Street, leaving Garrett and his flashlight to guard the shallow grave.

"Well, this night took an odd turn," Lawrence said. "Now what? I'm still jazzed up on the espresso, but Jay Cabo's right—we probably shouldn't go have a blast at the haunted houses. Respect for the dead, and all that. Right?" He looked around at the others. "Oh, no."

Cabo and Belma froze, staring at the ground near their feet.

Cabo said, "What? A hand?"

"Is it a skull?" Belma asked. "If it is-dibs."

"No, look at Jenna's face. She has that town-historian-on-a-mission look."

"That's a look?" Cabo asked. He turned to Jenna. "Oh yeah. I see it now."

Jenna ignored them. She was still riding high on the espresso too, but something else had her buzzing with excitement:

Another buried secret in Lost Haven.

———

They reclaimed their table at the Sanctuary Café, warmed by the patio heaters and the hot cider McTavish served with cinnamon sticks and a dollop of hand-whipped cream. Cabo had another green smoothie and requested that it be heated, which made everyone else at the table scoot away a few inches.

Word had already spread about the dead body, likely from the police dispatch center, which competed with Jenna's shop as the town's official gossip hub, and the café was humming.

One of McTavish's servers came back wide-eyed from dropping coffee off for Garrett's team, and the other patio dwellers peppered her with questions.

"Did you see the body?"

"Did it have on Chicago boat clothes? You know what I mean…"

"Is it Amelia Earhart?"

The poor girl just shook her head. "I put the coffee down about a hundred feet away and yelled for Garrett to come get it. I didn't even see the hole. Now I have to go wash my hands. Maybe my hair."

She disappeared into the café, leaving the poor folks outside bereft of rumor fuel.

"Well Jenna," Lawrence said, "I hope you're happy."

"Me? What did I do?"

"It was your idea to take the shortcut through the park. If we'd gone around, we'd be screaming, running, and trying not to get peed on by Jay Cabo. Instead we're sitting here with delicious cider and dry clothes."

Cabo frowned. "Hey."

"Inacceptable," Belma added.

Jenna said, "Guys, that's someone's wife out there, someone's sister, or mother. We're going to give them closure about a missing person."

Lawrence said, "Um, unless that someone is the one who killed their wife, sister, or mother."

"I hadn't thought of that." Jenna paused with her cider raised halfway, thinking. "Ah. If that's the case, we're going to give the poor dead body justice. There. Ha."

She sipped in triumph.

"But *we* didn't have to find the body," Belma said. "The exhumation crew was already digging right next to it. They probably would have seen it in the morning. But no, we had to go traipsing through the dark and scary park on our way to making Jay Cabo pee his pants."

"I wasn't going to pee my pants," Cabo insisted.

Lawrence said, "This isn't about you and your bladder, Jay Cabo."

"Then what's it about? Because that keeps coming up. Like, much too frequently."

"It's about the look in Jenna's eye," Belma said. "See? It's still there. That glitter, that spark, that guilty giddiness over some dark and sordid mystery that's just going to upset a bunch of people and disrupt everything."

The three of them stared at Jenna, who sat back in her chair with a completely innocent, shocked look on her face.

"You guys, I do not—"

Then she spotted Garrett emerging from the park and walking toward the café.

"Okay, you three shut up. I have information to collect."

—

The patio grew silent as Garrett approached. He stopped when he saw the dozen or so pairs of eyes on him, watching and waiting.

"What?" he said.

The patio exploded with more questions, the same batch thrown at the server and some newcomers:

"It's Amelia Earhart, isn't it?

"Is it my aunt Ethel? She said she moved to Florida but we never hear from her."

"Did the Kavanaughs kill whoever it is?"

Garrett swiped his hands like a conductor, cutting it all off. "I didn't touch anything. I saw a scrap of clothing, that's it. We're not doing a thing until Detective Olson and the forensics team gets here. So, no more questions, and someone please bring me some of those little pumpkin cookies. Thank you for your cooperation."

———

Garrett left with a white paper sack full of pumpkin cookies. The hushed speculations on the patio drifted back to mundane chatter, and eventually people began to head home.

"Well, that's it for me," Belma said. "I have a feeling tomorrow is going to be extra busy. An October Sunday is crazy enough around here, but people are going to gawk at the forensics team—and my amazing Halloween window display—and those people deserve better than the pumpkin dog treats we give our law enforcement officers."

"Are you going to put the diabetes right in the chocolate," Lawrence said, "or does that cost extra?"

"It costs extra." Belma stood and turned to Jenna.

"I assume we're doing the haunted houses tomorrow night?"

"Of course."

"What?" Cabo said. "I thought we were done with all of that."

Lawrence shook his head. "Just for tonight. Good taste expires after about twenty-four hours, much less if Belma's baked nonsense is involved."

"Unless..." Jenna said.

"No!" Belma cried. "No 'unless'."

"You don't even know what I was going to say."

"Oh yes we do," Lawrence said. "Unless that stupid dead body is wrapped in some mystery you need to stick your nose into. Even if that happens, you'll still have a few hours to run and scream and not get peed on by Jay Cabo."

"That's it," Cabo said. "I'm not going."

"Hush, you're just making it worse by denying the wet pants."

"I didn't wet my pants yet!" Cabo yelled.

The patio fell under another silence.

Wide-eyed, Jenna whispered. "Okay, we'll do the haunted houses no matter what. But if that body comes with buried secrets, you all have to help me uncover them."

"Absolutely not," Lawrence whispered.

"Not happening," Belma muttered.

Cabo burped and eyed his warm smoothie with suspicion. "I think I need a bathroom."

—

J enna went home slightly worried about the effects of the late-night espresso, but she changed, washed her face, and read a bit of *Sanctorum Subter* from the late Harrison Kavanaugh's personal collection, and sleep eased toward her just before midnight.

She turned off the light and tried not to think about what the forensic crew would discover about the body in Lilac Park. Not because it was scary or sad—it was certainly unfortunate for the body and anyone close to the deceased—but because it was exciting.

Jenna had come to slightly awkward terms with the fact that her curiosity about and devotion to Lost Haven's history sometimes nudged good taste and manners out of the way. If the dead body in the park unearthed big questions about who, what, why, and how, she hoped it wouldn't be necessary to completely offend anyone in her search for the answers.

She drifted off to sleep, blissfully unaware of the chaos that was about to erupt in Lost Haven.

# CHAPTER 4

Sunday morning, Jenna unlocked the Welcome Shoppe just before eight and got the coffee pot going, feeling incredibly sleazy for thinking about a new espresso machine the entire time.

Jimbo did not work on Sundays, a proclamation that made Jenna question what exactly made that day different than any other. Though it was nice to not be furious about his puttering, she did find herself missing his random humming, whistling, and occasional mild curse when he realized he'd misplaced another tool.

She flipped the sign on the front doors to Open and stepped outside. She'd briefly considered an electric sign, but preferred a hand-painted look to soften the new storefront a bit. And it cost zero dollars to operate, which was nice.

The sidewalk was still in shadow, chilly and hinting about the coming winter. The earthy smell of fallen leaves rolled out of the park on a damp breeze, and she wrapped her arms around herself. It was going to be one of those crisp autumn days where she'd need a fleece hoodie in the shade and a t-shirt in the sun.

In a word, perfect.

She looked north along Main Street and didn't see any forensics vans, police cruisers, or armored S.W.A.T. personnel carriers which was probably good, but slightly disappointing.

Winkle's Fine Chocolates & Sweets didn't open until nine, but lights were on inside and Jenna knew Belma would be working on the day's fresh treats. She tapped on the front door and Belma popped out of the back in a chocolate-smeared apron. Her brown and mint hair was slightly damp with sweat and her face was flushed. She opened the door for Jenna, looked both ways along Main Street, and shoved a small cookie at her.

"Try this."

Jenna fell back a step and looked down at the round, brown object.

"What is it?"

"Just try it."

Jenna made no move to accept the cookie. "Is this something you and Cabo are working on? Some sort of protein cookie that's supposed to be delicious and healthy, but is actually neither?"

"No, but that's a pretty good idea." Belma checked the street again—no one was within earshot or paying them any attention. "I'm testing pumpkin cookie recipes."

Jenna gasped. "Belma, that's Lawrence's thing!"

"Yeah, just like his Christmas almond cookies, and his New Year's champagne bars, and his Valentine's Day heartbreaker brownies—he has too many things! So try the stinking cookie and tell me if it's better than the ones McTavish serves."

Jenna hesitated, on the verge of what felt like a traitorous act, then took a bite.

There was a very thin crispy layer of baked sugar on the outside, and when that gave way, warm pumpkin, butter, and brown sugar melted in her mouth followed by a tang of cinnamon, cloves, and orange peel.

"Oh Belma."

"Good?"

"I could go on and on about how good this is, but I'll get right to the point: Lawrence is going to hate you."

Belma's face glowed. "Oh sweetie. I think I might cry."

"You can bawl your eyes out; just get me another cookie first."

They both went inside the chocolate shop and Belma put a small plate of the pumpkin cookies on the counter. Jenna took one to eat and a backup, also to eat.

"What are you calling these?"

"I'm debating," Belma said, "Either In-Your-Face Pumpkin Delights, because you want to put them in your face and I'll be delighted when Lawrence is humiliated, or Punkin Drops, because I'm dropping these babies on the café and making Lawrence my punk."

"Makes me wonder what Snickerdoodle really means," Jenna said.

"You don't want to know."

Jenna paused to focus on her taste buds. "The orange peel started out sweet, and now I'm getting a slightly bitter aftertaste. It's quite nice."

Belma pumped a fist. "I put that in there just for Lawrence. It represents defeat."

"Well, it's delicious." She popped the backup cookie in and talked with her mouth full of heaven. "Have you heard anything about the body?"

"The booty?"

"*Body.* The corpse."

"Oh," Belma said, "no, nothing. The police cars are still parked around the corner, so I assume someone is still standing guard."

"Can I take them some of these cookies? If the cops like them, you're golden. And they'll be so distracted by the deliciousness they might spill some info."

"Aha," Belma said. She slid the cookies off the plate and into a white paper sack. "I put eight cookies in here. How many are going to make it to the gravesite?"

Jenna did some quick math, dividing her self-control by the number of cookies.

"Four."

"Let's try for six. I'll keep an eye on your shop."

Jenna hefted the sack. It was heavy with the small but dense cookies, calling to her to make the bag lighter.

"I should probably run."

—

In the light of day the park was much less spooky and sinister, but the corpse buried in a shallow grave took on a stark reality. There was a heavy, respectful hush among the barren lilacs that Jenna didn't want to disturb.

She eased toward Garrett's POLICE LINE tape, which looked bright and brittle twisting in the breeze, and saw a white van backed into the small clearing next to the backhoe and statue of Marinus Mink. The rear and side doors were open, showing a crowded but orderly space of drawers, racks, and hooks.

Another Lost Haven deputy, Bub Thorp, was sitting with state police detective Olson in folding camp chairs. They both had aluminum travel mugs of coffee and watched the two forensics investigators working in the grave.

The forensics team wore light blue Tyvek suits with booties, hoods, and clear plastic face shields to avoid contaminating the scene, and they had removed the entire chunk of sod above the corpse in one piece and set it aside on a tarp. Now they were standing in the hole next to the body, carefully scooping soil and brushing it into a sieve, looking for…anything, Jenna supposed. She caught a glimpse of long white hair in the shallow grave before one of the techs blocked her view.

*Long white hair*, she thought.

*Who in Lost Haven is missing a grandmother and doesn't know it?*

*Or even worse, does?*

Everyone was so focused on the work being done they didn't notice Jenna until she spoke.

"I have cookies."

"Gaaaah!" Bub, who was closing in on sixty and had a few dozen pounds to spare, clutched his chest and tried not to spill his coffee. "Good lord Jenna Hooper, don't ever startle an officer of the law. That's a felony."

Detective Olson shook his head. "It's not."

Bub said, "And scaring the corpse nerds can seriously compromise evidence."

The forensics crew looked over and blinked at Bub through their face shields. It was Tina and Gino, the team that had processed Harrison Kavanaugh's murder scene and pretty much all of Main Street after Bart and Sherri were arrested.

"We aren't scared," Tina said. She turned to Gino. "But we might have to change the name of our improv group to The Corpse Nerds."

Gino peered at a small scoop of dark soil. "What about just: Corpse Nerd?"

"I like it. Let's consider." She turned back to Jenna. "Did you say cookies?"

Jenna lifted the sack.

"That bag is now official evidence," Bub said. "Please forfeit the bag to your nearest police officer."

He held his hand out without getting up.

Olson stood and walked over with a smile. He gave Jenna a quick hug over the crime scene tape. "How you doing girlie? Still trying your best to keep me working instead of golfing, obviously."

"Sorry about that. Here, these should help."

She handed him the heavy sack. He peered inside and sniffed.

"Oh my. Pumpkin?"

"I think so," Jenna lied. "Belma made them for you guys."

"Well, let's find out." He handed her a cookie, chose one for himself, and they both took bites.

Jenna, victorious in her ruse, feigned surprise at how delicious her fourth cookie of the morning tasted.

Olson turned to the rest of the team. "These are terrible. I'll save you the misery of choking them down."

Bub said, "Detective Olson, if you do not forfeit those cookies immediately, I will tell everyone who clogged up the toilet at the police station this morning at approximately oh four hundred hours."

Olson chewed and frowned. "That was you, Bub."

"Indeed it was. And trust me-no one wants to hear that story. Cookies. Now."

Olson held the sack out for him. Bub was surprisingly dainty in his perusal and selection. He nibbled the cookie and looked off to the side, examining the results.

"Well that's just delightful."

He threw the rest in his mouth, plucked two more out of the bag and settled into his chair.

"Move along. Nothing to see here, folks."

Olson said, "Thanks for the treat, Jenna. And thank Belma for us."

"Of course. I'm surprised there aren't more people here—the café was pretty fired up last night with questions about the body."

"Well, we have confirmation."

"You do?" Jenna said, perhaps a bit too loudly.

"Yep. I can confirm it is a dead person."

"Oh. That's it?"

"So far. That's a big step though. We've eliminated

the possibility that it's a bag of garbage, a buried campsite, or random pants buried in the park."

"That's a thing?" Jenna said.

"You'd be surprised."

Jenna tried to find an excuse to linger, but failed. "Well, if you need anything, you know where to find me."

Bub said, "Bringing more of these cookies every fifteen minutes or so would be great."

"You might be able to get them at the Sanctuary Café soon, if Belma gets her way."

"The café?" Bub said. "I thought they served Lawrence's cookies."

"They do. For now."

"Oh, boy." Bub glanced down, found his sidearm still in its holster, and patted it. "I might need this later."

———

Jenna returned to the Welcome Shoppe to find Belma behind the counter ringing up an elderly couple for a driftwood birdhouse with "Sanctuary" painted over the small access hole. Since the discovery of the buried town, Jenna was becoming more and more certain you could slap "Sanctuary" on a pile of leftover mashed potatoes and sell it for $19.99.

"Here she is now," Belma told them. "Jenna, these

nice folks are from Farmington Hills, browsing for a cozy beach house for their retirement."

"Oh, lovely!" Jenna said. "Have you found anything so far?"

"Not yet, but we have some appointments with our realtor today," the woman said. She was glowing with the excitement of it.

Jenna said, "If you have any questions at all, please come back and we'll have a chat."

"And don't walk through the park," Belma added. "There's a dead body in it."

The shop fell silent and completely still.

"A what?" the man said.

"*Dead body*," Belma shouted. "A corpse. Of course, there's a whole cemetery under the park, but this one is on top of that. And newer."

"Oh dear," the woman said.

Jenna cleared her throat. "Belma…"

Belma didn't hear, or didn't care. "It's the third one we've had in the last, what, four months? Does that qualify as a murder spree? Or does the same person have to do all of the killing?"

The woman said, "Well, I—"

"I guess we don't know when this new stiff was actually killed yet, so it could be much older than the two earlier this year. And whoever killed this one, heck, they might still be walking around town."

The man lifted the bag with the birdhouse in it. "Thanks for your help- we're running a bit late."

They hurried out of the shop, took a fast left, and disappeared around the corner. Belma watched them with a growing smile.

Jenna whirled on her. "What was that?"

Belma chuckled. "They'll go back to the east side, tell their friends about this horrible little murder town on the coast of Lake Michigan, and next thing you know we'll be drowning in Farmington Hills tourist money. People love death."

"And those poor folks won't buy a home here."

"Jenna, our main resource is *tourists*. If they move here, they aren't tourists anymore. And those two looked like the sort who'd get a bug in their butts about opening some sort of cutesy shop, selling sugar cookies from her family's recipe or some such nonsense. I'm not having it."

"Well, they seemed nice to me."

"Nice, huh? Then why are they sneaking across the street to Lilac Park, knowing there's a dead body in it?"

Jenna turned and sure enough, the couple was strolling across Main Street, peering into the lilacs and leaning close to whisper to each other. The woman pointed north and they headed that way, deliberately avoiding any acknowledgement of the Welcome Shoppe and the two women inside, watching them.

"Those nice, sweet, morbid folks," Belma said. "Spread the word, you ghouls! Cha-Ching!"

"Well, thanks for sort of taking care of them," Jenna said. "Hey, can you think of anyone who's gone missing around here and has long white hair?"

Belma crossed her arms. "Jenna, do not tell me you tampered with that crime scene."

"No no, they're already digging up the body. I just happened to catch a glimpse of the white hair."

"'Just happened,'" Belma muttered. "Like you're going to 'just happen' to find yourself in the morgue peeking at death certificates and checking toe tags."

Jenna didn't deny it. In fact...

"Stop considering!" Belma said. "It was supposed to be a joke."

"The town historian—"

"Yeah yeah, blah blah," Belma said. "I don't care who that body is or who put it there. I care about one thing, lady: did any of my cookies make it to the scene?"

"All of them, in fact. They were greatly appreciated and thoroughly enjoyed. Bub loved them so much he's expecting a small riot when you take them to the café."

"How great would that be?" Belma breathed. "Bub would eat the tires off a garbage truck, so I don't know how much his opinion counts, but I'll still take it. I'd better start making more."

She came around the counter and headed for the front doors.

"So, the white hair?" Jenna said.

"The only missing person I know with long white hair is my aunt Bertie, but I'm ninety-nine percent sure we'd find her if we checked the casino in Michigan City."

"So why don't you check?" Jenna asked.

"Because she's a horrible person and I prefer to believe she's dead. Ta!"

———

The Welcome Shoppe was busy that day, even for a fall Sunday in Lost Haven. Folks were out enjoying the color tours, cider mills, and final days of light jackets before the Michigan winter settled in.

Speculation about the body in the park was rampant, and people who pretended to be getting photos of the Sanctuary Cemetery exhumation project kept drifting toward the north end of Lilac Park, hoping to glean something about the corpse.

*Amateurs*, Jenna scoffed. *They don't even have any cookies to offer.*

She had about a dozen customers browsing the racks, poking at the haunted attraction displays and peering down into the roped-off Sanctuary staircase when Detective Olson wandered in.

"Welcome!" Jenna said.

"You might want to wait on that." Olson headed straight to the counter, checking to make sure no one else was within earshot. "I don't know if I'll still be welcome after I ask you this question."

Jenna waved him off. "You're always welcome here, detective."

Of course, she was thinking: *Ask the stupid question!*

Olson scanned the shop again and leaned in. "I know this is going to get out anyway, but I'm hoping to find a few answers before it does. If there's anyone I need to talk to, even bring in for questioning, maybe I can get to them before the gossip does."

"I hope you drive fast," Jenna said.

"As a matter of fact, I do. Now, I didn't even bring this up with Bub Thorp, since he has the ability to gossip via radio, and nobody can outrun that."

"I'm trying really hard to act like I'm not excited about this."

"I know, and I appreciate it. I would also appreciate it if you kept this between us for as long as possible."

Jenna nodded. "I won't say a thing until I hear it from someone else."

Olson looked around one more time. Satisfied, he pulled his phone out of his pocket.

"We've identified the body in the park. We think."

"You think?"

"Yeah, which is why I'm bothering you." He kept the screen away from Jenna and poked and swiped a few times. "We don't have the body fully exposed yet, but Tina and Gino were able to extract some ID from one of the pockets: a driver's license and a few credit cards."

"What's her name?" Jenna asked.

Olson stopped and looked up. "Why do you say 'her'?"

Jenna confessed: "I saw a bit of her long white hair when I brought the cookies."

"Ah. Classic detective work, though tradition calls for donuts. Well done."

Jenna blushed.

"And the hair is exactly why I'm here." Olson checked his phone's screen for a beat, and then turned it so she could see. "Any idea why this man would be wearing a long white wig when he got killed and buried in a shallow grave?"

Jenna looked at the driver's license photo.

It was Martin Ritter.

—

When she recovered, Jenna quickly filled Olson in on Martin Ritter's Lost Haven Morgue embezzlement scandal and how everyone thought he'd fled to some tropical island with a fake passport and new haircut.

When she was done, he said, "So this is kind of a big deal."

"Uh, yeah."

"Well, he didn't get a haircut."

"Can you tell how he was killed?"

"Not yet," Olson said. "Once he's out of the ground we'll get him straight to the medical examiner's office. Hopefully the cause of death can still be determined, but…the state of decay is pretty advanced."

Jenna gasped.

"Sorry," Olson said, "I should keep my mouth shut."

Jenna frowned. "What? Oh, no, who cares about a bunch of bugs and loose flesh? Have you seen the Halloween decorations around here? No, I just realized that whoever killed Martin is probably the person who actually stole the money. Wait, is the money buried with him?"

"Nope," Olson said. "Unless Bub Thorp pulled it out while everyone else was looking the other way, then carefully replaced every speck of soil around the body."

"So no," Jenna said. "Nobody else moved out of town when the scandal hit last year, so the killer has to still be here in Lost Haven. And they have to know his body is being dug up."

Olson said, "Over the past year, you haven't noticed anyone covered in dirt and blood, lugging around a million in cash?"

"I think I'd remember that."

"Probably."

Jenna said, "Do you think it's weird that the killer

left his wallet? I mean, if I was going to kill someone, I probably wouldn't leave their ID behind."

Olson studied her with a raised eyebrow.

"I said 'if,'" Jenna added.

"I'm making a note that you're even considering it. But it's not that odd. Murders happen in the heat of the moment, people aren't thinking straight. Chances are very good this person hadn't killed before, so it's not like they had practice at it. Or spent any time thinking about how they'd do it…"

He cocked the eyebrow at her again, and then continued.

"And who knows, maybe the killer knew we'd identify the body eventually anyway through DNA, so what's the point of stripping the ID? It's just one more thing to get rid of. But my best guess, something nasty went down in the park, the killer panicked and couldn't lug a dead body around downtown Lost Haven, so they dug a quick hole and dropped poor old Martin Ritter in it."

Jenna nodded. "And now they know his body has been found. But they don't know we know it's him."

"Not yet anyway. I'll check around, see if anyone has suddenly packed a bag and found a reason to fly to Mexico."

"I can help with that," Jenna said. "I'll—"

Olson held up a hand to stop her. "You'll continue to operate your lovely new Welcome Shoppe, because you are a small business owner and not a badge-carrying member of the law enforcement profession."

Jenna's heart sank. She already had ideas about who to talk to, who might have something to hide, and how she would document her first-hand account of everything for the Lost Haven historical record. If Olson was going to prevent her from helping, all of that would be impossible.

Well, extremely tricky and potentially illegal, which put it right next door to impossible.

Then Olson glanced over his shoulder, leaned in and lowered his voice.

"At least, that's what I'll tell the judge if this conversation ever becomes admissible in court. Between you and me, you have incredible connections in town. Anything you can find out—without putting yourself in any danger whatsoever—is greatly appreciated by me and my golf game."

Jenna bounced on her toes, fighting the urge to wrap him in a crushing hug over the counter.

Olson winked and straightened up. "And I mean it: don't do anything dumb and get yourself hurt-or killed. It looks really bad in my report."

"Of course," Jenna said.

Now this, it would turn out, was truly impossible.

# CHAPTER 5

As soon as Olson was out the door, Jenna texted Cabo to see if he could swing by. Twelve agonizing minutes later, he walked through the front door.

"What took so long?" she demanded.

Cabo stopped in the entranceway. "Good to see you too. I was running a class. I have another one in twenty minutes, so if this is about more haunted house stuff...I'd rather go stare at the sun for nineteen of them."

"No no no, come in, come in." Jenna checked the shop, making sure no customers were headed their way. "I have news about the body."

Cabo perked up and hurried behind the counter, bringing with him a strong aroma of spearmint and something Jenna couldn't identify, but did not like.

"What is that smell?"

"Recipe 8.2," Cabo said. "You're probably picking up the asparagus. It really comes through the pores, huh?"

"Maybe you should go back to your studio and call me."

Cabo checked his watch. "Nineteen minutes."

"Okay, okay. Detective Olson just left and they've identified the body. He also pretty much gave me his blessing to help figure out what happened and who the killer is."

Cabo was skeptical. "Did he say that? Or did he just, you know, nod and wave, and you took it to mean you've been deputized?"

"I'm basically an unofficial consultant," Jenna said. "But he asked for my help, and now I'm asking for yours. We made a great team during the whole Lost Haven resort thing, and you being semi-new to town will help a ton."

"So you're using me?"

"Do you want to be an assistant to the consultant to the detective or not?"

"Does it pay?"

"No. Well, it pays in justice. Does that count?"

"No."

Jenna was stumped.

"I'm just messing with you," Cabo said. "We do make a great team, and you can pay me in high-fives."

"Starting now," Jenna said, and held her palm out just above the counter.

Cabo tapped it with a fist, softly, so they wouldn't attract any attention.

"Oh, one part that sucks, temporarily," Jenna said.

"We can't say anything to Belma and Lawrence about it. Not until the body's identity is public, anyway."

"Why does that suck?" Cabo asked.

"You know…keeping secrets from friends?"

"The way I see it, the more they know, the more danger they're in. Like right now, because you're about to tell me who the body is, you're putting me on a very short list of people who know something the killer does not want known. That puts me in danger."

"I hadn't thought of it that way," Jenna admitted. "Should I not tell you?"

"'Well, you have to now. And I can take the danger. So by keeping this between me and you, we're actually protecting our dear friends from harm."

Jenna put her palm out again. "I like the way you sleuth, Jay Cabo."

He tapped it again, and then they got to work.

—

Jenna said, "The corpse in Lilac Park is Martin Ritter."

She braced for an explosive reaction, but Cabo's face didn't even twitch.

"Did I know him?"

Jenna blinked. "Yes. Well, you knew *of* him. I told you about him last night."

Still, nothing from Cabo.

She said, "Owner of the Lost Haven Morgue?" Zilch.

"Stole about a million dollars in cash on Halloween last year?"

"Oh, *that* guy," Cabo said. "Yeah, I remember. Wait—so he didn't get away with the money?"

"No, but someone else did."

Jenna pulled a legal pad from beneath the counter and plucked a pen from the jar next to the cash register.

"And I have a pretty good idea of who it could be."

—

Jenna said, "Before we start our list, I want to be clear about what's at stake here. It's very serious."

"Besides life and death? Because that seems pretty serious."

"Obviously, yes, life and death. Justice for crimes committed, peace for the deceased's family. Yada yada."

"You can't yada yada murder, Jenna."

"Listen to me. The names I'm about to write down are all linked to Halloween and haunted houses in one way or another. If Ritter's murder is somehow connected to the holiday, or the way we celebrate it, it could change everything. Halloween in Lost Haven is in jeopardy, Jay Cabo. No more window displays, no more haunted houses, no more skeletons and spider webs scattered through town. We'd just be another boring little town with some pumpkin cookies and dried cornstalks tied to the streetlights."

"Well, the cookies will still be good."

"The cookies will still be *delicious*. But Halloween in Lost Haven is about more than that, a lot more. And if Martin Ritter could rise from his shallow grave as a zombie, which I'm sure he'd absolutely love to do, he'd beg us to make sure nothing happens to his precious holiday, no matter what."

"So what are we going to do if solving the murder means the end of Halloween in Lost Haven?"

"Let's hope it doesn't come to that," Jenna said.

———

Jenna wrote five names on the pad:
  - Dave Kemp
  - Dina Polk
  - Preacher Hank
  - Unflappable Bob Wedell
  - Julian Vance
Then, after brief consideration, added a sixth:
  - Jimbo Gelderson
Cabo's eyebrows went up. "Isn't that the old dude working on your shop?"

"I don't see *anyone* working on my shop," Jenna said, with enough bitterness to flavor Belma's new pumpkin cookies for years. "But yes, that's him."

"You think he could have killed Ritter?"

"After what happened with the Kavanaughs, I try not to assume what people could or couldn't do. Right now I'm just going by who has a motive, or who would be very good at burying a dead person in Lilac Park without getting caught. Jimbo is one of the few people on the exhumation crew, and he *can* work quickly if he has to. I've seen it. Once."

"That seems a bit weak," Cabo said. "Do you think you might be, you know. Venting a bit?"

Jenna tapped the pen against the pad.

"Maybe. Okay, but if he actually did kill Ritter, I still get to say I told you so."

She scratched a line through Jimbo's name.

"Although…" Cabo said, and Jenna brightened, ready to re-add the name. "You mentioned motives. If Ritter had the million bucks on him, just about everyone in town would have a motive to take him out. If they knew he had the money."

"That's true," Jenna said. "But a list that says 'Everyone in town' doesn't help us much."

They both stared at the paper.

Jenna made the call. "For now, let's focus on haunted house motives. Who benefits most if Ritter is gone and his haunt goes out of business? If they got the money too, that's icing on the cake, but not the reason for the murder."

"Is that why Dave Kemp is at the top of the list? Who's that?"

"Dave Kemp, also known as Skull Monger."

Cabo blinked. "Skull Monger? Why is there anyone else on the list?"

"Kemp runs the No Sanctuary haunted house, and he demands that everyone call him Skull Monger from October first through the thirty-first. I think I mentioned that he and Ritter not only had a professional rivalry going, they had a fundamental disagreement about the best way to scare people."

"If you mentioned it," Cabo said, "I wasn't listening. Because it sounds absolutely ridiculous. And stupid."

"Well, to these guys it was worth getting into shouting matches over. One year during the Harvest Parade, Ritter's Lost Haven Morgue float collided with Kemp's No Sanctuary float. Ritter's was full of actors in full zombie makeup, prosthetics, the whole thing, doing the Thriller dance."

"Okay, I admit, that sounds pretty cool."

"Well, Kemp's float was all animatronics, run by a generator and air compressor. The collision knocked everything loose, so it turned into a rolling platform filled with limp props and droopy spider webs."

"Eh. Not as cool."

"Exactly," Jenna said. "Ritter's actors took a

moment to regain their balance, and then kept on dancing. Kemp screamed at Ritter that he ran into him on purpose, Ritter yelled back, 'That's what you get for trying to scare people with machines.' It was a big scene. And of course, both grown men were in full makeup. Ritter in his classic zombie wig and wardrobe, Kemp in his Skull Monger outfit, which looks a lot like the Grim Reaper, but with a chainsaw instead of a scythe."

Cabo took a moment to absorb everything. "This is all very alarming, but for a lot of reasons beyond the dead Ritter angle."

"Yeah. Parents were pulling their children away, the firefighters almost turned a hose on the two men to break it up...it wasn't a proud moment for Lost Haven."

"So you think these guys decided to settle things once and for all? They meet in Lilac Park on Halloween night, or just run into each other. Things get out of hand and Ritter ends up dead. Kemp panics and buries the body."

"Maybe?" Jenna said, knowing it was a stretch.

"How does the money come into play? Is Ritter actually stealing it and stumbles into Kemp? Are he and Kemp working together to steal the cash, but have a disagreement about the split?"

"I truly cannot see those two working together on anything," Jenna said.

"A million bucks helps make a lot of differences seem less important."

"It wasn't quite a million…"

"Jenna, even a thousand bucks might do it. When I was doing bodyguard work, I had clients with people threatening them every day, swearing they were going kill them no matter what, blah blah blah. The client goes, 'How about five hundred bucks to go away?' Every time, the sworn enemy took it and went away."

"And never came back?"

"Oh, no, they came back all the time. It's like feeding a stray, you do it once, and they know where to go for a free meal. It was a terrible plan and I always advised the clients not to do it, but who listens to me?"

Jenna frowned, not quite sure what they were talking about anymore.

"The point is," Cabo said, "money changes everything. Even a small amount can make people change their mind about something. A large amount, like not quite a million, can change everything."

"Well, if we're looking for someone who benefits from Ritter leaving the haunt business, and who will do questionable things for money, that brings us to the next name on my list: Dina Polk."

—

"Dina Polk is the stage manager at the Lost Haven Morgue. She hires and trains the other actors, coordinates with the makeup team, handles the wardrobes, everything to make sure the performers are ready to go every season, and every night. When the Morgue is open, she performs under the name Mistress Sara Moanies. She was Martin Ritter's girlfriend, and his second-in-command."

Cabo nodded. "You're guessing she wanted to be first-in-command?"

"I think it's a motive, for sure. I mean, she's running the Morgue this year without him around. And when you add in the money..."

"Oh, this must be good," Cabo said. "You're making that face."

"What face?"

"The one you make when things get a little spicy. You blush and your tongue sticks out, just a tiny bit."

"It does not," Jenna said.

"Remember the time you came to one of my yoga classes and Mrs. Lambert's boob fell out?"

Jenna blushed and her tongue peeked.

"I rest my case," Cabo said. He leaned closer and scanned the store. A few customers were drifting toward the front, but they didn't have anything in their hands.

"So ol' Dina Kemp is a bit saucy?"

"There are rumors," Jenna said, "that in the off-season, when the Lost Haven Morgue isn't open for haunted house patrons, it's open for…another kind of patron."

Cabo waited. "Like…sports fans? I don't know where this is going."

"People who are willing to pay for a certain thing, but it's illegal…"

"She sells drugs?"

Jenna blushed harder. "No. Well, maybe. Probably. But if you take her stage name…"

"Mistress Sara Moanies? Oh, I get it. Mistress of Ceremonies. Cute."

"I'm talking about the Mistress part."

Cabo frowned.

Then it hit him: "No way."

Jenna nodded.

"She's a *prostitute*?"

"Hush! The rumor is, she runs a secret brothel in the Morgue during the off-season. But the only people who would know if it's true are the people who either work there or go there, and they're not blabbing."

"Man, this is messed up on so many levels. I mean, in a *morgue*?"

"The rumors say it's very tastefully done. No cobwebs or skeletons, it's all very clean. Apparently the set design is very nineteenth-century Victorian."

Cabo said, "Rumors, huh? You've never seen the place in person?"

"Jay Cabo, I will toss you out of this investigation right now if you don't behave."

"Yes, Mistress Jenna."

She threatened him with a fist about the size of his ear. He was very kind and did not burst into laughter.

Jenna calmed down and said, "I'm not judging, but if the rumors are true, Dina will obviously go to…interesting measures…to get money. If she was stealing from Ritter and he caught her, or if they were planning to steal the whole pot together, maybe she saw an opportunity to have the Morgue to herself and all the profits, along with whatever she's doing in the off-season."

"Yeah, she definitely belongs on the suspect list. Maybe even above Kemp, or Skull Monger, or whatever. I mean, you guys keep acting like everything is so scandalous around here, while most of it is snoozeville. But this—a secret brothel in this little town? This is scandalous."

"You're not the only one who thinks so."

Jenna tapped the next name on her pad: Preacher Hank

—

"**P**reacher Hank," Cabo read. "Now, is he really a preacher, or is this another creepy Halloween nickname thing?"

"Oh, he's a preacher alright," Jenna said. "He'll stop people on the street and holler at them, say they're going to burn for eternity if they don't stop chewing gum, or looking at birds, or whatever it is he's decided to be offended by that day. I'm actually shocked he hasn't come into your studio yet to tell you yoga is the devil's work and stretching is the same thing as fornicating with the floor."

"That's actually a pretty good sales pitch..."

"I don't know if Preacher Hank has actually been ordained or not, but either way he's vowed to shut down all of the haunted houses in Lost Haven. He says they're an affront to decency and an abomination in the eyes of his church."

"Where is his church?"

"It's actually an RV, so...wherever he's parked right now. The Holy Roller, he calls it. All month long he'll be parking it outside the haunts, screaming at patrons through a bullhorn about how they're sinners and giving gold and silver to the devil. Then, of course, he offers to graciously accept that same money to save their souls."

"What a guy," Cabo said. "But is he a murderer? Sounds like he's a stickler for the whole sinner thing."

Jenna thought about it for a moment. "I've seen him get pretty worked up. I think if he was in that state of mind, and he and Ritter somehow got into it in the park last year, he might justify killing a fake zombie as a way to begin cleansing our horribly sinful town."

"But he wouldn't want anyone to know about it, so he buried the body."

"Well, yeah. I mean, he's nuts, but he's not crazy. He'd have to know he'd go to prison, and he can't whip Lost Haven into shape from there."

"And the money?" Cabo said.

"Certainly a factor. If Ritter had it with him, and Preacher Hank killed him—maybe because of the cash, or maybe it was just lucky timing—that's a lot of gas money for the Holy Roller."

"Does he know about Mistress Sara Moanies and her, uh, extracurricular activities?"

"I think the top of his head would blow off if he even suspected. That would…wow. Something to keep in mind, if we want to work those two off each other."

Cabo's jaw dropped. "Jenna Hooper. Maybe Preacher Hank is right—you're gonna burn."

"Hey, sometimes a historian has to make a little history happen, you know?"

"No, I don't. I also don't know why Bob Wedell is the next name on your list, or why he goes by *Unflappable* Bob Wedell."

"Only during October."

"Of course," Cabo said. "Please call me Confused Cabo. But only during every month of the year, for as long as I live in Lost Haven."

—

"So you know Bob Wedell as the owner of Wedell's Hardware," Jenna said.

Cabo nodded. "He's helped me many times. Who would have thought my simple studio space would need so many random trips to the hardware store? And that was just to get it open. The maintenance? A serious hassle."

Jenna swept a hand, presenting her unfinished shop. "Jimbo makes at least four trips per day. Sometimes he comes back with one screw. One. Sometimes, nothing. Don't get me started."

"Sorry."

Jenna took a deep breath. "Anyway. You don't know him as Unflappable Bob Wedell, superstar haunted house patron."

"I know what those words mean, but they make zero sense when you string them together like that. Superstar patron? Does he pay extra?"

"No, he never gets scared. Not even startled."

"And that makes him a superstar?"

"Oh yes," Jenna said. "It's an ongoing contest among the haunts to see who can get Unflappable Bob to jump. Or yelp, smile, blink, anything. But he just strolls through the haunts like he's out for a relaxing walk."

Cabo frowned. "Does he enjoy it?"

"Good question. Belma, Lawrence and I went with him through Ghost Ship once, and he sucked all the fun out of it, at least for us. We were screaming like lunatics and there's Unflappable Bob, no expression at all, just staring back at the nightmares to slaughter him. It made us feel like idiots."

"Well, like I've said, anybody who—"

"Yeah yeah, wait until you've gone through these haunts, then you can decide if we're ridiculous or not. Until then, shut it and don't distract me from my suspects. Now Bob, he might not enjoy the haunts, but he does enjoy the status of being the one person they can't scare. It makes him special. At least, it did, until last year."

"What happened last year?"

"Well, according to Martin Ritter, he scared Unflappable Bob Wedell so badly the poor guy wet his pants."

Cabo's eyebrows went up. "Really?"

"That's what Ritter claimed. Wedell denied it, of course, but he was in the haunt alone, so it was his word against Ritter's. And a lot of people wanted to believe Ritter. Because if it was true, it dethroned the king, in a way."

"The king of haunted house patrons," Cabo said, full of skepticism.

"Exactly."

"Dethroned by peeing his pants."

"You've got it. Even if it didn't happen, it took Wedell down a few pegs. He won't even talk about it."

"Okay, but would he kill over it?"

"That's the question, isn't it? And the money—maybe Ritter was stealing it and agreed to pay Wedell a chunk to let him tell the town he'd terrified the one and only Unflappable Bob. Or maybe he actually did scare him. They meet in the park, Ritter gets carried away, taunting Wedell, and *smack*. We know Wedell can dig a hole; he sells shovels for crying out loud."

Cabo nodded. "His store is right across First street, due north of where Ritter was buried."

"It will be a big help once we know how Ritter was killed. If it was a claw hammer to the head, Wedell's looking good. If it was something crazy, like poison or getting stabbed with a t-bone, maybe not."

"Stabbed with a t-bone?" Cabo said.

"Exactly. That would likely point to one person on my list: Julian Vance."

———

"Let me try this one," Cabo said. "Julian Vance. He's the owner of the Lakeside Grille restaurant."

"Correct," Jenna said.

"He's, what, thirty-five?"

"Close, maybe a year younger. He was a senior when I was a freshman at Lost Haven High."

Cabo said, "His October nickname is Boo-lian Dance, and he runs a secret Halloween disco in the restaurant's freezer."

Jenna was not amused. "I see what you're doing, and I suggest we take a moment of silence to mourn your prospects as an amateur investigator."

They stared at each other for a few moments.

"That should do it," Jenna said. "And no, that's not his nickname, and he doesn't run a secret disco. But..."

"Of course there's a but. No one in this town is normal."

"He is also the owner of Ghost Ship, obviously a competitor of the Lost Haven Morgue. Now brace yourself, because this story actually requires a bit of Lost Haven history."

"No wonder you saved it for the end of the list." He checked his watch. "I have seven minutes before the class. Should I go to the bathroom before you start?"

"Too late," Jenna said. "Now, you've seen Ghost Ship, right?"

"Uh, I think so. Giant freighter looking thing, docked out in the marina like some invading warship? Kinda hard to miss?"

"That's the one. It's an old Lake Michigan steam barge built to haul lumber from Sanctuary to Chicago and Milwaukee, back when the founding families were stripping the land bare. She was called *Gloria*, named after Marinus Mink's lovely wife."

"Wait, Marinus?" Cabo said. "Isn't that the statue in the park, right where Ritter's body was buried?"

"You're back on track for amateur status, my friend."

Cabo felt a tiny burst of pride. "So is the statue relevant to Ritter's death?"

"I have no idea, but the historian in me really, really hopes so."

Cabo just shook his head.

Jenna pressed on. "Once the lumber in Sanctuary was depleted, the *Gloria* was commissioned to transport Christmas trees from the Upper Peninsula to Chicago, despite that city's proven dislike for all things joyous, but then she disappeared for decades. No one knew where she'd gone, or what she did.

"Then, a few years ago, she went up for auction in some lot along Lake Superior. Julian Vance purchased the *Gloria* and had her refurbished into a floating Michelin three-star dining experience. He rechristened her *Julian's Journey*."

Cabo perked up. "Do they have good steak?"

"The best," Jenna said, "but you won't get any. Everybody in Lost Haven thought Vance would keep his new, exclusive water-borne restaurant in our marina, returning *Gloria* to her true home. I mean, you've seen the line for the Lakeside Grille on weekends. Even some weeknights, it's a forty-five minute wait to get a table. Docking *Julian's Journey* just down the shore would give ample seating at both places.

"But Vance had other plans. He chose to dock the restaurant in Chicago throughout the year and only bring her back to Lost Haven for October, when the ship is totally repurposed to be a haunted attraction. They don't even serve crackers."

"Okay," Cabo said, "I'm mildly offended that I can't get a steak from this guy's boat, but it's his, he can do what he wants with it. I'm guessing Ritter and the other Halloween maniacs around here feel a bit more strongly?"

"You guess right. Dave Kemp wanted Vance to sail back to Chicago and sink on the way, while Ritter called him a traitor and accused him of taking advantage of our town's holiday spirit. He told everybody that if Vance truly loved Lost Haven, he'd keep the ship here all year. He wanted patrons to boycott Ghost Ship until Vance promised to stay."

"Which Vance loved, I'm sure."

"He still gets customers, but of the three main haunts, his gets the least amount of traffic by far. So Ritter's boycott was probably costing him money."

"Are people still boycotting now that Ritter is gone?"

"I'd love to know the answer to that," Jenna said. "Hopefully we'll get a chance to ask him tonight when we go through his haunted ship."

# CHAPTER 6

J enna closed up just after seven, as did everything else on Main Street on Sundays except the café, which McTavish kept open later during peak holiday seasons. The evening was slipping into pre-daylight savings darkness, and the low clouds hovering over Lake Michigan gave the sunset an eerie orange glow that made the autumn colors pop.

Jenna barely noticed any of it.

Ever since Olson's visit, her mind had been bouncing around inside her head like a pinball, lighting up all sorts of questions and looking for angles, grudges, motivations, anything she may have missed that would make one of her murderous candidates stand out from the rest. The most maddening part about all of it was that she might already know the one nugget of information that identified Ritter's killer, and not realize it.

Not yet, anyway.

But she needed to find out, and soon. Even though it had been mere hours since she'd found out the corpse in Lilac Park was Ritter, it felt like time was already edging toward a cliff. The killer could be speeding out of town at that very moment, booking a flight to Romania, destroying all evidence that might possibly connect them to the crime.

Word hadn't gotten out yet about who the corpse was. Olson did call to let her know Ritter's body had been moved to the medical examiner's office, having been unearthed just after noon, and Dr. Taft was incredibly respectful when it came to the dead. This was usually a good thing, but Jenna couldn't talk to anyone except Cabo about Ritter until his identity was revealed. She took a brief moment to compel the medical examiner's ethics to crumble, just this one time.

That done, she considered visiting the gravesite again. It was still off-limits while Tina and Gino finished up their work, and maybe they'd found something new. Plus, they had to know about Ritter's driver's license. If they just happened to go to the Sanctuary Café and let it slip…

*Don't get those poor crime scene technicians in trouble with Olson!*

Yeah, she should probably leave them alone. Visiting the site also carried the risk of the techs trying some new improv comedy out on her, and she'd rather crawl into the open grave for the rest of the night.

Jenna wondered if she should share her suspect list with Olson. It would be good to have his professional eye taking a closer look at them, but if by some chance the real killer wasn't on her list, they could slip away while Olson was focused elsewhere.

He said he'd look for anyone who left town in a hurry once news of the body spread, which was great, but what about the folks who were still in Lost Haven? He might not recognize it if any of the locals were acting strangely—most of them were strange to begin with—but Jenna would.

She checked the time: 7:15.

*You've been standing in the twilight for ten minutes!*

*Note to self: It's getting cold in Michigan. Do all mystery solving indoors.*

She was supposed to meet the crew at the café around 7:30 so they could begin their postponed Lost Haven haunted house tour—not nearly enough time to have a casual chat with any suspected killers. Luckily, just about everyone on her initial suspect list was already at the haunted houses.

She headed north on Main Street, pulling her hoodie close against the growing chill and feeling slightly conflicted.

On one hand, she wanted the corpse's identity to get out so she wouldn't have to keep it a secret from Belma and Lawrence.

On the other, having Ritter's death out in the open might drive the killer to do something drastic.

Like, you know, murdering the town historian

who just happened to be asking questions at the wrong time.

—

"You're keeping a secret from us," Lawrence said.

Jenna blinked. "What? I am not."

"And now you're a liar. I don't even know you anymore, Jenna Hooper."

The four of them were sitting around what was quickly becoming their autumn table outside the Sanctuary Café, sipping hot ciders and whatever green disaster Cabo had convinced McTavish to create.

Belma squinted at Jenna. "Yeah, I see it-the beady, furtive eyes; the flared nostrils. Mouth pursed like an ugly belly button."

"Happy Halloween to you too," Jenna said.

Belma turned to Cabo. "Do you see it?"

Cabo took a gulp of the sludge and wiped toxic waste off his lips while avoiding looking anywhere near Jenna.

"Maybe she just has to go to the bathroom."

"Do you?" Lawrence said. "And don't lie."

"No, now knock it off," Jenna said. "We have haunted houses to prepare for."

Lawrence turned to Cabo. "Ah, on both subjects,

did you wear an adult diaper for your inevitable bladder failure?"

"Don't need it," Cabo said, holding his green smoothie aloft. "Not if this baby works like it's supposed to."

The table fell silent.

"I asked McTavish to add an anti-diuretic," Cabo bragged. "I may be as bloated as a dead fish, but I won't have to pee for about twenty-four hours."

He smirked in triumph.

"So bring on these dumb haunted houses and do your worst. I'm middle wedge, and my crotch is dry as a desert."

After a few moments, Lawrence said, "What have we done with our lives?"

"Enough chatter!" Jenna finished her cider and thumped the mug down on the table. "Ghost Ship. No Sanctuary. The Lost Haven Morgue. Let's go!"

She stood and tugged her hood up to hide her guilty face. She didn't know how long she could hold out if Belma and Lawrence kept needling her about a suspected secret, even if not knowing made them safer. She couldn't believe it had come to this, but she was grateful for Cabo's disgusting, distracting smoothie. As long as everyone stayed focused on that and the potential for Cabo to wet his pants, she'd be fine.

*Boy, Lawrence was right. What have we done with our lives? A great question to ponder later, when you're not about to confront and interrogate Julian Vance at Ghost Ship.*

No, "interrogate" is the wrong word.

*Gently converse, with the goal of determining innocence or guilt.*

Much better.

*And a slightly more important goal: If Vance is guilty—don't be his next victim.*

—

Jenna hustled back down Main Street and was surrounded by the time she got to Cabo's Bodyworks.

Lawrence hooked one arm and Belma took the other. Cabo hovered slightly behind. To any observer, it would look like a group of friends sauntering arm-in-arm along the sidewalk. But Jenna had no such illusions—this was a temporary abduction.

"Don't think we've forgotten," Lawrence said. "What's the secret?"

"Nothing."

Belma whispered, "Did you meet someone?"

"No."

"Make out with a random customer?" Lawrence asked. "Don't worry, no judging."

"What? No."

"Honestly Jenna. You are terrible at being dishonest."

"I know. That's why I'm practicing. And I didn't make out with anybody."

Jenna glanced back at Cabo, simmering a bit that he wasn't getting any of this grilling. His face was flat as a manhole cover; probably due to the extensive security training he'd gone through to make sure he could look and act like a robot when he needed to.

But he did give a small, helpless shrug, like he wanted to help but couldn't without spilling the secret.

"Are you and Garrett back together?" Belma said.

"Belma, no. How come, if you two think I have a secret, it's all about men and making out?"

"Wishful thinking on your behalf?" Lawrence tried.

"Well, you keep your wishful thoughts away from my love life, thanks very much."

"Love life?" Belma scoffed. "Sweetie, if you can find it, let us know, and we'll stay away."

"Hmm, maybe I left it next to your new cookie recipe," Jenna said.

Belma's eyes popped in alarm.

"What new cookie recipe?" Lawrence asked.

"Nothing," Belma said.

Jenna pressed a bit more. "What are they called again, Belma? Something bitter…"

"Nope. Dunno. I don't even like cookies anymore."

Lawrence frowned. "I heard a rumor about some new pumpkin cookies going to the police in Lilac

Park today, but I know you wouldn't have anything to do with that. Right?"

"Obviously!" Belma shouted. "Ha ha!"

Lawrence narrowed his eyes. "Wait a minute…"

Belma puffed her cheeks out, waiting for it.

Lawrence whirled on Jenna. "You know something about the dead body!"

Belma gasped- her near fistfight over cookie betrayal completely forgotten.

Jenna considered denying it, but they were coming up on the western edge of Lilac Park, then it would be a left turn on Shoreline Drive and a quick hop onto the boardwalk. She couldn't have these two hyenas barking at her when Vance was around, so…

"I know exactly one more fact than you all, and Olson made me promise not to tell anyone. It will come out soon though, so just be patient."

Lawrence scoffed. "Be patient? The last time dead bodies started showing up around here, you almost died a dozen times and we were all suspects."

"I think it was only twice that I was in actual mortal danger," Jenna muttered.

"Don't change the subject! I suppose you don't have to be a decent friend and tell us everything you know, but at least tell us this: Is anyone in this group a suspect? Or in danger?"

Jenna laughed. "No way."

"Not even Belma?" Lawrence asked.

"Hey," Belma said.

Jenna shook her head.

"You're sure? She's very murder-y."

"I don't see how she could be involved at all," Jenna said.

"Well that's disappointing."

Jenna clamped her mouth shut. She wanted to tell them just how blown their minds were going to be when they found out who the corpse was, but she knew the more she talked the easier it would be to let Ritter's name slip.

"Okay, are we done grilling Jenna?" Cabo asked from behind.

"Not even close," Belma said.

"Well, too bad, because I can see Ghost Ship over there in the marina, and something is very, very wrong."

Jenna's head whipped up. "What? Where?"

"Right here," Cabo said. He gently—but firmly— pried Belma and Lawrence off of Jenna and eased her to the front of the pack. Then he put his arms around the two interrogators and pulled them close.

"Much better. I am middle wedge."

—

Ghost Ship loomed in the Lost Haven Marina like a three-story iceberg that had broken off from some cursed land and drifted into the harbor.

Red searchlights burned through the fog pouring from her smokestacks. Eerie green and blue light seeped from portholes and hatches, and dark shapes scurried along her walkways like overgrown rats.

"Well, that's good enough for me," Cabo said. "Next."

Lawrence and Belma tugged him forward.

"Not so fast, buddy," Lawrence said.

They were in the marina now, on the spacious boardwalk with thick poles bracketing the entrances to the wide docks stretching into the harbor. The docks were mostly empty, it being October, but a few lingering yachts hunkered in the still waters, their dim walking lights casting odd shadows across the planks.

Because of Ghost Ship's size she was moored at the end of the dock along a stretch of boardwalk usually reserved for visiting boats that didn't have a slip in the marina. Her presence created a wall of steam barge that sealed off the view of anything else. She was nearly two hundred feet long with three-story structures at the bow and stern and an open deck between for stacking lumber. She towered over the nearest yachts, whose owners no doubt wanted to relocate to the Gulf as quickly as possible so they wouldn't feel quite so…inadequate.

Hidden speakers played a slow, ominous orchestral song filled with moaning foghorns and screeching gulls, but it wasn't loud enough to mask the bangs, thumps, cackles and screams coming from within Ghost Ship's hull.

"Do you hear that?" Jenna asked Cabo.

"What, the screaming?"

"Yes."

"Yeah, I hear it."

Jenna's eyes widened. "Isn't it fantastic?"

"I need new friends."

"I'm sure Jenna filled you in on the legend of Ghost Ship," Belma said.

"Yep," Cabo said. "All set."

Jenna frowned. "Actually..."

"Oh man," Cabo groaned.

Jenna ignored him. "The legend says one hundred years ago, Ghost Ship was lost at sea carrying lumber for coffins. She sank to the bottom of Lake Michigan, but her drowned crew was steadfast and determined to finish the job. So they hacked the lumber apart and built the coffins, and used them to float Ghost Ship back to the surface."

"This makes zero sense," Cabo said.

Jenna was undeterred. "Now, every October she returns to port in Lost Haven, seeking to fill the empty coffins so her crew can finally rest in peace."

"So if I stuff you three into some coffins," Cabo said, "we can call it a night?"

Jenna shook her head. "You're having fun, Jay Cabo. I can tell."

Cabo grumbled, but he smiled while he did it.

The four of them eased toward the bottom of the gangway, where a short line of people shifted and chatted nervously in the chilly lake air. Maybe it was best that Saturday night hadn't worked out—the line would have stretched all the way back to Shoreline Drive—but a crowd like that can add to the fun as well.

Jenna noticed Cabo's feet doing a nervous tap-dance on the dock and she decided that a shorter line was definitely better: less time for him to create and execute an escape plan.

A tall man dressed in a thick peacoat and a captain's hat stood at the entrance to the ship's gangway, slashing a red lantern into the crowd and muttering about fathoms and rip currents.

When he spotted the newcomers he clumped toward them in an aggressive limp, fixing them in place with his red beam.

"Who that be! Some fresh chum for me hungry crew?"

Cabo eyed the dark waters bobbing around the dock. "If I jump in, do you think I'll freeze to death?"

Lawrence said, "Probably, because we're not coming in to save you."

"Quiet on the deck!" the Captain bellowed. He smelled unease on Cabo and leaned in close, making sure everyone could see the barnacles and tiny crabs clinging to his face.

Cabo saw, and then looked away.

The captain leaned closer.

Cabo looked again, turned away. Groaned.

Jenna, Belma, and Lawrence could not have been happier.

"What's the matter?" the Captain asked Cabo. "Don't ye like me skin treatment? They tell me it'll have me looking young again—I'm hoping for a fresh hundred and fifty years old, har har!"

Belma whispered, "Is he a pirate or a Navy guy?"

"Shush," Jenna said.

"Did Lake Michigan have pirates?"

"Please. You're ruining my suspension of disbelief."

The captain whirled on them. "Did I not order silence?! Keeping you mortals in check is like trying to herd guppies, and you jabber more than two gulls fighting over a scrap of flotsam! Now do ye have the silver needed to enter Ghost Ship, or should I cast ye overboard and let the lake have her way?"

"We have it!" Jenna said, giddy with nervous delight. She held out a stack of bills, collected from Belma and Lawrence. She was treating Cabo, since making him pay for something he hated seemed rude.

The captain snatched the money away and held it near his lantern for review. After grumbling about the feel of newfangled paper money he grinned at Jenna with stained teeth, the crabs jiggling on his face.

"Ah, exact change. Ye know the way to me heart, Jenna."

Jenna froze. The use of her name was unsettling—was the Captain singling her out for some reason?

His mad gaze burned into her for a long moment, then he whispered, "I think I'll be seeing ye inside, me lassie."

He broke away and clumped back toward the gangway, pausing to stop next to a young woman staring at her phone as her thumbs poked out a text. Jenna recognized her from Bloomers, the floral shop in town...Hannah something. She didn't notice the Captain waiting about an inch from her ear, though everyone else in line did, and the dock grew silent.

Her boyfriend sidled away.

Hannah finished texting, glanced at her boyfriend, and frowned. "What?"

He nodded to her left.

She turned, her nose brushing one of the crabs dangling off the Captain's cheek, and screamed directly into his mouth. She flailed backward into her boyfriend's arms and he wrapped her up, laughing like a loon.

"Yum yum yum!" the Captain crowed. "Fresh screams! Tastier than any rum on a winter's night! I want more!"

He stomped away, grinning as the line shied away like a rope drifting on a current.

"Just so you all know," Cabo said, "I won't be speaking to any of you after tonight."

They huddled around him, squeezing him into the

middle wedge position and hopping with the anticipation of more terror.

But Jenna felt something else creeping in: true fear.

Because she'd recognized the Captain as Julian Vance, and for some reason he was going to be waiting for her inside Ghost Ship.

——

As the line grew shorter, Jenna grew more and more nervous.

And not in a good, fun, Halloween-in-Lost-Haven way.

More like a murder-suspect-just-possibly-threatened-her way.

They were the third group from the front of the line. Next up was a party of six, none of whom Jenna recognized. Her mood lifted slightly knowing that tourist money was flowing into Lost Haven.

Behind them were Hannah and her boyfriend, then the Main Street crew. Hannah had recovered from her ordeal with Vance and was texting again, which seemed to be irking her date.

"Can you put that away?" he said.

"I know, I'm sorry. It's for work. We're getting a bunch of orders; I have to go in early tomorrow."

A short, stocky man dressed in a baggy vintage

diving suit complete with the bowl-shaped brass helmet appeared at the rail of Ghost Ship.

He opened the hatch on the front of his helmet and bellowed, "Next!"

Jenna grabbed Cabo's sleeve and let Lawrence and Belma drift forward, distracted by the group of tourists finding all sorts of reasons to delay climbing the gangway and beginning their terrifying tour.

"That was Vance," she whispered. "The Captain."

"Really? He was good."

"Oh, his haunt acting was superb. But he said my name. *That* part can't be good."

"Well…everybody in town knows you. Maybe he's just picking on a familiar face?"

"Maybe. Hopefully. I mean, even if he killed Ritter, nobody else knows it was his body in the park. Or that we're helping Olson. So Vance might be panicking, but that's no reason to single me out. Right?"

"Exactly," Cabo said. "He's just being a weird, freaky haunted house actor, which is perfectly normal for your weird, freaky town."

"It's your town now too, buster."

"Eh, we're still on a trial basis."

Jenna smiled and shook her head. Cabo was a Lost Haven lifer now, even if he didn't know it yet. They caught up to Lawrence and Belma, who were heckling the tourists.

"Hurry up and faint already," Lawrence yelled.

Belma called, "The longer you wait, the worse it is. You're just making them mad!"

In front of them, Hannah stared at the blazing screen of her phone.

"Oh, no way!"

Her boyfriend rolled his eyes. "What now?"

"All of these orders, they're flowers for the Lost Haven Morgue."

"Like, the haunt?"

"Yeah."

Jenna moved closer, hoping she wasn't hearing the girl correctly.

"That body they found in the park," Hannah said. "It's Martin Ritter. The guy who stole all that money."

"Martin Ritter?" Belma crowed. She turned on Jenna. "Is that the secret you knew?"

"Hush!" Jenna whispered. She looked at the line behind them. People were on their phones, texting or talking with hushed urgency and shock.

The word was out.

Hannah glanced over and did a double-take. "Hey. Didn't you guys find the body in the first place?"

"Sure did," Lawrence said. "But we didn't know it was him until you just told us. Wait, I take that back. It seems *one* of us knew."

He glared at Jenna but she barely noticed.

"We're going to talk about this later," he said.

She barely heard that as well.

Her mind was reeling with how this changed pretty much everything...

———

Jenna wanted to run.

Hannah and her boyfriend were next, hopping up and down at the bottom of the gangway, and then it would be their turn. Vance was already planning something for her, though she had no idea what.

She scanned the ship's rail, the walkways, and the dark portholes for a hint or a glimpse of Vance.

No luck.

*Anything could be waiting in there for us*, Jenna thought. *If Vance had something to do with Ritter's death, and now he knows the body has been identified, things just got very dangerous for him. And if he somehow knows Cabo and I are helping Detective Olson...what will he do?*

Calm down. You're getting way too far ahead of yourself. Julian Vance is a nice, very successful guy. Why would he kill Martin?

*Ships are expensive.*

True.

*Restaurants are expensive.*

Also true.

*Julian has a restaurant ship.*

I see what's happening here.

*Martin may have had close to a million dollars in cash. That pays for a lot of tablecloths. And his death gets rid of a major haunted house competitor.*

But the Lost Haven Morgue is still operating…

*It's only been one year. How long will it last without its creator, and with a loss of close to a million in cash?*

That's it. Julian Vance killed Martin Ritter.

*Now, now, you don't know anything for sure yet. There's plenty of time to—*

"Next!"

The deep-sea diver's face was just a dark shape within his brass helmet. He peered down at them and laughed- a deep, hollow sound that made the hair on Jenna's arms stand up.

*Run.*

No. Vance is on the suspect list. I need to talk to him. I need to find out if he was involved with Ritter's death.

*Olson can do that.*

Not like I can. Olson doesn't know the tension between these haunts. He doesn't know the drama among the people involved. He doesn't know…

*Go ahead. Say it.*

He doesn't know the history.

*Fine. But you can still run—just do it inside Ghost Ship when Vance tries to murder you too.*

Deal.

Hopefully.

—

The four of them walked up the steep gangway. Lawrence and Belma were quivering with nervous energy.

Cabo was hyper-vigilant, checking all angles and sides as rapidly as he could.

Jenna's hands were balled into fists and she really hoped she didn't punch anyone who didn't deserve it. But if it happened, she'd apologize. Tomorrow.

The deck was about the size of a basketball court and was typically filled with outdoor dining tables draped in white cloth, candles, and shining silver, but now it was a labyrinth of narrow passageways created by temporary walls made of pallets and heavy canvas tarps.

The maze led back and forth between the two towering ship structures at the bow and stern, and the portholes staring down at them were either pitch black or burning with red light.

They turned right at the top of the gangway and shuffled toward a dark hatchway leading into the warren of the ship's bow. At the threshold, they froze.

"Go, Lawrence," Belma said.

"I'll stand here until Christmas, you cowards. You go."

He tried to nudge Cabo forward, but the man was rooted to the deck like he'd grown there.

"I will physically pick all of you up and use you as human shields if I have to."

"We haven't even started yet," Belma said. But she didn't step forward.

Jenna was frozen as well. She had no idea what waited for her inside Ghost Ship, and that was usually the best part about a haunted house: the unknown.

This time was different.

And potentially deadly.

Inside Ghost Ship, Vance and his crew had full control.

But guilty or innocent, he also might have answers.

Jenna plunged ahead, dragging the rest with her.

—

The inner passageway was jet black and completely silent. Jenna reached out to the sides and touched steel walls before her arms could completely straighten. Cabo was right behind her, with Lawrence on his left and Belma on his right.

She could tell, because they were screaming directly into those ears.

"Quiet!" she yelled.

They screamed.

"Guys! Nothing happened yet!"

Belma stopped, her scream cut off like she'd hit the pause button.

Lawrence petered out into a soft whimper, then nothing.

They stood in the darkness, waiting for…what?

"I smell asparagus," Belma said.

Cabo grunted. "Sorry. That's me."

"Holy ghost," Lawrence said, "did you pee already?"

"Nope. Just sweat." Cabo was doing some sort of breathing exercise, something from yoga or Pilates or millennia of genetic survival.

Jenna said, "Okay team, let's get it together. Belma and Lawrence, we've been through Ghost Ship before. It's our job to make sure Cabo survives."

*Because if Vance tries anything, we might need him to punch an exit through the wall.*

"But it's already different from last year," Lawrence said.

"We've only seen one room so far, and it's completely dark," Jenna said. "Come on. Just stick close and we'll be fine."

Two inches from her nose, Vance whispered: "No you won't."

———

Jenna broke formation.

She screamed and flailed and kicked, then bounced off the left wall, bowled into the right wall, and spun forward into darkness so complete they could have been at the bottom of Lake Michigan.

"We lost Jenna!" Lawrence yelled. "Houston, we have lost Jenna!"

Belma howled, "What is happening?"

Cabo repeated a mantra: "Middle wedge always survives, middle wedge always survives…"

Jenna punched at the darkness, waiting for a fist to connect with the crabs dangling off Vance's face. Instead, she hit a heavy canvas tarp that parted, allowing a sliver of weak, flickering orange light to slip through.

Jenna dove into the opening, slapping the oil-cloth to the side and gasping for air that was never lacking in the first place. The others flew to her and huddled close.

"Whoa," Lawrence said. "This is a *lot* different from last year."

He was right. Vance had obviously invested in the haunted version of his ship, because he'd managed to turn the world upside-down.

They were in a large ballroom lit by a massive crystal chandelier sprouting from the floor. Only half of its lights worked, and those were flickering. Even though it was on the floor, it still swayed gently, as if suspended from above, and the tiny crystals clinked an irregular tune.

Large oil paintings hung upside-down on the walls. One showed men in a traditional English hunting party, but their faces were skulls and the horses breathed fire. A giant, vengeful fox ran among them, slashing and biting.

Another was a simple portrait of a young woman, but as Jenna moved her head to scan the rest of the room the painting shifted, aged, and became a dry, gray corpse.

On the floor—or ceiling—directly in front of Jenna's feet, someone had scrawled "Don't look up" in blood.

Jenna looked up.

Ornate chairs and tables clung to the ceiling around a polished dance floor, where dead bodies were strewn and heaped on top of each other. A single hand moved, reaching toward them from within the pile and pleading to be pulled free.

"Help me," a muffled voice called. "The ship is alive! She'll kill you all!!"

"I believe the hand," Belma whispered. "We need to get out of here."

A crack ran from the chandelier to the far wall, near the corner, where it expanded into a door-sized hole.

"There," Jenna said.

They shuffled forward as one, stuck to the wall as they edged around the chandelier, waiting for something or someone to fall out of the pile of bodies above them.

Which is why they never saw it coming.

They were sliding along the English hunting portrait when the entire canvas dropped away, crashing down to reveal a man in a blood-soaked tuxedo, his face ruined and bloated.

He lunged for them, bellowing "Abandon ship!"

And that did it.

Jenna forgot about Julian Vance, Martin Ritter, and all of the other trivial real-world problems like pumpkin cookies, unfinished shop construction, and murderers.

She ran for the hole in the far wall, somewhat aware of her friends clinging to her like a life preserver in a vast ocean, but mostly just trying to survive.

And she couldn't help laughing hysterically the entire time.

—

They fled into another black hallway, careening off the walls and stumbling into a stainless steel galley that was thankfully oriented correctly, with the floor on the floor and the ceiling where it should be.

Unfortunately, they interrupted Ghost Ship's head chef while he was preparing a bisque of severed human limbs and wriggling fish, and he was not happy about it. He wore a blood-soaked apron and a surly pig mask under his greasy chef's hat, and as the group tried to edge around the far side of his narrow island he pulled an electric knife and a frying pan off the counter and came after them.

They ran, of course.

Two laps around the island, screaming like fools, until Belma darted into the pantry and through a secret door behind one of the shelves, which led to a dark, twisting hallway with uneven floors and invisible spider webs that brushed against their faces.

One plucked at Jenna's eyelash and she recoiled, clunking her head against Belma's.

"Sorry!"

Belma pulled away and got her face buried in Cabo's armpit.

"Gah! Asparagus!"

"It's not pee!" Cabo yelled.

He stepped to his left and drove Lawrence into the wall, smooshing his face against the cold steel.

"My nostrils!"

They all spilled out of the spider web hallway into Ghost Ship's boiler room, where, obviously, they were going to die.

———

The boiler room was a nest of rusted pipes, valves, and hoses, all of it seeming to move in the shifting firelight coming from the boiler's front grate. The cramped space was about twenty degrees hotter than the hallway, and Jenna immediately broke out in a sheen of sweat.

Someone was thunderously banging on the pipes, but she couldn't find the source. The deafening sound came from the left, then the right, then immediately ahead—was the maniac moving, or was there more than one of them?

"It's too hot!" Belma yelled.

Jenna tugged her and the rest of them along. "Just keep going!"

They cut back and forth through barriers made of pipes and barrels, the temperature getting even hotter and the banging closer until they stood facing the simmering boiler. It was a dead-end.

"Which way?" Cabo yelled.

"What?" Jenna said.

"I said, which—"

Then the boiler's door flung itself open, revealing a glowing, gaping maw large enough for them to walk through if they bent down. Heat poured from within, and Jenna couldn't see how deep the passage-way went, or where it led.

"Nope," Lawrence said. "No way!"

Jenna pulled him close. "What are you going to do, stay here?"

"It's nice here. Cozy. I think I'll open a second store right there, next to the barrel of sludge."

Then the barrel stood up. Human legs in greasy coveralls and heavy work boots stomped toward them, the barrel wobbling above like a demented Jack-in-the-Box. Arms sprung from of the sides and clanged on passing pipes with a huge wrench, and before Jenna could react, Cabo's bodyguard training took over and he swept everyone up in a bear hug and shoved them into the boiler.

"Now I smell like asparagus!" Lawrence bawled.

"Move!" Cabo yelled.

They scampered through the boiler passage and spilled through another hatchway into the cool night air. They were on the deck between the two ship structures, in the maze of pallets and tarps that would take them to the ship's stern and whatever—or whoever—waited for them. Above, the fog pouring from Ghost Ship's bow did its best to obscure the stars, but a few managed to twinkle through.

"What have you idiots gotten me into?" Cabo said.

Belma shook her head. "It wasn't like this last year, we swear."

Jenna breathed deeply, grateful even for the faint smell of fish and seaweed that came with every inhale. The short lull finally gave her a moment to think, and she wondered if Vance had used Ritter's cash to upgrade Ghost Ship. If so, the haunt would take on a whole new level of macabre: literally built upon a man's murder.

She wondered where Vance was at that moment—on the boardwalk terrorizing more patrons?

Stalking her and the rest of the group through the ship?

Lurking somewhere ahead, waiting to fulfill his promise to see Jenna again?

Then, from somewhere in the maze of wood and oilcloth, someone began stomping toward them. Red lantern light flickered through creases and cracks in the walls as it came closer.

No, not someone.

The Captain.

Vance.

He bellowed: "I can see you, Jenna Hooper!"

———

"**R**un!" Jenna yelled.

"Where?" Cabo said.

"Just run!"

She led them into the maze, where a quick left immediately brought them closer to Vance. She took the first right she could, then another, and immediately hit a dead-end.

Lawrence piled into her back, then Cabo and Belma.

Jenna poked at the wood and cloth, searching for another secret exit.

No luck.

The red light from Vance's lantern oozed above

the maze from somewhere—she had no idea where—but it seemed to be getting closer.

"We need to turn around," she said.

Belma turned and commanded, "Follow me!"

Then she didn't do anything else.

Lawrence said, "You have to go somewhere to be followed, Braveheart."

"Shut up, I'm strategizing."

"Oh, good. I hope they serve breakfast here."

While they bickered, Cabo whispered to Jenna, "Captain Vance is kinda stalking you."

"I noticed."

"Do you think he knows that you know? About… you know…"

"I don't see how he could."

"Me neither. I mean, I know too, and he isn't stalking me."

"Maybe Olson already talked to him as a suspect, and Vance somehow knows I'm helping?"

"But that would mean Olson told him. We're the only three people who know about it, and it wasn't me. I'm pretty sure it wasn't you. What would Olson get from telling him?"

Red lantern light stabbed through a crease in the wall to their right.

"I'm coming for ye, lassie!" Vance yelled. The only thing keeping him away was a few slats of wood draped with tattered fabric.

That got Belma moving. She took off, dragging

Lawrence with her. Cabo grabbed the back of his belt and hooked an arm around Jenna.

Before they dove back into the maze, Jenna got close to Cabo's ear and said, "I'll tell you what he gets: If Vance tries anything to stop me, Olson will have a pretty good idea who killed Ritter, won't he?"

———

"**H**ar!" Vance yelled. "Toss those cold fish you're with overboard, Jenna, they're dead weight!"

The maze twisted, turned, and wrapped them in circles. Lawrence briefly tried to find their way by using the North Star, but the light turned out to be a jet, likely flying between Detroit and Minneapolis.

At every corner it seemed like Vance's red lantern got closer: two turns behind them, then one turn ahead, then just on the other side of a wall again. The entire time, Vance continued to laugh and bellow and taunt.

"Why are you running, lassie? Sure, I have crabs, but they're the cute kind!"

"Ghost Ship has the best cruises—straight to the bottom, no stops! Har har!"

Jenna felt relatively safe with her friends, but the maze offered too many blind spots and dead ends. Vance obviously knew the layout—if he had a secret door and his timing was right, he could snatch her away and disappear before anyone knew she was gone.

It's not like she would go easy, and she almost welcomed the idea of being alone with him so she could ask point-blank questions about Ritter.

*You're assuming he won't just conk you on the head and chuck you into the harbor.*

That's true. I'm expecting at least a little humanity.

*From a murder suspect. This is going to turn out very well.*

So each time Vance drew closer and called her name, she burrowed into the group and used them as anchors should the Captain try to drag her out to sea.

She had her face buried in Lawrence's back and her arms wrapped around Belma's neck when Cabo said, "Left, no straight! We're out!"

Jenna popped up like a periscope and saw the hatchway ahead, leading into the stern's structure. She didn't care what waited inside. The doorway was like a cold drink after crossing the desert, a hot bath after falling through ice.

It was glorious.

It was salvation.

Then, it was blocked by the Captain and his lantern.

———

"I'll need some payment before ye pass," the Captain said.

"We already paid!" Belma whimpered.

"Oh no lassie, not silver or gold. I'll be needing something much more precious."

He stroked his ravaged face, making the crabs wriggle and dance. He stood nearly as tall as Cabo, and when he stretched his arms out to the sides the hatchway behind him completely vanished.

"I think I'll be taking one of yer party. Just for a spell, a bit of Captain's courtesy, then I promise you'll get 'em back good as new. Maybe just a bit drowned, but that's to be expected."

"Take me," Cabo said.

"Take him," Lawrence agreed.

The Captain grinned. "Oh, you think you get to pick? Tis the luck of the lake who chooses, and she's a fickle lady."

He pointed at Belma.

"Eenie…"

At Cabo.

"Meenie…"

At Lawrence.

"Minie…"

At Jenna.

"You."

"No way," Cabo said.

The Captain unlocked a hidden panel in the wall

to his left. He swung a hinged pallet open, exposing a doorway that led back into the maze.

"Then it's back to the madness for you all."

Belma and Lawrence both shoved Jenna forward.

"Here you go," Lawrence said.

Belma added, "She likes red wine. It doesn't matter what kind or year,. Or if it's white."

"Hey!" Cabo tugged Jenna back into the group. "Nobody gets left behind."

"Just hold on!" Jenna yelled. She pulled free of everyone and straightened her hoodie, trying to regain some dignity. "I will decide where I go, thank you very much."

The Captain watched, thoroughly amused, as Jenna took a deep breath, gathered herself, and stepped closer to him.

"Jenna," Cabo said.

"I got it."

She stood right in front of the Captain, looking up at the dangling crabs.

"You got something to say to me, buddy? Something you want to try?"

The Captain's bravado faltered. "Er, no, you'll just have to wait and see what lies in store for you, lassie."

"I don't think so pal. I'm onto you. Just come clean, Vance."

Jenna's heart was pounding. This was a huge risk. If Vance was involved with Ritter's murder, she was deliberately letting him know—or confirming, if he already suspected—that she was on the case. If he had plans to stop her, they were about to go into full effect.

The Captain blinked. "Uh, har. Right here?"

"I'm waiting."

Jenna felt about one-tenth as brave as she sounded. If that. Her friends certainly offered confidence, but until that moment she hadn't considered the possibility that all of Vance's Ghost Ship crew could be involved. If they swarmed from the maze and treated all four Main Streeters as a threat, McTavish might just have the whole block to himself.

The Captain glanced over Jenna's shoulder. Gauging, she assumed, how quickly he'd have to move to yank her into the maze and slam the secret door shut behind him.

"Fine then, lassie. Here we go."

Jenna braced herself.

Then the Captain completely broke character and became Julian Vance, restaurant and steamship owner.

"Jenna, will you have dinner with me this week?"

———

Jenna felt like she'd been smacked with a boat oar. "Dinner?"

"Yes," Vance said. "At my restaurant. I know it's

super lame to ask you on a date to my own place, but it really is the best in town. We can go anywhere you like, though."

Jenna was baffled. "Have you been flirting with me this whole time? Yelling my name and everything? This is flirting?"

Vance shuffled his feet and winced. "What can I say? I specialize in lame. But people get a lot more frightened if you get specific like that. We try to do it with every group, if we catch a name. That Hannah girl in front of you, man. She was a mess. Sorry if you and your friends got too freaked out."

"Why would we be freaked out?" Lawrence said. "You only tried to massacre all of us and abduct Jenna."

"Guilty."

"Yeah, what's with the kidnapping?" Jenna asked. "Is that flirting too?"

A high-pitched scream from somewhere in the maze behind them made everyone turn.

"Duty calls," Vance said. "Tell you what—you guys wait by the exit when you're done, I'll come find you. I mean, I'll come get the lot of you, lassie! You and your landlubber losers! Har!"

And he was gone, through the secret door and back into the maze to cause more havoc.

"What just happened?" Belma said.

"I have no idea," Jenna replied.

But she thought: *Did I just get asked out by a murderer?*

A GRAVE HALLOWEEN IN LOST HAVEN · 127

The rest of Ghost Ship was a blur.

Jenna stumbled through with the group, barely registering the characters and animatronics that leaped, banged, hissed, and stomped toward them. Her mind was reeling from the encounter with Vance and what it could mean.

What she did notice:

Lawrence's screams were a constant soundtrack, though his voice had grown hoarse since the encounter with Vance.

Belma got startled by a man dressed like a killer squid and hip-checked him through a piece of flimsy paneling.

In a room decorated like a decrepit captain's quarters, something touched Cabo's neck and he dove across the bed, did a full somersault, and landed on his feet before disappearing through a doorway, forcing everyone else to sprint to catch up.

Then they reached a hallway with a curtained doorway at the end. A glowing "Lifeboats" sign hung above the drapes, and the opening was only wide enough for one person at a time.

Lawrence yelled, "Lifeboats! Remember what the picture guy said? Abandon ship!"

"Wait, what?" Jenna said. "Are you sure? Be careful!"

But he was already gone. Lawrence pulled loose from the group and ran ahead, slapped through the curtains and disappeared.

His raspy scream dwindled before ending with a grunt.

"I am so torn right now," Belma said. "I really want him to be in terrified agony, but I also really want that to be the friggin' exit. Either way, I gotta know."

She eased up to the heavy curtain and poked a finger through.

"Lawrence?"

Nothing.

She pushed her hand through and flapped it around to deter any lurking monsters.

"Lawrence, don't you be waiting to scare me! I will knock you flat out!"

Silence.

"Want me to go?" Cabo said.

Belma scowled. "No way. If you get there first and he's messed up, you'll help him. I want to make fun of him. So wait your turn."

She took a deep breath and stepped through.

Her scream dwindled and got cut off with a grunt.

Jenna and Cabo looked at each other.

"This is going to sound chicken," Cabo said, "but you go. I don't want to leave you here by yourself."

"Normally I might bristle at the possible sexism of that, or argue that you should go first because I want to make sure everyone makes it through."

"But…"

"But I'll be honest. I'm a little freaked out right now."

"Yeah," Cabo said. "Vance…"

"Not here—anybody could be watching and listening. And you come through right behind me, got it?"

"I'll probably knock you down on the other side of the curtain."

"Deal."

Jenna crept toward the curtain, positive that Lawrence, Belma, or somebody with a fire-spewing chainsaw was going to burst through. She jabbed the heavy fabric as a decoy.

Nothing.

"Here I come!" she tried.

Complete and utter stillness.

She steeled herself and was preparing to take a step forward, maybe, when Cabo grabbed her shirt from behind and leaned close.

"Hey," he whispered. "If Vance is waiting for you through there, shout a code word."

"What code word?"

Cabo paused. "Say, 'Vance is here.'"

"Brilliant. Now can you do me a little favor? And never tell anyone about it?"

"Sure."

"Can you give me a push?"

"A push?" Cabo said.

"Yeah. Otherwise I'm going to stand here until November first when they take all of this down around me."

"Uh, okay. But don't get mad at me if you don't like what's on the other side of this curtain."

"No promises."

Cabo shook his head. "Ready? One. Two."

He shoved her on two, knowing she would resist if he waited until three. Jenna flew through the curtain with her hands raised in the official karate-chop position, though she'd never karate-chopped anything in her life except maybe a mosquito, by accident.

She took one step into total darkness.

On the second step, the floor fell out from under her. She landed on something soft and slid down, screaming as she plummeted along a steep slope through a pitch-black shaft, bursting through another curtain into blinding light.

She bounced to a stop in a little corral at the bottom of the inflatable slide, then rose, confused and blinking, to find Lawrence and Belma standing on the boardwalk with Julian Vance, all of them laughing hysterically at her graceless exit from Ghost Ship.

"Six-point-five," Lawrence scored. "I gave you the point five for the ladylike grunt when you hit the wall there."

"You want ladylike?" Jenna said. "Well f—"

Then she froze as the slide shuddered beneath her. Foregoing dignity, she scrambled off the landing pad just as Cabo tumbled through the final curtain, screaming and cursing.

"Like a true sailor," Vance laughed.

Cabo thundered down the slide, arms and legs akimbo, and crashed to a stop in the inflatable catch basin. He lay with his face wedged into the corner and didn't move.

Jenna reached in and tugged his shoe. "Cabo? You okay?"

He slowly rolled onto his back and stared up at the October sky.

"I seriously hate all of you for making me do that. Mostly because you were right. It was a lot of fun."

—

The five of them sat at a wooden picnic table near the end of the dock below Ghost Ship's towering stern. The slide exit was about forty feet away, and every time someone plummeted into the crash pad they all cackled with delight.

"I could watch this all night," Lawrence said. "Maybe all year."

Vance nodded, the crabs on his face dancing. "We talked about setting up a camera so people could go to our website and watch a live feed, but it would ruin the surprise ending for anyone who saw it, then came through. I'd still love to have the footage though."

Lawrence brightened with an idea: "You could use Belma's clip to blackmail her! She came out of that thing cussing like a drunken hockey player."

Belma shrugged. "I swear at my customers too. They're used to it."

They all stopped to watch a twenty-something man somersault down the slide with little high-pitched *Eeeps!* escaping with every impact. He landed in a pile and immediately scrambled to his feet, checking his waxed mustache to make sure it was still there.

"Hipsters," Vance mumbled. "Oh, how I love scaring hipsters."

"Did one of your people try to abduct him too?" Jenna asked. "Or was that just for me?"

"Oh, him too," Vance said. "Him or someone in his group. But your abduction was special. And…now that I've said that, I realize how creepy it sounds. But it was special. Well, it was *supposed* to be, until you called me out."

He smiled a genuine, non-crazy Ghost Ship captain grin.

"I wanted a few minutes alone so I could ask you out with a little more, ah, privacy, which we still don't have. But yeah, my crew and I do the whole 'pay the price' bit with every group. We separate one of them out for a short trip alone through a couple rooms, and then they get reunited with the rest."

"Why?" Cabo said. "Other than to be a complete maniac, of course."

"Because it's scary," Vance said. "The solo person is scared, of course, and the rest of the group is freaked because their friend is gone. It also helps with resells. The people in the group all want to know what it was like getting nabbed, and the solo person wants to see what they missed with the group."

He rubbed his fingers and thumb together.

"Cha-ching, my friends."

"Well," Jenna said, "you obviously put a ton of work and money into the whole thing since last year, so I hope you do get some repeat customers."

Vance beamed. "You noticed the changes?"

"Uh, yeah," Belma said. "The upside-down room? The secret boiler door? The squid man? He's not allowed to sue me, by the way—I hip-checked him out of self-defense. And I'm sure we missed a bunch of other stuff because we were too scared to look at it."

"Music to my ears," Vance laughed.

Jenna looked up at the towering ship, shook her head, and turned to Vance. "It had to be a huge investment."

"I found some backers in Chicago who see the potential in it. I'm not sure which is scarier—my haunted house, or answering to a group of folks who lent me money. So, since you missed a bunch of stuff, and speaking of repeat customers..."

Cabo groaned. "I'm gonna need a month or so to get my heart rate back to normal."

"Ah, the haunter's dilemma," Vance said. "Sometimes the scares are *too* effective."

Jenna said, "We were scared, but not as scared as the other haunts should be. Do they know how intense Ghost Ship is this year?"

"Come on, you know this town. They probably knew before I did. Watch, Kemp will have a slide added to No Sanctuary before the month is over. Animatronic, of course."

Jenna laughed. "If Martin Ritter was still alive, he'd probably steal the idea along with the cash."

Vance frowned. "Ritter? What do you mean, 'still alive'?"

It was hard to tell with the makeup and lack of light, but Jenna didn't notice any nervous tics or glances. Was he truly confused, or faking it?

"You didn't hear?" she said.

"Hear what?"

"Ritter…he's the dead body we found in the park last night. Apparently it's all over town. I'm surprised your phone isn't blowing up."

Vance blinked, seemingly stunned. "Ritter? You're serious?"

"Unless the medical examiner finds out otherwise, but…yeah."

"Oh, man," Vance said, his voice distant. "I'm sure my phone is blowing up, but I don't carry it during operational hours. Nobody here does, it's policy. Too distracting. We use radios to communicate, but nothing from the outside. Ritter? Wow. I thought he was a total scumbag, turns out he was, well…what? Murdered?"

"They're investigating that now," Jenna said, watching Vance closely. He was either being completely honest, or he'd upgraded his acting skills along with Ghost Ship. "If he was murdered, it's scary to think the killer might still be around."

"Yeah, jeez. I wonder if it was because of who Ritter was—I mean, I don't want to say he had it coming, but there are quite a few people in town who are probably celebrating the news—or the money."

Cabo asked, "Was he a scumbag before he allegedly stole the money?"

"Oh, yeah," Vance said. "I don't want to speak ill of the dead…Look, the guy put on a good haunt, but he was a fanatic about what he thought was the 'right' way to do it. And it's fine to advertise how well you scare, but to go around bragging about how badly you got one particular person? That's just tacky."

"You mean Unflappable Bob?" Jenna said.

Vance nodded. "Between you, me, and the table, I'm going to get him this year. The dude is not a fan of fire, apparently, and I had the whole boiler room set designed just for him."

Belma's mouth fell open. "All that for one person?"

"Let's say it's *inspired* by him. It's *for* everyone,

because it works, obviously. And the abduction thing won't work on him, because he goes through alone. I actually love the guy—he forces me to get better at terrifying people. But if you're looking for someone with an itch to kill Ritter, old Unflappable Bob was pretty steamed about his legend being ruined."

"Steamed," Jenna said. "Nice."

Vance shrugged. "Like I said, I specialize in lame."

Another victim tumbled down the slide, screaming and grunting.

"Perfect timing," Vance said. He pulled a large pocket watch from somewhere within his layers of dusty, tattered captain's garb. "And I need to get back at it. Thar be souls to shudder and bones to rattle, yar, yar, etcetera, etcetera. And Miss Jenna, I'll be stopping by yer shop tomorrow to chat about our fancy pants date, if ye don't mind."

Jenna couldn't help smiling. "I open at eight. But I might be a little late—we have two more haunts to hit and I'm already keeping the lights on tonight. Sleep may be limited."

"Then I'll be seeing you tomorrow, me fine lass, but not too early after the red sky in the morning." He stood and tipped his captain's hat at the table. "Folks. Thank ye for visiting Ghost Ship and leaving yer screams behind. We'll take good care of them. Next time, maybe you'll decide to stay...forever! Har har!"

———

Vance whirled away into the fog and red light, pausing next to the slide's landing pad to crouch down, wait for a middle-aged woman to struggle to her feet, then popped up and startled her so badly she tried to climb back up the slide.

"I am so happy right now," Lawrence said. He turned to Jenna. "So?"

"So, what?"

"Don't 'so what' me. Are you going to go out with him?"

Jenna glanced at Cabo, the only other person at the table who knew Vance was on the suspect list. He gave a tiny shrug, absolutely no help at all.

"I think I need to sort some things out first."

Lawrence caught the glance. "Wait a minute. You and Cabo?"

Jenna's mind immediately finished that question like so: 'You and Cabo are working together to solve Ritter's murder and you didn't include us?'

But that's not the question he was asking.

"Well…" she started.

Lawrence's eyes boggled.

Belma grinned like a wolf.

Cabo raised his hands. "Hold on! Jenna, he's asking if you and I are, you know."

"Yeah, I know. With Olson. And Ritter."

Lawrence made a choking sound, like he might hack out the last month of meals.

Belma gripped the table to keep from spinning off her seat.

"No, no," Cabo said. "We're helping Olson solve Ritter's murder. That's it. We're not doing anything else that would prevent Jenna from going on a date with Vance. We're just friends."

"Oh!" Jenna said. "What? No. Come on. I mean… Huh?"

She was so flustered, caught between not offending Cabo and the revelation about Olson and Ritter, the words fell out before she could approve them.

"I mean, Vance is pretty much our number-one suspect in Ritter's death, right? It would be stupid of me to go out on a date with him. Right? Oh! Unless it's to gather information. What do they call that?"

"A slut?" Belma offered.

"A honeypot! A woman spy who's all, hubba-hubba, and the guy is like, hey baby, and he tells her everything. I guess I could try that, but what if Vance catches on and tries to kill me, like I thought he was doing this whole time at the haunt?"

Lawrence closed his eyes. "Jenna. Stop talking. My crazy can't keep up with yours."

"You guys think Vance killed Ritter?" Belma said.

Cabo shrugged. "He's on the list."

"Along with who else?"

Jenna, blushing hard enough to feel like she had a sunburn, pulled the folded legal sheet from her back pocket and smoothed it on the table.

"You're carrying around a list of murder suspects?" Belma asked.

"Yes," Jenna said, like it was as normal as wearing a watch.

Lawrence touched the paper. "Okay, this is probably the best way to be the next person on the list of murder victims, but we can talk about that later."

He and Belma dropped over the sheet and began mumbling to each other.

"Yep," Lawrence said. "Yep."

Belma nodded. "Mm-hmm. She's a black widow for sure." She glanced up at Jenna. "But look, it makes sense that Vance is on this list, but if he murdered Ritter, he's not going to massacre you on a date at his own restaurant. I say it's worth the risk, just in case he's innocent."

"She's not *that* desperate," Lawrence said.

Belma looked at him, eyebrows raised.

"Okay, maybe she is," he said. "I can see you two together. The owner of Lakeside Grille and Ghost Ship with the owner of the Welcome Shoppe? You'd be *the* Lost Haven power couple. Assuming, of course, he isn't a psycho. But listen, all of you: Ritter's nasty corpse isn't going anywhere. He'll still be dead tomorrow. Right now, we're missing the most important part of this whole situation."

Jenna pulled her notes back and extracted a pen, ready to go.

"What are we missing?" she asked.

Lawrence stood at the end of the table and leaned on both hands, looming over the rest of them.

"Jay Cabo: Is your underwear dry?"

———

**H**is underwear completely dry, Cabo led the way off the boardwalk and onto Shoreline Drive, which would take them east and south along the edge of the marina if they turned right. Instead, he kept going straight and stopped at the entrance to the Lakeside Grille, which was closed this late on a Sunday, and peered through the window.

"So this is all Vance's, huh?"

"Soon to be Jenna's," Belma cooed.

"Stop it," Jenna said.

But she was suddenly intrigued.

The restaurant's exterior was white brick with black trim and ornate light fixtures. Inside, dim security lights showed a large waiting area with plush chairs and couches, and then a wall made of semiopaque glass with a wide opening that led to the dining room.

Beyond that, Jenna could see the silhouettes of the huge windows and deck overlooking Lost Haven harbor.

She had to admit, it was slightly thrilling to imagine walking through the front doors, waving at the host, and cruising straight to a reserved table on the deck, which typically needed to be claimed weeks in advance and even then required a certain level of social status in Lost Haven.

She could sit there for the Sunday brunch, enjoying her coffee and stack of books while taking her time with the amazing buffet of omelets, waffles, bacon, prime rib, crab legs, and enough desserts to feed a fleet. And the bread!

*Uh, is Julian Vance there too?*

Oh yeah…

Jenna mentally replaced the stack of books with Vance to test it out.

Verdict: Not as exciting.

*Maybe he likes to sit and read and not talk to anyone too?*

Now we're getting somewhere.

"Jenna!"

She snapped out of it to find the rest of her group walking away along Shoreline Drive. Lawrence stood with his arms crossed.

"Stop fantasizing about Vance's pants and let's go. No Sanctuary awaits."

Jenna followed, grumbling, "I wasn't fantasizing about Vance's pants…"

"Of course you weren't," he said. "Let me guess: Books. And the brunch buffet."

"Shut up," Jenna said.

"And bread. You know what? I think we're on to

Vance. His devious plan is to take you on a date and kill you with carbs."

Jenna considered it, and then shrugged. "There are worse ways to go."

# CHAPTER 7

No Sanctuary was south of downtown along the eastern curve of Lost Haven Harbor, overlooking the water and Shoreline Drive which, aptly, followed the shoreline. The haunted house crouched like Cerberus on the main road into downtown and collected all of the incoming Halloween traffic, snarling Shoreline and the side streets every October.

As they navigated through the vehicles crammed into front yards and wedged along the curb, Cabo said, "Doesn't this upset the neighbors a bit?"

"Oh, they despise it," Lawrence said. "They try to shut Kemp down every year."

"Lawrence..." Jenna said.

"What?"

"It's October..."

"So? Oh, wait, sorry: They try to shut *Skull Monger* down every year."

"Thank you," Jenna said. She turned to Cabo. "He's right. The neighborhood hates it, the Lost

Haven Historical Society thinks it's an atrocity, and Preacher Hank calls it an abomination."

"Seems like Kemp—er, Skull Monger—has made a few enemies."

"And he loves it," Belma said. "He likes stirring the pot almost as much as I do. He totally embraces the whole 'no such thing as bad publicity' approach."

They reached the sidewalk across from No Sanctuary and stopped to take it all in.

"I can see that," Cabo said.

The Victorian mansion was five stories high and took up half of the residential block. It was set back from the road a bit, allowing enough room in the front yard for a small cemetery complete with open graves oozing mist and a sickly green light.

Years ago, after months of arguments with the Lost Haven Historical Society, Kemp had gotten approval to renovate the attic windows. He'd built exact replicas of the frames from The Amityville Horror, and now they glared down at the street like furious red eyes.

An animatronic zombie stood near the sidewalk, its head lolling in an erratic pattern. It held a hand-scrawled sign dripping with blood-red paint, offering NO SANCTUARY with an arrow pointing toward the mansion, and SANCTUARY, pointing down into the graves.

More ragged and rotting zombies held signs declaring:

## REVILED BY NEIGHBORS

## CURSED BY THE HOLY

## CONDEMNED BY HEALTH INSPECTORS

"That last one, there," Cabo said. "Is that true?"

"Maybe," Belma said.

Cabo frowned.

Jenna said, "The plot of land beneath this mansion was unused since the founding of Sanctuary, even when the town was at its busiest. No one would set foot upon the soil, let alone build upon it."

"Why not?" Cabo said.

"Because it was cursed."

Cabo rolled his eyes. "I never thought I'd be disappointed that you *weren't* talking about real history."

"Oh, this is real," Jenna said, trying to use her most foreboding voice. It came out sounding like she had a bit of a cold.

"The founding families knew it was cursed, so they stayed away. But when an outsider came to town, flashing his money and bragging about how one day he'd own the town, the families wanted to teach him a lesson. So they sold him this prime real estate, overlooking the harbor, and watched as he started to build what was supposed to be the largest mansion in Sanctuary."

"Bigger than Horizon House?" Cabo said.

Jenna nodded. "That was the plan. But the man couldn't spread out, since his plot was only half a block, so he went up. The design called for eight stories, enough square footage to stake his claim as the biggest house in town, but as soon as they broke ground strange things started to happen."

"Strange things?" Cabo said.

"He had to bring in workers from out of town, because no one here would take the job. But the outsiders started getting sick. And injured."

"Tools were thrown at them, and into the harbor, by invisible hands," Lawrence said.

Cabo was unconvinced. "What?"

Belma pointed at the yard. "The ground opened up and swallowed construction materials. Sometimes even workers."

"Come on."

"The land was cursed," Jenna said. "Evil. One of the few places on earth where the barrier between our world and hell is extremely thin. A gateway. The founding families eventually told the man, figuring their point had been made. But he continued to build. His laborers started leaving or disappearing, one by one, until it was just the owner and a last remaining worker. The house was only five stories high, and the man swore he'd get to eight if it took him the rest of his life. Well, the worker knew something terrible was going to happen to him if he stayed, so he gathered all of the survivors who'd already abandoned the project and brought them back to town for one final night.

"He also summoned a priest, who blessed the men and the construction materials as the sun was setting. The owner wasn't on-site, so the workers had no interference as they put a roof on the fifth floor as quickly as they could. The priest performed a ceremony that sealed the evil inside the house, but just as he finished the owner returned."

"What did he do?" Cabo asked, his skepticism shoved aside by morbid curiosity.

"He demanded that they tear the roof off and keep working," Jenna said. "The workers refused, and the man became violent. They had to subdue him and tie him up, and fearing his wrath and the Lost Haven constable, they locked him inside the house and left town."

Cabo looked at the mansion. "So he decided to stop building?"

"I wouldn't say that," Jenna said. "No one saw him again after that night. He was locked in the house all night with pure evil, and when the sun rose the next morning he was gone. The house was still locked from the outside, and the ropes used to bind him were coiled neatly at the top of the basement stairs."

Cabo swallowed. "How much of that is true?"

"All of it," Jenna said. "And now, every October, the gateway opens again and the evil comes out to play, led by the man who built the house on cursed ground. He continues to build his nightmare home, stretching the floor plan into hell to become the largest mansion in Lost Haven. And that man's name... is Jay Cabo."

"Aww, shut up!" Cabo cried.

Lawrence cackled with delight. "Oh, she got you good."

"Yeah yeah, I was a little sucked in," Cabo said.

"A little," Belma scoffed. "Your mouth dropped open halfway through and kept going until the end. Now come on. Those pants aren't gonna wet themselves."

———

A line of patrons stretched from the front door, across the porch and down the walkway to the street. A group of teenagers scampered down the cobblestone driveway from somewhere behind the mansion, having survived the ordeal, and disappeared into the night laughing and gasping for air.

"We should do our haunt tour on Sunday every year," Lawrence said. "On Fridays and Saturdays this line goes all the way to Main Street."

Jenna wasn't so sure anymore. "Sometimes the actors are worn out by Sunday night and the experience isn't as good. Obviously not the case with Ghost Ship, and not a factor with No Sanctuary, since it's all animatronics. But I sort of like waiting in line. It builds the anticipation."

Lawrence shook his head. "Can I get you a shirt that says, 'I sort of like waiting in line'? It would seriously tell everyone everything they need to know about you."

"No," Jenna said. "And here comes another group down the road, so get in line, smarty, unless you want to wait even longer."

They scrambled through the parked cars toward the mansion, jumping into line.

Cabo tugged them all in close for a private conversation. "You guys see Kemp anywhere?"

"Skull Monger," Jenna corrected.

"No. I'm not calling him that anymore. It's silly, and it takes too long to say. Kemp. One syllable. And it's his name, so…that's what I'm calling him. Do you see him?"

Feeling somewhat chastised, Jenna scanned the front yard. "Not unless he's disguised as one of the zombies, which he totally could be."

"The haunt's still running, so I guess he didn't leave town when word got out about Ritter," Cabo said. Then, to Lawrence and Belma: "We figured whoever killed him might freak out and try to disappear when the body was identified. We just didn't know his name was going to come out this quickly."

"Vance has a hot date," Lawrence said, "so he's not going anywhere. Well, maybe after he kills Jenna."

"Thanks," Jenna said.

"No Sanctuary is all animatronics," Belma said. "Skull Monger—or, um, Kemp—could turn it on, let it run, and bail. He'd be gone for hours before anyone realized it."

Jenna leaned into the group. "Listen, I really appreciate everyone jumping in to help, but I don't want to put you at any risk. I know what I'm getting into, and so does Cabo. If you two want to stay out, not get involved, it might be best if you weren't with us going through the haunts."

"Are you out of your mind?" Belma said. "This jacks up the haunted house experience by about a million. And if one of these crazy haunters is involved with Ritter's death, it could put a serious damper on Halloween in Lost Haven. I want to get this solved as soon as possible, ideally with a murderer who has nothing to do with our haunts, or Halloween in general, so we can get back to normal and scare the crap out of each other."

Lawrence nodded. "What she said. But with much, much less spittle."

"Okay," Jenna said. "Welcome to the team. The priority here is spotting Kemp. Skull Monger. You know who. We need to ask him a few careful questions. If he's still around, he's either innocent, hasn't heard Ritter's name yet, or he thinks he can get away with the murder."

"Let's go see if we can find out which," Cabo said. "Without getting killed, preferably."

"Preferably," they all agreed.

—

The line moved quickly.

Maybe a little too quickly for Jenna, who was hoping to catch a glimpse of Kemp outside the haunt and save a trip through, at least for tonight. She'd be more than happy to run and scream and laugh once Ritter's murderer was caught and stashed away, rather than potentially lurking and plotting to thwart anyone involved with the investigation.

The risk didn't seem to bother Belma and Lawrence. They were relishing the amped-up fear, clutching at Cabo's arms and hopping up and down as they approached the wide front steps of the mansion's porch. A constant, dreadful bass rumbled from the house, punctured by woeful moans and pleas for mercy. Jenna assumed—hoped—they were part of the soundtrack.

The deep porch stretched the entire width of the house, and during the summer it was tastefully decorated with wicker furniture, massive ferns and lazy ceiling fans.

For October, hundreds of burned, ragged clown dolls were heaped on both sides of the entrance, forming a funnel from the stairs to the front door. There was literally no way to go but forward once they were on the porch. A single, bare yellow bulb dangling from the ceiling flickered and made the dolls seem to move.

The wooden stairs creaked beneath Jenna's feet as she led the way. The clown dolls watched, silently mocking her growing terror.

Behind her, Lawrence repeated a mantra: "They're not real. They're not real."

"Yes they are," Belma said. "Look, I can touch them."

"They're not real. They're not real."

Belma asked Cabo, "Do you like clowns?"

"Nobody likes clowns," he replied through clenched teeth.

"Oh, I think they're cute," Belma said.

"Psst."

The four of them stopped.

"Did you hear that?" Lawrence said.

Jenna frowned. "I thought it was you."

Lawrence shook his head.

"Psst. Help me."

Belma pointed. "It's coming from the clown dolls. That one, the one with the pacifier."

"Come closer." The voice did seem to be coming from the pacifier clown, but not from its mouth. More like its belly, or from just behind it.

"Uhh," Belma said.

"Chicken," Lawrence muttered from behind Cabo.

That was all it took. Belma leaned closer to the clown wall and reached for the one with the pacifier. When her finger was an inch away a sharp burst of air horn blared from one of the dolls' mouths. Belma shrieked, fell back against Cabo, bounced off him and smooshed her face into Jenna's shoulder.

Lawrence screamed with her, clutching his heart and trying to decide what to stare at: Belma's humiliation or the horrendous clowns.

When Belma finally spun to a stop, Lawrence tried to high-five the dolls.

"Worth it. So worth it."

"Okay," Jenna breathed. "We're okay. Wow. The haunted house hasn't even started yet. Okay."

A touch-screen tablet was mounted next to the front door with "VICTIMS:" on the screen. Jenna tapped the 2 button and held her buy-one-get-one-free coupon up so the tablet camera could scan it.

The cost for a single admission showed as the amount due, and Jenna swiped her card through the heavy-duty slot mounted next to the tablet.

A moment later the tablet displayed:

## 2 MAY ENTER

## ONE AT A TIME THROUGH THE DOORWAY TO HELL, PLEASE

"So polite," Cabo said. "And I'm impressed by the use of technology."

"Kemp will do anything to avoid working with people," Jenna said. "Who's first, you or me?"

Cabo eyed the entrance. It had been customized with a tall, narrow revolving door. Each compartment of the door was barely big enough for one person, and it served multiple purposes. One person per compartment allowed the system to match the number of purchases with the number of patrons, but most importantly it forced people to separate from their group and step through the door alone into whatever was on the other side.

"I'll go first," Cabo said, sounding like he expected to encounter a firing squad on the other side.

He stepped into the revolving door and had to wriggle a bit to make his shoulders fit, then disappeared.

The tablet changed:

### 1 MAY ENTER

"See you on the other side," Jenna said, trying to mask her anxiety by laughing maniacally as she followed Cabo.

Belma had her own coupon ready. "She sounds like a terrified hyena."

—

The crew regrouped just inside the revolving door. They stared down a long, dark hallway toward the far end, where a set of rickety elevator doors stood open, the interior illuminated by another flickering bulb. A huge man in black hooded robes waited inside for them.

*Skull Monger?* Jenna thought.

There was only one way to find out.

The hallway seemed to stretch for a hundred yards, far beyond the actual depth of the mansion.

The high walls were stained, peeling wallpaper hung with portraits of grim-looking ancestors. One showed a man with huge muttonchops, a severe frown, and glowing eyes that followed Jenna and her crew as they shuffled past. Having learned their lesson about haunted portraits at Ghost Ship, Jenna kept to the center of the hallway and the other three fell into single-file behind her.

"Hey, I'm in the back!" Belma yelled.

"Let us know if you get massacred!" Lawrence replied from the relative safety of third in line. "And let go of my belt!"

"Never!"

They passed a large frame featuring a woman holding a small dog in her lap. Both seemed happy enough, until black blood oozed from their grinning mouths.

Jenna sped up, each step taking them closer to

the elevator and the man waiting within, about ten miles away.

Then something touched her head.

She looked up and saw the ceiling, about three inches from her nose. The hallway seemed to be closing in and she had a moment of true panic when she thought her vision was warped, as she reached out and touched one wall, then the other, alarmingly close. It wasn't an optical illusion—the hallway was collapsing in on them.

"What's the hold-up?" Belma hollered. "I can't see anything from back here!"

"The hallway is shrinking!" Jenna yelled back. The elevator was ahead, though she had no idea how far away it truly was.

The huge robed man waited for them, watching and unmoving.

She glanced behind her. Cabo was nearly doubled-over, Lawrence was hunched, and while Belma didn't seem to notice the encroaching room, her eyes were wide with fear.

"Something is behind me! It's getting closer!"

"Are you one-hundred percent sure it's not just your butt?" Lawrence laughed at his own joke, but terror made it sound like a whimper.

"Go!" Belma screamed.

Jenna went, straight into the elevator to hell.

—

J enna pulled the group into the elevator where they huddled in the back corner as far from the robed figure as possible. A few laws of physics may have been broken as four objects—people in this case—managed to occupy the same corner simultaneously.

The doors groaned shut. The only light came from sickly green fluorescent bulbs recessed along the edge of the ceiling, flickering and bickering with each other in an erratic pattern. Jenna scanned the walls for any possible hidden escape—or attack—routes, and only found crusty red grooves where fingernails had clawed at the wood.

The robed figure didn't move. It had to be a man Jenna figured, under the piles of black, dusty fabric. The person loomed taller than Cabo and the shoulders seemed to take up half the elevator. Kemp wasn't that big, but with the right wardrobe choices and boots, he could be.

Lawrence plugged his nose. "Cabo. How have you *not* sweated all of the asparagus out by now?"

"It was a lot of asparagus," Cabo said. He stared at the robed figure like it was an ornery snake found under his pillow.

Something shifted under the robes, and then an arm emerged. It was wrapped in filthy bandages, the hand sheathed in a black leather glove. Huge fingers jabbed into the elevator's control panel and caused a series of flashes inside the works. A wisp of smoke curled out as the elevator rumbled to life, shaking everything from Jenna's toes to the tips of her hair.

The floor shuddered and cables shrieked. Random bands of red light rose in the narrow gap between the doors, moving faster and faster as the elevator plummeted.

Jenna's heart thudded. They were locked in the tiny space with a possible murderer, one who could be desperate to keep his involvement with the crime hidden at any cost. Her breath caught in her throat, tainted by the acrid smoke and palpable fear in the elevator.

"Was this thing here last year?" Cabo whispered.

Belma and Lawrence both shook their heads. Neither one of them wanted to disturb the robed man, whoever it was.

Cabo said, "Does this place really have a basement this deep?"

"Shut up," Belma hissed.

The robed figure turned, slowly and silently, the black folds barely shifting. He looked down at them from deep within the dark hood, which hid his face completely.

"It was him," Belma said, pointing at Cabo.

Cabo studied the shadowed hood. "I don't even think there's a person in there."

"Why risk it?" Lawrence asked. He was staring straight into the corner behind them, employing the questionable theory that if he didn't see something, it didn't exist and therefore couldn't get him. He was terrified, along with Belma.

Cabo was definitely uneasy, but his response was to face the potential danger, even if he didn't like what he was seeing.

Jenna, near panic, took a different approach altogether.

"Hey, Kemp!" she shouted.

Lawrence moaned, "Oh, good lord…"

"Kemp, is that you?" She deliberately used his real name rather than Skull Monger, knowing it would eventually provoke him.

"Are you trying to get us killed?" Belma whispered.

"I'm trying to get this over with—I can't do another haunt trip like Ghost Ship, it was too much."

Then, without really thinking about or planning it, she blurted, "Kemp, did you kill Martin Ritter?"

"Jenna!" Cabo yelled, and then muttered, "Well, if he didn't know we were helping Olson, he does now."

Jenna ignored him. "Come on. Speak up, buddy."

She poked the robes in the general area of the stomach and her finger thumped against something hard. She poked again, unembarrassed about invading Kemp's personal space. This time her finger traveled into the abdominal cavity, deep enough that it should have been touching his spine.

"Hold on."

She dove into the robes, pulling and lifting the

heavy fabric over her head like she was about to take a photograph in the eighteen hundreds.

"It was nice knowing Jenna," Lawrence said. "Most of the time."

"It's okay, it's an animatronic," she hollered from inside the robes, where she could barely make out the steel framework and pneumatic hoses. She escaped the drapery and looked up at the still-hidden face, or whatever was in there under the hood.

"Not Kemp," her voice a mix of relief and disappointment. She wanted the anticipation and tension of encountering him to be over, but she was glad her brief meltdown hadn't done any damage to the investigation.

"Sorry everybody. I kind of lost it there for a moment."

"Kind of?" Belma said.

"I'm okay now. I got it out of my system, and Kemp is none the wiser. He should be completely unaware that we're looking into Ritter's death."

Then the fluorescents flickered just right—or wrong, depending—and she caught a small glint inside the hood.

"Oh, no..."

"What?" Cabo said.

The elevator ground and whined to a halt. The doors creaked open, revealing a subterranean passageway made of glistening stone walls covered in mold, fungus, and heavy with cobwebs. A faint, ominous green light permeated the area, its source unknown. All other sounds were drowned out by the constant, throbbing bass that made their clothes vibrate.

Jenna didn't notice any of it.

She reached up and pulled the hood open, revealing the video camera mounted within. Her heart began thudding again. She let the hood fall back into place and dropped to her knees, rooting around in the piles of black cloth pooled at the base of the animatronics.

Behind her, Lawrence said, "What on earth are you doing?"

"Looking for ...this!" She found the video and power cables stapled to the elevator floor. They ran next to a slightly larger pneumatic hose into the corner with the control panel and went up the wall, painted the same dingy, rusty gray and brown as the rest of the small room. All three disappeared through a hole in the top corner.

Jenna stepped out of the elevator, waving for the others to follow. The passageway went straight for a couple yards then took a sharp turn to the left, where a barrier of rolling fog blocked any further vision.

She peered up and found where the two cables and hose emerged from the elevator. They followed the top of the stone wall before flowing into a gray pipe secured to the upper corner of the foggy passageway. More cords and hoses joined them, coming from terrors still unseen.

The Main Street crew huddled together at the turn.

"Guys," Jenna said, "I may have just tipped off Ritter's murderer. We have to find where that camera goes."

"In here?" Belma was incredulous, gesturing at the fog, darkness, and certain chaos that awaited them in the passageway and beyond.

"In here," Jenna confirmed. She pointed at the gray pipe. "We just have to follow that. I hope. If Kemp hasn't seen the footage yet, we can erase it."

"And if he has?" Cabo asked.

"Then we hope he didn't kill Ritter. And, if he did, that he has a really, really good sense of humor about it. Ready?"

"Are you kidding me?" Belma said.

Lawrence hugged himself. "You're out of your mind."

"This is not a good idea," Cabo said.

Jenna waded into the fog, hoping they would follow.

And that Martin Ritter's killer wasn't creeping toward her, invisible until it was too late.

—

The crew did follow. They piled in behind Jenna and clung to her in the fog, battling for the relative safety of middle wedge despite Cabo's demands that his reserved position there be honored and unchallenged.

They argued and shoved while Jenna eased forward, searching for glimpses of the pipe through the shifting fog. The passageway stretched for ten hesitant, shuffling steps before curling to the left.

Jenna peeked around the corner, checking first for Kemp waiting to smack her in the head with an animatronic leg, then for the pipe. It was there, still in the upper-left where the wall met the ceiling. It traveled out of the passageway and into the next room, which had a thin veil of fog but nowhere near the impenetrable curtain of the passageway.

Jenna stepped forward again, to the threshold of the room, and only then did she look down to examine the space they were about to enter.

Fifty sets of eyes stared back at her.

She frantically tried to undo her last step but backed into her three companions, who hadn't seen the next room yet.

"Uh, guys?"

She had to shout over the throbbing bass. When she didn't get a response, she glanced behind and saw Belma with the top of her head planted against Cabo's ribs, trying to drive him to the side.

"You only get middle wedge for one haunt, rookie! Ghost Ship was yours, No Sanctuary is mine!"

Cabo, unmoving, shouted, "You're going to hurt your head!"

"Guys," Jenna called, her gaze locked on what waited for them ahead.

"Both of you, spread out!" Lawrence demanded. "I'm gonna be the glorious wedgie between you two butt cheeks!"

"Guys!" Jenna yelled.

The other three finally looked ahead. Belma gasped, and then gasped again when Cabo released a burst of obscenity that ruffled Jenna's hair.

"We are so dead," Lawrence said.

The room was of an unknown size, painted completely black—floor, walls, and ceiling. The only light came from red, archaic symbols and words glowing upon the black surfaces.

"Look." Lawrence pointed a shaky finger at the only words in English, two feet tall in buzzing neon red on the far wall:

## YE SHALL BE JUDGED

The rest of the room was packed with human figures in blood-red robes, standing shoulder-to-shoulder along a narrow path winding through the space. Each of them wore a spotless white mask with small openings at the mouth and nose, and large oval holes for the eyes.

All of the heads were turned so the eyes could stare at the Main Street crew.

Lawrence spoke just below shouting level. "Belma, is this your fan club?"

"Uh, no."

"They all kinda seem like they're into Satan. I thought maybe they're just confused about who you are."

"You're not fooling anybody. I can hear the whimper in your voice."

Cabo pulled Jenna closer, from two inches away to one inch. "Any one of those could be Kemp."

"I know," Jenna said. "Or none of them."

"So which way are we betting?"

Jenna stared back at the blank faces. "You remember the chainsaw?"

Cabo frowned in the red light. "The what?"

"At my shop, the chainsaw. And the first rule of haunted houses."

"Jenna, if this is about me wearing a diaper, or asparagus pee..."

"Not this time, pal. The first rule: Always go forward."

"Is there a caveat to that? Like, 'Unless a real murderer might be in front of you'?"

"The rules don't get that specific," Jenna said. "But definitely something to bring up at the next meeting."

—

Jenna hunched her shoulders and waded into the crowd of white-masked judges. The red robes were close enough to brush against her elbows, and she braced for the inevitable hand waiting inside one of the folds, ready to clamp on her arm and pull her into the group.

The bass continued to pound, covering any other sounds that might tip her off to approaching danger like footsteps, breathing, somebody conking Lawrence with a frying pan. She would need to rely on her eyes, which seemed to be working fine in the thin veil of foggy mist tinted red by the neon.

So, as unsettling as it was, she forced herself to stare into every set of blank, empty eyes for any sign of Kemp lurking within. When the masks all turned to follow her and the other three as they scuttled along the narrow path, she refused to believe it.

Then Belma said, "They're moving!"

"They're staring into my soul!" Lawrence bawled. "Go faster! I can't take the judgment! It's like Thanksgiving with my family!"

Jenna tried to resist the panic, but she was like a bug stuck to the front of a freight train. Belma pushed, then Lawrence, and when Cabo kicked in Jenna had to speed up just to keep from getting trampled.

They battered their way through the twisted route, slapping at red robes and cowering away from the glaring, bottomless eyes. Jenna tore her attention away from the judges long enough to spot the pipe, painted black now, running above the giant neon letters.

The pipe was also larger, fed by more hoses—also black and barely noticeable—snaking up the wall and running into the conduit. It led toward a curtained doorway in the far corner of the room, and Jenna was eternally grateful the narrow path they were on seemed to be heading that way as well.

She turned a sharp corner, and another, the bass deafening and the empty eyes following, and then the door was there, just beyond one more left turn.

Jenna made the turn and found herself, face-to-face with the final judge, whose appearance brought her to a sudden, skidding halt. He wore a white robe and blood-red mask, like a negative of the others, and he stood with his right arm stretched across the doorway, blocking the exit.

His black eyes stared at her, and Jenna forced herself to lean closer, staring back, searching for a real person behind the mask.

Then a deep, recorded voice informed them: "You have been judged."

The arm rose with a slight hiss of air, barely audible beneath the bass, and Jenna pushed into the curtain with her heart in her throat.

"Wait!" Cabo yelled.

Jenna froze.

"There might be a slide."

At this point, the idea of tumbling uncontrollably

into the unknown was enough to make her stomach turn inside-out and dump ice into her lap. Jenna poked her foot through the drapes like a probe and tapped solid floor on the other side.

"No slide," Jenna yelled to the group.

Her stomach returned to its normal orientation, at least for the time being. It was a small comfort to know she'd be staggering somewhat controllably into the unknown.

She stepped through the heavy curtain and crossed the threshold into pure chaos.

—

The blacklight strobe hit first. It was an endless, rapid-fire blast of purple light that illuminated the horrors of the room in staccato frames, catching the hellish demons in their approach before cutting off and cloaking them—to some relief—in total darkness.

But then, when the strobe flashed again, the creatures were closer.

The throbbing bass was still present but muted, replaced by rapid clicking and skittering and something else Jenna couldn't quite place. She tried to focus on the noise and regretted doing so when she realized what it was: chewing.

One word repeated itself in Jenna's primal brain,

the one that had kept her ancestors alive through the cold nights when something prowled outside the cave and made them pile fire at its entrance.

The word kept time with the strobe, warning her every time the blacklight flashed:

Spiders.

Spiders.

Spiders.

Their thick, glistening webs glowed in the brief blacklight and the patterns were seared into Jenna's eyes, refusing to fade even when she briefly squeezed them shut. The webs covered every surface and hung like curtains from the ceiling. Cable-like strands stretched between the walls, heavy with struggling, cocooned victims.

The spiders clung to all of it, too numerous to count. Some were giant, as large as Labradors and bristling with furry spines, their eyes a mass of clustered orbs pulsing with milky green light. Some were just large enough to wrap their eight legs around a human hand.

For Jenna, the worst were the tiny ones, darting too quickly to follow across the walls and into caverns of web, tunneling through to emerge who-knows-where.

*The back of my neck, probably,* she thought, and shuddered.

Lawrence peeked around Cabo at the room and

caught one flash of the strobe. That was enough for him.

"Nope."

"Come on Lawrence," Jenna called. "You can do this. We need to follow the video camera cables."

"I'd rather go back and be judged again. Forever."

"Always go forward," Belma said. "Always go forward."

Jenna appreciated the words of encouragement, then realized Belma had her eyes squeezed shut, and was repeating the phrase to herself.

She looked at Cabo. "Are you okay?"

He shrugged. "I actually like spiders. These are a bit on the large size for my taste, but so far so good. And they're just animatronics. Right?"

"Uh, sure?" Jenna failed to convince him, or herself. She pulled the group closer.

"Okay, Lawrence is middle wedge for this room. I'll lead, then Cabo. Lawrence, keep your head down and bury it in Cabo's back. Don't worry about the asparagus, it'll wash off. I think."

"Wait, that puts me last!" Belma said, her lower lip and chin quivering.

Jenna put a hand on her shoulder. "Just hold on to Lawrence and follow the train."

"Until a spider falls on me and I burst into flames!"

Jenna pressed on. "If a web touches you, keep going. If a spider touches you, keep going. If something else comes out of these webs—"

"Something else?" Lawrence said. "Like what? What do you know?"

"Nothing," Jenna said. "Just...if anything else happens, keep going. That's the key. Are you ready?"

"No," Lawrence said.

Belma shook her head violently.

Cabo cracked his knuckles.

Jenna turned and took her place at the tip of the spear. "Ready?"

"Wait!" Lawrence cried.

While she waited for the others to tremble and slide into position, Jenna glanced up and saw the black pipe tucked into the angle of the wall and ceiling behind a scrim of web. She traced its route, tracking it about ten feet into the room.

Then it disappeared.

"Okay, go!" Lawrence said.

Jenna planted her feet. "Hold on!"

"Don't take too long, I'm holding my breath!"

Jenna examined the pipe for a moment, and then turned to see Lawrence's cheeks puffed out like he had a mouthful of mashed potatoes.

"Why are you holding your breath?"

"Spiders love mouths! Just whatever you're doing, hurry!"

He gasped and the cheeks expanded again.

Jenna pulled the group forward, glancing from the pipe to the dozen or so spiders close enough to be darting in and out of striking range. Webs brushed at her face and hair and clung to her shoulders like unwanted scarves. After a few alarmingly big steps, she was beneath the spot where the pipe disappeared.

Her eyes scoured the area for unseen nooks and crannies where the conduit may have dipped before reemerging, but it was hopeless. The pipe took a ninety-degree turn into the wall and was gone. The wall was completely covered in web, a mixture of thick strands and vast, wispy curtains crowded with spiders. A few dangled from the threads surrounding the pipe's exit point, mocking her as they danced in the strobe and bass.

She pointed up. "That's where our video cable goes."

"So what's on the other side of this wall?" Cabo asked.

"I was afraid you'd say that."

It was Jenna's turn to hold her breath as she leaned toward the wall of webs and let her fingers slide between the glistening strands. The curtains resisted at first but she pushed her fingers through, fully expecting an eruption of spiders to flow up her arms and quickly cover her entire body.

Instead, she felt a blanket.

Not a blanket of web, or spiders, or spider eggs—just a blanket. She brushed it with her fingertips to make sure, and it felt like some sort of padded quilt.

"Standby everybody," she called over her shoulder.

"If I pass out, please drag me to a designated

non-spider area," Lawrence begged before going back to holding his breath.

Jenna moved to her right, poking through the webs to find the edge of the quilt. After two steps she felt the seam and gently pulled, drawing the blanket and all of the webs covering it away from the wall like a heavy drape. It was a brilliant design—she never would have noticed the seam if she hadn't used her fingers to find it.

The quilt was light gray with spider shapes and web patterns worked into the fabric to give even more depth to the room's appearance of endless spiders and webs. Jenna spent a brief moment appreciating the attention to detail Kemp put into terrifying everyone who shuffled through the No Sanctuary haunted house, then got back to business.

Because the pipe was there, going through the wall, and directly beneath it was a door.

—

Jenna stepped toward the hidden door. It was completely flat and blank with no hardware, but in the pulsing strobe she could see a patch of dirty smudges along one edge at about shoulder height.

Someone with grimy hands had pushed on the door in that spot enough times to leave a trail.

"Come on everybody."

"I don't think we're supposed to go through there," Cabo said, leaning in so he could be heard without bellowing.

Jenna stopped with her fingertips pressed against the stain. "Of course not. But this is where the camera cable goes."

"My point is, what do we say if we run into somebody? Like Kemp? That we're just sneaking around in forbidden areas long enough to delete yet another batch of awkward statements and questions from Jenna Hooper?"

"That could be a full-time job," Belma said.

Jenna took a moment to scowl at her, and then said, "It's a haunted house. I'm sure people get confused and lost all the time."

Cabo shook his head. "I think we need a better plan. We—"

Lawrence, who had been holding his breath with his eyes clamped shut the entire time, let out a desperate screaming gasp and plowed forward, knocking Jenna aside and blasting through the door. He left Jenna, Belma, and Cabo behind, mouths open and staring in astonishment, as he screamed his way onto a small dimly-lit landing and all the way up a narrow set of stairs.

The stairs went up one floor to another landing, which had an opening on the right wall into a room bathed in red light.

Lawrence got to the top of the stairs, still screaming, and took the hard right into the red room. Two seconds later another man shouted and Lawrence's shriek was cut off.

"Uhhh," Belma said.

Jenna grinned. "There's our plan."

Cabo smiled too, and then all three of them pounded up the stairs.

"Lawrence!" Jenna called. "Where are you going?"

Cabo hollered, "Get back here!"

"Jump out a window, you idiot!" Belma yelled.

When Jenna and Cabo looked back at her, she shrugged.

"Sorry. Habit."

They got to the top of the stairs and gathered on the landing to peer into the red room. Lawrence stood in the center, chest heaving and eyes wide, next to Dave Kemp, aka Skull Monger. Kemp was in his standard black flowing robes, but his death's head mask was missing. His wide face and blonde hair was slick with sweat. He held a huge wrench above his head, ready to swing it down onto Lawrence's face.

"Freeze!" Cabo said.

Jenna reached desperately for Kemp. "Don't do it!"

"I'm sorry about the pumpkin cookies!" Belma wailed.

Kemp frowned at all of them. "You're not supposed to be up here."

"Well, we're here all right," Belma said. "Witnesses to your terrible crimes. So go ahead, bash his head in. You're busted, buster."

Kemp was obviously confused. "Crimes? Bash whose head in?"

"Lawrence's," Belma said. "He's right there. Go for it."

Kemp glanced at Lawrence, and then at the pipe he still held. He let go of the handle and the pipe stayed in place, clamped onto the pneumatic fitting he'd been tightening when the Main Street crew barged in.

"Just a tap?" Belma suggested.

"You guys aren't supposed to be up here," Kemp said again, "but I guess I'm glad you are."

He was irritated and flustered, but beneath those Jenna picked up on a growing amount of embarrassment. He swept an arm around the room.

"I've got a serious malfunction in progress and nobody to help."

They were in some sort of control hub. The constant racket from the haunt was muted, though the floor still vibrated from the throbbing bass. Dozens of air hoses and electrical cords ran along the walls and ceiling, gathering inside large plastic boxes with access panels built in. Several laptops were open on a long table displaying numbers and graphs, some of them with apparent warnings. Along the wall on the right, a bank of monitors showed feeds from security cameras scattered throughout the haunt.

Jenna scanned the monitors, each of which had a screen quartered to show four feeds. Her eyes flicked over one showing a giant sagging clown prop in a pool of water, another with what looked like an embalming chamber with a wall of cold storage drawers, and then finally found the elevator feed on the second monitor from the top left.

A group of teenagers was huddled in the corner as far away from the robed operator as they could get, scrambling over one another to limit any possible exposure. They obviously had no training.

Kemp either hadn't witnessed Jenna's elevator rant, or he was doing an excellent job pretending he hadn't. Whether or not he knew it was Ritter's body in Lilac Park was also unknown, and it would be good to see his reaction if it happened to come up. You know, in casual conversation...

"How can we help?" Jenna said.

——

Kemp said, "First thing, I need somebody to turn this wrench when I say so."

Lawrence reached up and gripped the wrench like he was on a subway, which was perfect, because he was swaying and shuddering from the trauma of the spider room.

Kemp eyeballed him. "You okay buddy?"

"I don't like spiders."

"Ah," Kemp grinned. "That room gets 'em every time."

He was a large man, wide across the shoulders and belly under the black robes, and his default expression could be categorized as "mild to moderate disapproval." But his face lit up when he smiled, and he showed genuine glee over Lawrence's misery.

"I spent three months getting that room right. I'm really glad it frightened you—do you feel like you got your money's worth?"

"I do," Belma said. "I'd pay double to have him go through it again. The silence while he held his breath was...like Christmas on Halloween."

Kemp looked at Lawrence. "That's new. Why did you hold your breath?"

"Spiders love mouths. Everybody knows that." Lawrence seemed to be slipping into shock, so it came out as a slurred mumble.

"Huh," Kemp said. "Good to know."

Lawrence frowned and looked at Belma. "When you idiots thought Skull Monger was going to smash my head in, did you yell something about pumpkin cookies?"

A flash of panic crossed Belma's face before she composed herself. "Nope."

"I thought I heard that too," said Kemp. "Something like, 'Sorry about your pumpkin cookies,' or close to it."

"Nuh-uh," Belma said.

Lawrence said, "Jenna, did you hear her say that?"

Belma's face pleaded with Jenna to lie. Lawrence waited, clinging to his wrench and slowly recovering from spider overdose.

"Well…" Jenna said, and then pointed at one of the laptop screens. "Is that supposed to be flashing red like that?"

Kemp whirled. "Samhain's butt! Okay, get ready with that wrench, Spiderman."

He pointed at Belma. "I need you to click on that flashing red alarm message when I say so, got it?"

"Can do!" She rushed toward the laptops, tipping Jenna a grateful nod.

Kemp turned to Jenna. "And you."

Jenna tried not to wince. This is when it would happen.

If Kemp had witnessed her elevator tirade, accusing him of killing and burying Martin Ritter in a shallow grave…

If she'd tipped off the real killer and possibly ruined any chance of him being caught…

"Watch that video monitor over there, third one over, upper-right corner. Let me know if Chuckles starts moving."

"Oh thank goodness," Jenna exhaled, earning a raised eyebrow from Kemp. "Third one over, upper-right, got it."

She hurried over to the security feeds before any further conversation could be had.

Cabo asked Kemp, "What camera system are you using, the Sentry Five Thousand?"

"Four Thousand," Kemp said, raising the eyebrow higher. "You know security systems?"

"I used to do bodyguard work, we liked Sentry a lot. I can help Jenna over there."

"Fine. Listen everybody, I gotta tell you, with the mouth spiders, the pumpkin cookie thing, Jenna saying a prayer about staring at monitors, and the big guy here coming from the Secret Service or whatever, you people might be the weirdest thing in my haunted house right now."

The Main Street crew all looked at each other in the red light, unable to argue.

Kemp said, "Now everybody get ready, battle stations!"

———

Kemp moved to one of the largest control panels near the top of the stairs, his back to the rest of the room. He opened the panel, revealing a massive set of pneumatic valves and connections, and started fiddling.

Jenna scanned the monitors and had a brief moment of concern when she wasn't sure she'd be able to identify what Chuckles was, let alone when it started moving, then she found the right screen and was instantly relieved.

Sort of.

The camera looked down from an upper corner into a room with a U-shaped path around a misty pool. Chuckles was the torso, arms, and head of a massive, demented clown emerging from the water. His springy hair was plastered to his lumpy skull, and his soggy makeup melted down his face to make severe lines of unhappiness. His head and arms drooped, seemingly waiting for someone to get close enough to pounce upon, which made him even creepier.

Cabo arrived next to her and spotted Chuckles. "Yikes. Better you than me."

"I'm trying not to look straight at it." She glanced over her shoulder. "Okay, I'm watching Kemp back there and Chuckles here—you know what to do?"

"Already doing it," Cabo said. He used the keyboard and mouse to highlight the elevator's camera feed, then pushed some buttons to make it rewind. On the screen, the point of view turned inside the hood, scanning groups of patrons as they jumped, fell, panicked, and ran in and out of the elevator, all at 3X speed.

"Is there sound?" Jenna whispered.

"There is, but it's not on, and it's not being recorded. We are so lucky. But dang, I'd really love to have that footage. Just for entertainment value. Your face…"

"Don't you dare," Jenna said. "Is the video being saved anywhere?"

"Yeah, but just on a local drive. So no cloud storage to worry about."

"Any movement?" Kemp yelled.

Jenna checked the monitor. A group of patrons was hugging the wall to stay as far away from Chuckles as possible, terrified as they waited for him to pounce, dance, explode—whatever he was supposed to do.

Chuckles remained slumped.

"We have no Chuckles movement, repeat, no Chuckles movement!"

"I am not in the mood, Chuckles!" Kemp bellowed from inside the panel. "Keep watching!"

Jenna stared at the huge, drooping clown, fighting every instinct to look away and scrub him from her memory forever. She wanted the thing to move so she could avert her eyes, but Cabo needed more time, so she willed the soggy clown to remain still.

"How about now?"

"Nope!"

Kemp cursed into the panel. "Stop acting like a human clown! Get to work!"

"I recognize some people who were in line behind us," Cabo muttered. "We might be the next group…"

"What are you going to do?" Jenna whispered.

"I'm just going to rewind it to before we get in, then let it record the rest of the night right over us. Easy peasy."

"Will Kemp notice?"

Cabo thought about it. "If he checks the time stamps, or wonders why the overall recording is shorter than the time his haunt was open tonight, yeah. So let's hope he doesn't do either of those things."

"We're doing a lot of hoping tonight, Jay Cabo."

"I could smash the whole console and rip out the drive. But he'd probably notice that too."

Jenna nodded. "Let's stick to hope."

"Now?" Kemp shouted across the room.

Jenna turned to the monitor and watched a young couple huddled together, neither one of them daring to look anywhere near Chuckles. The clown remained limp.

"Nothing from Chuck—"

The clown's arm moved, up and down, and then stopped.

"Wait! He's moving!"

The couple had noticed it too. They both sprang straight up into the air as if they shared reflexes, then they fell against the wall directly in front of Chuckles.

"Keep doing whatever you're doing!" Jenna yelled.

"Yah!" Kemp hooted. "Lawrence, tighten the wrench!"

"Tightening!" Lawrence declared. A burst of

pressurized air escaped into the room from the over-head hoses.

Kemp turned from the panel but kept his hands buried inside. "The other way! Lefty loosy, righty tighty!"

Lawrence panicked, his hair flapping in the jet stream. "It's overhead, I thought it was righty!"

"Just turn it!"

Lawrence cranked the wrench the other way, cutting off the escaping air.

"Keep going!" Kemp yelled. "Jenna, talk to me!"

She watched the monitor. The couple was scrambling to their feet as Chuckles sprang to life, his arms flailing and his head lifting to show the gaping mouth with rows of jagged teeth. His entire torso seemed to rise out of the water, looming over the hapless young man and woman.

Kemp said, "Now, Belma! Slam it!"

Belma hit the flashing red alarm on the laptop.

On the security monitor, Chuckles crashed his huge mouth shut, spewing water in all directions and causing the man to abandon all hope.

And his date.

He fled around the last corner of the path toward the room's exit, leaving the woman behind. She lunged for him and managed to grab both of the back pockets on his jeans, which tore loose in her hands and left her standing, alone with Chuckles, holding two denim pocket flaps.

She screamed and shook the pockets at the clown as if they were some sort of Wrangler talismans, then followed after her date, who was probably not going to have a good rest of the night.

Kemp shut the panel door and took the wrench from Lawrence. He checked the fitting along the ceiling and grunted his approval.

"Great job everyone. If I thought you could show up every day and perform this well, I'd almost think you were automated."

"Uh, your robot clown doesn't seem too interested in working tonight," Belma said.

Kemp shrugged. "He just needed a little encouragement. A tap here, a twist there, and he's back in business. But people? You gotta pay them, feed them, give them breaks, and they still don't do the work right, assuming they don't just call in sick."

He hefted the wrench, seemingly satisfied with its weight.

"Sometimes they even steal your money and dump your dead body in a shallow grave in Lilac Park."

He looked over at Jenna.

"But you already knew that, didn't you?"

———

Cabo took a step closer to Kemp, his eyes flicking from the man's face to the wrench.

"You know about Ritter?" Jenna said.

"Of course. Vance texted me about the conversation you all had."

"*Vance?*" Jenna was floored. "You two text? I thought you were rivals."

"We're in a semi-friendly competition to see who can scare more people, but I don't consider him a rival. Ghost Ship is rather...pedestrian in its tactics, don't you think? I mean, a slide? Come on."

The Main Street crew shared glances, assuring one another that no one would admit to being terrified by the inflatable bouncy slide.

Kemp said, "But we both know how Ritter stealing a bunch of money and getting himself killed could impact Halloween in Lost Haven, so he told me about the body in the park; and that you're the one who told him."

The words were heavy with suspicion, almost an accusation.

"It's all over town," Lawrence said. "Phones were blowing up while we were in line at Ghost Ship."

"How long was the line?" Kemp snapped. "Longer than mine?"

"Nooo," Jenna said, sensing an opportunity to soothe the man a bit. She looked at Cabo. "Maybe, what, about half as long?"

"If that," he said - picking up on her ego stroking.

"He's lucky to get that many," Kemp grumbled. "I mean, the kidnapping ruse? What a waste of time."

"You sure know a lot about Vance's haunt," Cabo said.

"Of course I do. I need to make sure he isn't ripping off my ideas, and from what I've seen and heard he couldn't do it, even if he tried. That stupid boat would shake itself apart if he ran even a tenth of animatronics I have here."

"What about the Lost Haven Morgue?" Jenna asked.

"What about it?"

"Did you and Vance let them know it was Ritter's body in Lilac Park?"

"He may have. I sure didn't."

Cabo nodded. "So they're more of a less-friendly competitive rival?"

"They wish," Kemp scoffed. "But they *do* have the potential to steal my ideas, so if Ritter kicking the bucket means they finally close down, it might sting our town's festivities temporarily, but it'll be worth it. Good riddance."

"Good riddance to Ritter," Jenna said, "or the Morgue, if it shuts down?"

"Both. Ritter was a thieving scumbag, and that Dina Polk is no better. When I heard he'd stolen the money, the first thing I thought was they were in on it together."

Jenna looked at Lawrence and Belma. "I don't think word about Ritter and the money hit Main

Street until what, mid-afternoon the day after Halloween last year?"

"I heard it from Morrie Nelson after he finished brunch," Belma said, "and I came straight over and blabbed it to you."

"And I could hear you all the way from my shop," Lawrence said.

Jenna smiled at Kemp. "I'm guessing the Lost Haven Haunted House Network moves faster than that?"

Kemp pointed at the bank of security monitors. "I was standing right there when I heard. It was probably around three in the morning, just a few hours after closing for the season."

"Halloween night?" Jenna said. "You had to be exhausted!"

"Oh, I was, but a true haunter never rests. Things to repair, new props to design and build for the next year. It never ends."

"Who called you with news like that at three in the morning? Vance again?"

Kemp studied her for a moment. "I don't know what Vance was doing at that time, but he wasn't calling me. Maybe he was in Lilac Park."

Jenna leaned in, eyes wide, trying to act like she wanted juicy gossip instead of investigative facts. "With Ritter?"

Kemp shrugged. "Only they would know that. And as for who did tell me, that's none of your business. And they didn't call me, I called them. I think we both found out Ritter was missing at the same time."

Jenna frowned. "I don't understand."

"At three a.m., the morning after Halloween, I was standing right there reviewing the security footage so I could find out which townie punk sprayed pink UV paint all over my black light room on the last night of the season."

"Did you find out?" Cabo asked.

"Oh, sure." Kemp said. "It was Martin Ritter, zombie mask and all."

———

Jenna's confusion turned into befuddlement.

"Wait, what? Ritter came through No Sanctuary on Halloween night last year?"

"That's right. And he defaced my wonderful props and set design."

"Why?" Belma asked. "I mean, I know you think he was a scumbag, but that seems…"

"Stupid?" Kemp offered.

Belma nodded. "I was going to say risky, but stupid works."

"My theory," Kemp said, "is he was planning to leave town with the cash and didn't care what sort of wreckage he left behind. He wanted to get one last dig in, one last middle finger, before he was gone forever and I couldn't retaliate."

"I guess it sort of worked," Jenna said. "Unless, well. You know."

"Unless I killed him?" Kemp said. He smiled. "I can have a bit of a temper, as you and Chuckles the clown witnessed just now, but killing Ritter over some spray paint would be a bit too extreme, even for me."

"What about spray paint and a million bucks?" Lawrence said.

Cabo chimed in. "And you two had a classic feud going. These guys told me about it, and I thought it sounded ridiculous. It wasn't just the spray paint—it was years of trouble waiting to boil over."

"Well, you got me there," Kemp said. "He was a pain in the butt, and he'd probably say the same thing about me, if he could. But like I said, I was in here watching camera footage around three in the morning, and that's when I saw the tape of Ritter with the spray paint."

"Do you still have that footage?" Jenna asked.

"Of course."

Belma saw where Jenna was going. "Oh man. I gotta see that! Can you spool it up, or whatever you do?"

"Of course not."

"But...why not?" Belma said.

"Because I have no desire to showcase some buffoon's supposed moment of glory, when he ruined my lovely art."

"Did you tell the police about it when Ritter went missing?" Jenna asked.

"Nope. I didn't tell anyone."

"Why not? There was a pretty intense search going on for him last year. I don't know if the footage would have helped, but it seems a little suspicious not to tell anyone."

"You're exactly right, it wouldn't have helped. As far as I was concerned, it was an insult between haunters, and it would be handled that way if and when Ritter ever showed his face in Lost Haven again."

Cabo rolled his eyes. "Now there's a haunter's code? Eye for an eye?"

"More like empty eye socket for empty eye socket, but you're on the right track."

"But you called the Morgue looking for Ritter after you saw the footage," Jenna said. "So you told them about it."

"Wrong. I called them hollering for Ritter, but I didn't tell them why. They hadn't seen him for hours. That's when they realized he was gone, along with the money."

Jenna chewed her lip. "So by the time you found out about his paint job, he was probably already dead."

Kemp shrugged. "I have no idea what time he died, obviously, but it seems so. The killer may have been throwing fresh dirt onto Ritter's zombie face right when I made that phone call."

"Well that's…" Lawrence wrinkled his nose, and then blinked. "I was going to say disgustingly morbid, but looking at you, and where we are, it's totally fitting."

Kemp said, "I hope he died fast. He was a scumbag and a vandal, but he didn't deserve to suffer. Not too much, anyway. Now if you'll excuse me."

He reached inside his hood and pulled the leering skull mask over his face, instantly becoming Death himself.

"All of my props are animatronics, but I still unfortunately need people as patrons, and they are an endless source of grief. I must patrol. And you must re-enter the spider room and find your own way out."

Lawrence immediately began to dry heave. He leaned over the row of laptops, his torso spasming with each convulsion, and Kemp scrambled to slide the computers out of the danger zone.

"Stop that! Stop that! Okay, never mind! You don't have to go through the spiders again. I'll escort you all out, unless the others want to keep going?"

The last part came through the mask as a gleeful challenge.

"We'll stick with Lawrence," Jenna said. "I think we all might need a little break from the terror."

Kemp shrugged inside his flowing black robes. "Suit yourself. But remember, in here, the scares are all carefully planned, and they won't hurt you. Out there? Just ask Martin Ritter."

———

**K**emp led them to a door near the security monitors, taking a moment to scan the screens for any misbehaving props or patrons. Grunting in satisfaction, he took the Main Street crew through the door and into a short hallway, lit by a single red LED bulb.

Belma said, "I'm not complaining—this light makes my skin look great—but why all the red?"

"It saves your night vision," Kemp said over his shoulder. "You can go from red light into darkness and your eyes don't have to adjust. If I had regular lights in here, every time I went out into the haunt I'd be blind."

"Huh," Lawrence said. "And here I thought you were just being creepy."

"That's fine too."

He pushed through a narrow black curtain running floor to ceiling. To Jenna it looked like he'd just stepped out a window, but when she followed she realized they were inside the walls of No Sanctuary, sliding through a tight space between two rooms. Cabo came through behind her, his toes probing for hidden slides, and the relief on his face when the floor was flat and intact made her smile.

Intentional gaps and holes in the walls showed glimpses of a room on the right half-buried in sand with grasping hands bursting out of the grit. A group of patrons leaped and darted through the room, laughing and screaming every time a withered hand came near.

On the left, the young couple from the Chuckles camera feed staggered through the weird purple haze of a blacklight room, going in the same direction as Kemp and the crew. The walls and ceiling were covered in leering masks painted neon green, yellow, orange, and blue, and they glowed with feverish intensity in the blacklight. The man had his arm draped over his date's shoulders so she could help drag him forward.

Over the constant bass of the haunt, Jenna heard him say, "Just leave me. Save yourself."

"Shut up," his date said.

Then several of the masks moved, turning to watch them come closer, and the man sprang onto her back.

"Go go!"

"I can't, you're too heavy!"

"Ahh! They're looking at me!"

Jenna was so enthralled she bumped into Lawrence, who had stopped to keep from running into Belma. Ahead of her, Kemp waited by a closed wooden panel, watching the continuously eroding date. He still wore his mask, but Jenna assumed his grin matched the skull's.

The couple survived the blacklight room and turned right, and Jenna realized Kemp was waiting for them to pass by on the other side of the panel. He leaned down and said something to Belma, who muttered to Lawrence.

Lawrence turned and said, "We're crossing through the haunt. Go fast and don't stop."

Jenna repeated the orders to Cabo, who nodded.

Kemp peered through a hole in the wall on the right. When the couple appeared in the sand room, he pulled the panel open and rushed through, crossing a narrow hallway and disappearing through another hidden panel on the far side. Belma followed, and then Lawrence and Jenna skipped across holding the far panel open for Cabo.

He stepped out, looked left and right, and froze.

Jenna waved him forward but he didn't notice. He was staring at something in the sand room.

She leaned out and saw that the man, half-cata-tonic, had turned to look back at the glowing masks and found Jay Cabo standing there instead—all six-feet-five inches and two hundred fifty pounds of a person who had not been standing there mere seconds earlier.

The man's legs locked up completely. His eyes boggled and his mouth flapped, trying to warn his date, but nothing came out. The woman continued to slog ahead, attempting to dodge the clutching corpse hands while dragging him along.

Cabo, at a loss said, "Boo?"

The man finally found his spine, and his feet, and he hoisted his date over his shoulder and bolted for the far end of the room, kicking up a rooster tail of sand in his wake. Before they disappeared Jenna heard the woman burst into laughter.

"Wee!"

Cabo shrugged and stepped through the open panel. Kemp, Belma, and Lawrence were pressing ahead through the passageway, visible only by the sparse light poking through more cracks and holes.

"Nice work," Jenna said. "You may have saved that relationship."

"Just call me the Halloween Cupid. Listen, we gotta talk about Kemp."

"Oh, we will, trust me. Once we get out of this madhouse it's straight to the café."

"Do you think he killed Ritter?" Cabo asked.

Jenna paused. "I really don't know. We have to verify some of the things he said first, but I'll tell you this: if he didn't kill Ritter, he knows who did."

———

Kemp led them through more passageways—more than it seemed the old mansion could possibly hold along with the entire haunted house—and eventually stopped at a door marked EMERGENCY EXIT / CHICKENS.

"Chickens?" Lawrence said.

Kemp nodded in the skull mask. "Some people just can't continue past a certain point. Like that poor sap getting dragged around by his date back there, or you when you came out of the spider's nest."

"I was absolutely fine," Lawrence said.

When the laughter subsided, Kemp opened the door onto an exterior second floor balcony with a staircase leading down to the driveway. The fresh, cool night air flowed in, making Jenna close her eyes and shiver with delight.

"Don't just stand there, you're letting my fog out," Kemp snapped.

"Sorry."

Lawrence led the way down, his head held high while scanning for any cruel spider traps Kemp may have set. Belma and Cabo followed, and when Jenna started down Kemp tugged on her sleeve. She stopped and turned, looking up into the black, empty eyes of the Skull Monger.

"I want you to consider something," he said. "What's more important? One idiot's life, or Halloween in Lost Haven?"

Jenna swallowed. "That's not a fair question."

"Just think about it. Because the more you dig, the more you find. You already found the body. I think that's enough, don't you?"

He slammed the door, leaving her alone on the stairs and suddenly much colder than the chilly night warranted.

# CHAPTER 8

The walk back to Main Street was brisk and mostly silent. With groups of people roaming between No Sanctuary and Ghost Ship, the sidewalks were just busy enough that a private conversation between four people (two of them helplessly loud) would be constantly interrupted and overheard, so the crew made a quick pact to remain silent until they could huddle together at the café and whisper.

Lawrence put up a brief fight. "But people at the café don't whisper—they bray at each other and into their phones like no one else is around. I think whispering will draw more attention to us."

Jenna had to acknowledge the truth in what he said, especially in Lost Haven.

"Tell you what. You and Belma have a separate conversation, like a cloaking device, to mask what Cabo and I are whispering about. Then we can rotate to make sure everyone chips in."

Lawrence and Belma eyeballed each other.

"A conversation, you say?" Belma said, making it

sound like she and Lawrence were going to be walk-ing on hot coals while carrying buckets of gasoline.

Lawrence sniffed. "Never mind- let the whole town wonder what we're whispering about. Unless you want to talk about pumpkin cookies?"

"Whispering's good!" Belma whispered.

They were just turning the corner of Shore-line Drive onto Main, and Jenna saw a lone figure passing under a streetlamp coming toward them from downtown.

Tall frame, long arms, a brisk, rangy gait that indicated he had no time for nonsense or interrup-tions of any kind.

*Well*, Jenna thought, *too bad for Unflappable Bob, but I have some nonsense and interruptions just for him.*

———

Unflappable Bob strode into the pool of the next streetlamp and looked up at the Main Street crew heading toward him. He was likely coming from his hardware store or the apartment above, and he had an envelope-sized package in one hand which he tucked into his back pocket as he stepped off the concrete to cut around them.

Jenna eased left to stay in front of him.

"Bob!" she called. "Are you going to No Sanctuary?"

"Yep." He didn't break stride.

"You think Skull Monger will scare you this year?" Belma asked.

"Nope."

Lawrence said, "Watch out for the spider room."

"Yep."

"And the water clown," Cabo added.

Bob said nothing but took a moment to peer at Cabo, and his toe caught the turf a little too early in stride. His pace hitched just a bit, and Jenna took the opportunity to stop right in front of him so Bob either had to stop or bowl her over. He stopped, but the look on his long face told her it had been a coin flip-at best.

"We just came from there," Jenna said. "Kemp and his, uh, staff? Animatronics? Anyway, they all did a really nice job. We were freaked out."

Bob nodded like he expected no better from them and tried to slip around. For him, apparently, the conversation was over.

Jenna and the others spread out to put him in the middle of the group.

"We're headed out to the Morgue now," she said.

Bob sucked a tooth and kept walking.

"We weren't sure if you were planning to lift your boycott of that establishment."

"Nope."

"Not even with the news of, well…you know."

Bob raised an eyebrow at her. "What news?"

"You haven't heard?" Belma said.

"Been doing inventory since I closed today. Don't like interruptions during inventory, so I take the phone off the hook."

"And turn off your cell?" Cabo asked.

"Don't have one of them. Microwaves."

Cabo blinked; unsure they were still talking about the same thing.

"So what haven't I heard that's so important?" Bob said.

Jenna said, "The body in the park."

"Which one?"

"The new one, the one we found. It's Martin Ritter."

Bob stared at her. "Ritter?"

He spat the word the way most people say *taxes*.

Lawrence nodded. "Dead and buried with his zombie mask on."

Bob turned and scowled toward Lilac Park. "Somebody murdered him?"

"Unless he killed himself," Belma said, "then managed to scrape a couple feet of dirt and a layer of sod over his body."

"After stashing close to a million dollars some-where no one could find it," Jenna added.

Bob seemed to glaze over for a moment, focused on something internally, and then he snorted. "I wouldn't put it past that charlatan to do exactly that. One last foolish prank, and close enough to my store to cause me trouble."

"You?" Cabo said. "Why would you have any trouble?"

"Because everybody in town knows I despised him for the lies he spread about me right before he went missing last year. Now he turns up dead, and I guarantee you I'm on the short list of suspects."

Jenna fought the urge to check her pocket to make sure her list was still there "Oh, yeah, that whole thing about him scaring you last year. I'd forgotten about that. I wonder if it would be the first time somebody got killed because they alleged someone else wet their pants."

"He may as well have called me a Democrat. There are some things you just don't say about a man, and one of 'em is that he got scared when you know full well he didn't. Martin Ritter nearly ruined my reputation. My legacy!"

Cabo glanced at the others, then said, "Your legacy of...being the guy who can't be scared?"

"Damn right. Unflappable Bob. They work their tails off trying to come up with something that will make me jump, squeak, hesitate, run, and, of course, the pinnacle: soak my drawers. Well son, I'll tell you—it ain't happened yet, and it never will."

"There's no shame in getting scared at haunted houses," Belma said. "I mean, Jay Cabo almost wet his pants on Ghost Ship."

"I did not!"

Bob's mouth twitched in what may have been a

smile. "You see? Don't like being accused of coward-ice, do you? Now imagine you have entire teams of people trying to prove you can be broken, and a whole town counting on you to stay strong."

"The town doesn't care, Bob," Lawrence muttered.

Bob pressed on, unaffected by Lawrence's real-ity. "Then one of your enemies realizes he'll never beat you, so he lies. He lies right through his cheap zombie mask, spewing filth and deception, and then disappears, leaving you to deal with the fallout of your tarnished reputation. Poof! So you can't just grab him by the neck and shake him until he tells everyone he's a dirty liar."

"That seems extreme," Jenna said.

Bob was rolling. "Oh, sure, you offer to show people your pants under UV light, proving that they're urine-free, but no one wants to deal with that truth. They'd rather believe the lie because it lets everyone know you're human. Knocks you off that Halloween pedestal everyone has you up on."

Belma shook her head. "That's not why nobody wants to look at your blacklight pants, Bob."

"So yes, my legacy," Bob told Cabo. He took a deep breath and straightened to his full height, look-ing at all of them. "I hope my name is on the short list of people who may have killed Martin Ritter and put him in a shallow grave. If it isn't, it would mean I'm not seen as a man of integrity. One who will stand up for himself and what he believes in, and defend those things to the death."

"Things like not wetting your pants in a haunted house," Cabo confirmed.

"Exactly. Long live Halloween in Lost Haven!"

That sank in for a few moments, and then Jenna said, "Who else should be on that list?"

"If it's made up of people with my sort of integrity? No one. I'm surprised there are any diapers left on the store shelves with all of the cowards running around these days. But if it's just people who hated Ritter and wanted to see him gone, one way or another... we ain't talking a short list anymore. I know he made Dave Kemp's life miserable, always taunting him and using his Maniacs to wreak havoc. And Fancy Vancy, trying to keep up with that rickety, part-time haunted ship of his even though it's pathetic. And that's just the haunted house crowd."

"What other crowd would there be?" Jenna asked.

Bob looked at her for a moment, and then checked the analog watch on his wrist. "You people are making me late. I gotta get through No Sanctuary before it closes, otherwise folks will start thinking I'm too yellow."

Belma sighed. "No one will think that, Bob."

"I'm leaving." He turned and took a few steps, then stopped and took a moment to look at each of them, burning the truth in. "But not because I'm scared."

—

I t was nearly eleven o'clock on a Sunday night, but the Halloween festivities in Lost Haven had the Sanctuary Café full inside and half of the patio tables occupied. Jenna, Belma and Lawrence reclaimed the corner table while Cabo darted inside to use the restroom.

"So close," Belma lamented. "I bet if we'd gone all the way through No Sanctuary, Jay Cabo would be on his way home to change his underwear right now."

"Unflappable Bob would be so disappointed," Lawrence said. "Although after our little encounter, I'm thinking about a formal petition to change his nickname to Unhinged Bob. Would you guys sign that?"

"I'll forge your name," Belma offered. "No way am I getting on his bad side after that spectacle of loony. I can totally see him getting spun up and losing it if he ran into Ritter last Halloween."

The three of them looked across the street at Lilac Park. Almost a year ago, at some point on Halloween night, someone had killed and buried zombie Martin Ritter less than one hundred yards away from where they sat.

Jenna shivered. "Are you guys still up for the Lost Haven Morgue tonight?"

"For fun," Lawrence said, "or as part of our little investigation?"

"Both. We're onto something, and I think all three haunted houses are involved. Or somebody is flat-out lying."

"Who?" Belma said.

"Vance. Or Kemp. Or both."

"So we don't know anything," Lawrence said.

Jenna held up a finger. "We *suspect*. That's the first step, right?"

"No, *this* is the first step," Lawrence said, smacking his lips as McTavish brought a round of hot cider and pumpkin cookies to the table. Belma shared a quick glance with Jenna, recalling the near miss at No Sanctuary.

"For the valiant patrons of all things haunted," McTavish proclaimed. "I'm overjoyed you've survived so far and wish you further success as you offend the dead and tempt fate."

Jenna frowned at the mugs. There were four, one of them in front of Cabo's empty seat.

"No smoothie?"

"Mr. Cabo has requested a brief reprieve from his regimen. It seems the asparagus isn't agreeing with his activities, and we don't have time right now to fiddle with the formula."

Lawrence raised his mug for a toast. "It's a Halloween miracle."

———

Cabo sat and sipped his cider, nodding at the complete absence of anything green and disgusting. "That's the stuff."

"Yeah, we know," Lawrence said. "That's why we drink it all the time instead of whatever you squeeze out of somebody's compost pile."

Cabo was intrigued. "Compost?"

"Focus, people," Jenna said, leaning in to keep the conversation somewhat private. "We've got a lot to cover, and we still need to hit the Morgue tonight. In fact, we should be there right now, trying to stay ahead of any information coming from Vance, Kemp, or Unflappable Bob, but we need to figure out exactly what we know."

"It's probably too late anyway," Cabo said. "If Vance and Kemp are communicating, is it safe to assume one or both of them are passing information to the Morgue as well?"

Jenna nodded. "I'd say so. And Vance and Kemp are first on my list to discuss—did you guys catch it when Kemp said how he found out about Ritter's body?"

"Yeah, that Vance told him," Belma said.

"But how?"

Cabo stared into his cider, and then snapped up. "Text."

"Right. And Vance told us he doesn't allow phones on Ghost Ship, not even for himself. They use radios. So either Kemp's lying about how he found out it was Ritter's body in the park, or Vance is lying about his phone."

Lawrence frowned. "Why would he lie about that? I mean a phone? It seems like a dumb thing to lie about."

"Not if it takes us off the trail of something else," Jenna said.

They all pondered that for a moment, but there just wasn't enough information yet to even begin speculating.

"Sticking with phones," Jenna said, "Kemp called the Morgue last Halloween looking for Ritter after he saw him on the security footage."

Cabo interrupted. "Yeah, about that security system. That's a very serious setup for a haunted house. I mean, it can handle multiple sites, hundreds of camera feeds, motion detection. It seems like overkill."

Lawrence said, "Did the grown man in a skull mask talking to a pneumatic clown on TV strike you as particularly logical?"

Cabo acknowledged the point with a nod. "I guess his line of work encourages a certain level of paranoia. Jenna, sorry—you were talking about when Kemp called the Morgue."

"Yes! When I asked Kemp who he talked to, he said, 'None of your business.' Why would he say that?"

"Because he's a prickly goon," Belma said.

"Possibly. But I think he spoke to someone specific, and he doesn't want us—or anyone—to know who."

After a moment, Lawrence gasped. "You don't think...?"

Jenna shrugged. "Maybe."

"What?" Cabo said.

Belma's mouth fell open. "No way."

"It's worth considering," Jenna said.

Cabo shook the table. "Come on!"

"Dina Polk," Jenna said. "What if Kemp is one of her clients?"

—

They piled into Jenna's Jeep at 11:20 and headed east out of downtown toward the Lost Haven Morgue. It was in what used to be a small industrial area on a fast two-lane road built for carrying tourists toward the lakeshore. Now the nearby businesses, all of them spread out with several acres each, were comprised of a junkyard trying to be an auto body repair shop, a heavy equipment rental store, and a landscaping company.

On the way, the crew jabbered endlessly about

the possibilities of Kemp and Dina Polk conspiring to murder Ritter.

Jenna said, "Maybe Kemp and Dina are in love, and Kemp killed Ritter during a passionate battle for her heart, trying to free her from Ritter's ruthless grasp."

Belma scoffed. "Have you been reading bodice-ripping romances instead of Lost Haven histories? I think they wanted to split a million bucks, needed Ritter out of the way, and put him in a hole."

"Now *that's* romantic," Lawrence said. "But no, you both have it wrong. Kemp and Ritter were working together to steal the million, and Dina found out. She killed Ritter and kept the money, blaming Ritter for the theft, and what's Kemp going to do about it? Nothing, that's what, because he was poised to steal it himself."

"What about Julian Vance and Unflappable Bob?" Cabo said.

Belma shrugged. "What about them? Unflappable Bob obviously killed Ritter because of irreparable harm to his—what did he call it?"

"Legacy," Cabo said.

"Right, his legacy, and then he walked a couple dozen yards to his hardware store, got a shovel, and buried the body in front of Marinus Mink's statue. Case closed."

No one could argue with the possibility of it, but no one had any proof to add either.

"As for Vance," Belma continued, "he and Jenna are going to get married and we're getting free lifetime entry into Ghost Ship and meals at the Grille because we're her besties."

"Yay," Lawrence cheered.

"Wrong," Jenna said. "Probably. Stop distracting me. Anyway...all that money Vance put into his haunted house since last year, plus the possible cooperation with Kemp...I think Dina will help us shed some light on the whole thing, if we ask the right questions. And maybe all this does is clear some of these names off the list, which would be huge progress."

"Speaking of light," Cabo said, "is that the Morgue ahead?"

As they rounded a curve, the blacktop about a half-mile down the road was bathed in a halo of white light. It highlighted the mist settling into dew—and possibly frost—in the chilly night air and drowned out the flashing yellow arrow sign for the Lost Haven Morgue.

"Oh no," Lawrence said.

Belma sighed. "We do not have time for this."

"What is it?" Cabo said. "Time for what?"

With no traffic coming from either way, Jenna let the Jeep coast to a stop a few hundred yards from the entrance. The Lost Haven Morgue Haunted Attraction was set back from the road with a short driveway that opened into a large parking lot, previously used by the employees of the slaughterhouse. The lot was over half-full, not bad at all for a haunted house this close to closing time on a Sunday night.

The blinding white light came from a bank of halogen bulbs perched atop an RV squatting on the shoulder of the road. It had an airbrushed scene on the side showing a man in flowing white robes, striking a heroic stance as he stood between a roaring inferno and a grateful flock of adoring people dressed in what looked like burlap sacks.

An actual man in flowing white robes strutted around the RV with a bullhorn, blaring an endless stream of words toward the Morgue's parking lot.

"Preacher Hank," Jenna grumbled. "I was hoping he took Sundays off."

"That...doesn't make any sense," Cabo said.

"Neither does he. Remember, he's not a real pastor. Or reverend. Or anything."

"He's just real annoying," Lawrence said.

Cabo watched the man jumping and spinning as he bellowed into the bullhorn. "So let's just ignore him. Pull in, park, and head straight for the Morgue."

"Oh, Jay Cabo," Jenna sighed as she rolled toward the driveway. "If only it were that simple."

—

As Jenna tried to hustle the Jeep past the RV and into the driveway, she muttered, "Don't make eye contact. Don't make eye contact. Shoot!"

"What happened?" Cabo asked.

"I made eye contact."

Preacher Hank bolted into the driveway and skidded to a halt directly in front of the Jeep, which was now caught directly in the blinding RV spotlights. Jenna had to stomp the brakes to keep from running him over.

"Do it," Belma urged. "I'll testify he dove under the wheels."

"I heard that!" Preacher Hank bawled through the bullhorn. "Who said that?"

He was short and lean under the robes with a dark, bristly crew-cut going gray at the temples. Heavy black-rimmed glasses framed his wild, beady eyes, which searched the Jeep's windshield for confessors. He was a man who enjoyed nothing more than an uncomfortable argument, and his face reflected his constant mission to find the next one.

He scampered around the fender and peered through Jenna's window, then turned his fist in a circle, mimicking a crank.

Jenna didn't move.

"He wants you to roll it down," Cabo said.

"I know."

She still didn't move.

Preacher Hank tapped on the glass with the edge

of his bullhorn. "My foot is in the destructive path of your rear tire, heathen. Roll thy window down, or run me over and suffer the litigious consequences!"

"Good lord," Lawrence said.

Preacher Hank pressed the barrel against the back window. "Blasphemy! How dare you speak that way in my presence as you prepare to enter this den of sin and iniquity!"

"How did he hear that?" Cabo mumbled.

"I hear all, you monstrous lump of vanity! Put down the weights and pick up your morals!"

Lawrence finally caved and rolled his window down. "You have a mustard stain on your robe."

Preacher Hank shoved the bullhorn through the gap. "That's nothing compared to the stain upon your soul, candy man! You rot the decency of Lost Haven with your delicious temptations, just as you rot the teeth of those sheep who partake! Shame on you, and do you have one of those pen thingies for getting out stains when you don't have immediate access to a washing machine?"

"Uhh, no," Lawrence said.

Preacher Hank shuffled back to Jenna's window. "How about you, keeper of false histories? You read all of the books except the one that matters, so do you have a detergent pen as an offering to get into my good graces and possibly save your eternal soul?"

"You know what?" Jenna said. She reached over

and rooted around in the glove compartment, emerging victoriously with a Tide pen.

"Why on earth do you have that in here?" Cabo said.

Jenna sniffed. "I may or may not occasionally enjoy a completely sloppy take-out burger and fries, and I may or may not spill ketchup on my lap. Every time."

She cracked her window and slipped the pen out to Preacher Hank, who clamped the bullhorn between his knees and feverishly attacked the mustard stain. Having decimated it into a damp splotch that was now gray instead of yellow, he handed the pen back and rearmed himself with the bullhorn.

"Thank you very much, I appreciate that!"

"You're welcome," Jenna said.

"But you shall not tempt me with your witchcraft! My virtue cannot be compromised by your gifts, sorceress! I do not suffer from the trappings of greed like all of you! Martin Ritter was consumed by greed, and look at what it got him!"

Jenna was lifting her foot off the brake to ease forward half-hoping he stayed where he was and got his toes crushed, but then pressed it back to the floor.

"What did it get him?"

Preacher Hank paused, unprepared for engagement, then pulled the bullhorn's trigger again. "Have you not heard the news, sinners?"

Jenna played dumb. "What news?"

"Ah, witness as Preacher Hank enlightens

the masses once again! That dead body buried on unhallowed ground in Lilac Park is none other than Martin Ritter!"

He pulled the bullhorn down and pressed his face against the half-open window to take in their reactions of astonishment and disbelief.

Jenna gasped, playing the role, and turned to give a look to the rest of the crew. "Whaaat? Guys, did you hear that?"

"It can't be," Lawrence said.

Belma covered a yawn. "I am stunned."

"I'm sort of new in town," Cabo said, "so my quiet and confused reaction is appropriate. And you said unhallowed ground—isn't Lilac Park actually a graveyard?"

"No!" Preacher Hank barked through the bullhorn. "The people of Sanctuary may have used pagan ways! Until it is confirmed they were truly people of good faith and part of my flock, I shall consider that land cursed. Cursed!"

He dropped to a conversational tone, but kept the horn going.

"And besides, they blessed the ground underneath, and then the sand and topsoil came in, so that stuff on top doesn't count as hallowed. Obviously."

Lawrence was skeptical. "Doesn't count?"

"You heard me, heathen! Are your ears shut to words of righteousness?"

"They're pretty much shut to everything, thanks to your megaphone there."

"This is my truth amplifier! Oh how I wish I didn't need it, but the earplugs of sin are thick and comfortable, and they are truth-cancelling, like those expensive headphones. Another example of sinful greed!"

A minivan leaving the Lost Haven Morgue veered off the driveway and skirted behind Preacher Hank, who turned and pointed his bullhorn at them.

"You're lucky I'm busy saving these souls, you grimy Fergusons! Next time I see you, prepare for thy reckoning!'

Everyone in the Ferguson van gave Jenna and the Main Street crew thumbs-up through their windows, grateful for Preacher Hank's fixation on the Jeep.

When Preacher Hank turned back, Jenna said, "I have some truth for you. The people of Sanctuary weren't pagans. Well, the founding families weren't, anyway, and they ran the town. I can assure you the cemetery is consecrated ground. I can even show you the books where the ceremony was recorded."

"I'm not falling for that trap, Jenna Hooper! You'll draw me in with false promises of revelation, and the next thing I know you're flapping your gums on and on about how the Minks and Gallaghers worked together to supplant the Kavanaughs in some dusty days of yore. Yawn! Pass!"

Jenna's mouth fell open in stunned indignation.

Belma snorted in the back seat. "Man, if Preacher Hank thinks your conversations are tedious…"

Jenna rolled her window down the rest of the way.

"Uh-oh," Lawrence whispered, relishing the epic battle about to ensue.

———

**P**reacher Hank spread his feet and licked his lips. He held the bullhorn at the ready position across his chest—he didn't need it now that Jenna had taken the bait, but it was close at hand in case she changed her mind and tried to flee.

She said, "You call us heathens and pagans, but it sounds like you think Martin Ritter got what he deserved," Jenna said.

"Hallelujah, even heathens can be observant sometimes," Preacher Hank said.

"He didn't kill anyone. He didn't even hurt anyone. He maybe—and this hasn't been proven yet—stole some money from his own business. That's worth getting murdered?"

"It's worth justice," Preacher Hank said. "Whatever form that takes isn't up to you and me."

"Who is it up to?"

"Darlin', if you have to ask, you and I need to have a much longer talk."

Jenna nodded toward his RV. "That painting

makes it look like you're the one handling things down here."

Preacher Hank glanced back at the airbrushed scene of biblical fire, fury, and salvation with him standing tall among all of it.

"I only asked the artist to paint what he was called upon to share with the world."

"Who's the artist?" Jenna asked.

Preacher Hank cleared his throat. "Me."

"It's pretty good."

He shrugged. "I took some art classes at the community college. Again, I was called upon."

"And what if you were called upon to serve so-called justice to Martin Ritter? Would you do that?"

Preacher Hank swallowed.

The man was in a pickle.

If he said no, he was nullifying everything he'd ever claimed about his complete and utter devotion to serving a righteous higher power.

If he said yes, he could be implicating himself in Ritter's death.

"Would you?" Jenna asked again.

Preacher Hank stared at her from behind his heavy black frames. Then he stepped back and lifted his bullhorn.

"Move along, now! You're hopelessly beyond redemption!"

"You don't want to answer the question? It seems pretty simple."

"I said move along! There are better souls more worthy of my time!"

Jenna checked the driveway, then up and down the road. "Looks like it's just us heathens right now. So what's the good word, Preacher Hank?"

The man's robes flowed majestically as he whirled and ran to his RV, climbed the two tiny steps, and disappeared inside. After a moment the spotlights on the roof died, and in the sudden dimness of the Jeep's meager headlights Jenna could see the faint shape of Preacher Hank's head peeking at them above the RV's dashboard.

She took her foot off the brake and let the Jeep roll forward.

"Oh my goodness," Belma breathed.

Lawrence was pressing his palms against his temples to keep his head from exploding. "Did you just discover a way to shut Preacher Hank up? Is this *another* Halloween miracle?"

"You think he did it?" Cabo asked.

Jenna smiled at her driver's side mirror as the RV fired up and spewed dirt and gravel from the shoulder, tilting away from its station outside the Lost Haven Morgue.

"I don't know yet. But I think he moved up a few spots on the list, don't you?"

Cabo shook his head, trying to clear it. "I think

all we've managed to do is put everyone we've talked to in the number-one slot. So far nobody's innocent."

Jenna eased into the Morgue's parking lot and killed the Jeep. "So let's go into an abandoned slaughterhouse that is now a haunted morgue and talk to a possible madam about her relationships with a dead man and one who calls himself Skull Monger. That ought to clear things up."

"Happy Halloween in Lost Haven," Lawrence said.

Belma grinned. "Amen."

# CHAPTER 9

From the parking lot, the Lost Haven Morgue haunted house looked like any other outdated light industrial building. It had a low brick structure with a flat roof in the front for offices, and a larger two-story building rising from behind, where the real work was done.

A tall chain link fence surrounded the building and an inner lot that wrapped around to the rear building, where the loading docks were. The large rolling gate in the fence was chained and padlocked shut, but the smaller entrance for workers was unlocked and open.

On the other side of that fence was when things got weird.

Cabo was watching the groups of people flowing out of the exit gate, off to their right, and didn't seem to notice what was waiting for him until he was about to step through the opening.

He stopped. "Uh, guys?"

"Yes?" Jenna said, feigning innocence and smiling wider than Belma and Lawrence combined.

"There are some, uh, people up ahead."

"There sure are."

The three shop owners snorted and nudged each other like third-graders with a hidden whoopee cushion. For the moment, Preacher Hank, Skull Monger, Julian Vance, and Martin Ritter were blissfully forgotten.

"Is this the start?" Cabo said. "What's going on?"

Jenna gave an exaggerated shrug. "I don't know. What does the sign say?"

Cabo looked at the large wooden sign, white with black lettering, bolted to the fence to the left of the entrance. It took a moment for him to ignore the filthy fingers that curled around the edges of the sign from the other side and dug at the wood with yellow fingernails.

"'The Lost Haven Morgue'," he read. "'Official Institute for Cutting-Edge Research into Post-Mortem Potential'."

A massive smear of thick red blood obscured some of the letters, and someone had used the blood to scrawl "GO BACK" across the bottom of the sign. The lower leg of the K trailed off the wood's edge.

"Post-Mortem Potential?" Cabo said. "What on earth does that mean?"

Jenna could barely contain her glee. "Well, I'm just speculating here, but it seems like they've been conducting some unethical experiments on the dead and things have gone horribly awry."

Cabo side-eyed her. "Just speculating, huh?"

"Absolutely. You could ask them."

She pointed to the far side of the fence, where at least a dozen zombies pressed against the chain link, glaring at them and trying to push through. They groaned and hissed, their brown teeth clacking with some hideous instinct to bite, rip, chew.

Beyond the gate, more fencing had been formed into a rough tunnel leading to the front doors of the building, which were propped open to show a pitch-black interior. A few more zombies wandered along the outside of the tunnel, one of them standing on top and swatting wildly at something only it could see.

"And these fine individuals would be Martin's Maniacs?" Cabo muttered, quietly enough to not be overheard by the undead horde.

"Just a sampling," Belma said. "Well, not Martin's Maniac's anymore, I suppose, since he's beyond any sort of post-mortem potential himself. Now they're what...Polk's Folks?"

Lawrence shook his head. "Like your caramel truffles, that is alarmingly bland. They are obviously Dina's Demons."

"Dang it," Belma said. "That is better."

"Oh, how you must get tired of saying that about everything I say, do, and bake."

"Maybe you should ask Bub Thorp about that," Belma mumbled.

"What was that, sweetie?"

"Nothing."

Jenna said, "I think we should have a blind taste test with the zombies. Let them take a chomp out of both of you and let us know which one is better."

"I'm much too salty," Lawrence said. "But we'd both beat Cabo, that's for sure. Everybody knows zombies hate the taste of asparagus."

He slapped the larger man on the shoulder.

"That's why you should go first."

"Oh, no. I'm middle wedge. I don't care what anyone says about it only counting for Ghost Ship, or rotating positions, or whatever. I don't need any zombie fingers creeping on me—I can't be responsible for the specialized bodyguard training that might kick in."

Jenna frowned. "You specialized in zombie defense?"

"Paparazzi. Pretty much the same thing."

"I'll go first," Belma said, sounding much less confident than she'd intended. "When Martin ran this place there was a rule that the Maniacs couldn't touch you. I think it's safe to say that's still in effect... right?"

Lawrence nodded. "Oh, sure."

"I can see you rolling your eyes."

"Sorry. That's just an automatic response every

time I hear your voice. Of course you'll be fine and no Maniacs will touch you."

"You just rolled your eyes again!" Belma cried.

Lawrence turned to Cabo. "I see what you mean about the training. It just takes over."

"Alright, follow me," Jenna said. She wasn't thrilled about leading the way into the zombie infestation, but it was getting late and she didn't want to risk the Morgue closing before they got in.

"Now remember, if we see Dina, she may be upset. She may have just found out her boyfriend was killed and buried in Lilac Park. Or, she may have just found out the boyfriend she killed and buried in Lilac Park has been identified."

"Is there a Hallmark card for that?" Lawrence said.

Cabo grunted. "There should be, just for this loony town."

"Either way," Jenna pressed on, "I think Dina may be the linchpin in all of this. Whether she's a killer or not, something was going on between her, Kemp, and Ritter. Maybe it still is."

Belma wrinkled her nose. "Gross."

"What I'm saying is, Dina could be in a highly emotional state."

"So we go easy on her?" Cabo said.

"Oh, no way. If she's on the brink of a total meltdown, we give her the final shove."

With that, Jenna hunched her shoulders, making herself as small as possible, and stepped into the zombie gauntlet. Belma followed, and then Cabo and Lawrence, and the four of them became temporary residents of the Lost Haven Morgue.

They hoped, anyway.

—

All semblance of discipline in the Main Street crew shattered as soon as the zombies began gnashing from mere inches away, clutching and shaking the chain link tunnel.

Jenna ran first, sprinting toward the open doors of the Morgue while the zombie on top of the tunnel scrambled above her, dripping something thick and heavy. She had no idea what waited for them beyond the threshold, but it couldn't be worse than a dozen zombies scraping their faces along the fence and battering the links, making a terrible amount of hacking, hissing, and slurping noises as they tried to get through.

It couldn't be worse.

Right?

Lawrence would find out first. He blew past everyone, high knees and tucked elbows pumping with the determination of a survivor.

Cabo couldn't edge around Belma and he wasn't quite at the point yet when manners failed and he could justify shoving her aside, so he cupped her elbows and lifted, carrying her the rest of the way to the entrance.

He screeched to a stop on the linoleum just inside the doors and set Belma down like a potted plant. She stood there, frozen, while the zombies howled and gnashed about their lost meal just outside the doorway.

"Did I just levitate?" she asked.

"Sorry," Cabo said.

Jenna blinked in the sudden darkness. They were in a small vestibule that served as an airlock between the outdoors and interior. The next set of doors was draped with a curtain of heavy, semi-transparent plastic, the sort used to keep cold air inside walk-in freezers. There was light on the other side, and shapes moved in that light, but Jenna had no idea what they were.

If they turned out to be more zombies, with their zombie teeth and milky zombie eyes, Dina Polk might be off the hook for the night because Jenna was on the verge of a brisk about-face and double-time back to the Jeep.

"Ready?" she asked the crew.

"Ready to go home and curl up and die," Lawrence said.

Cabo shook his head.

Belma said, "Only if Jay Cabo carries me."

Jenna took a deep breath and dove through

the flaps like ripping off a Band Aid—fast and briefly excruciating.

The room on the other side was a small lobby with two hallways going left and right. Past those, a built-in receptionist's counter spanned the width of a shallow space with a few doors on the back wall, leading further into the building.

The hallway on the left was barricaded with a chaotic pile of desks, chairs, and office printers the size of compact cars.

The hallway on the right was open, and from somewhere further along a light flickered.

The receptionist's area was not empty.

A woman stood there, lit from below to give her face harsh, dramatic lines. She lifted her arms and let the sleeves of her black, lacy gown flow like dark wings around her.

"I am Mistress Sara Moanies," she said. "And I've been waiting for you."

———

Jenna resisted the urge to address the woman as Dina Polk. Martin Ritter had been notorious for never letting himself or his Maniacs break character, and Dina was the enforcer who made sure everyone—including herself—obeyed.

"Hello, Mistress," Jenna said, feeling semi-foolish but willing to play along. "You've been waiting for us?"

The Mistress gazed at each of them from behind thick black lashes. Her face was narrow and pale with red slashes beneath her fine cheekbones. She was beautiful and ageless, in a haunting, gothic way.

"That's right."

"Us, like personally? Or just…anyone?"

The Mistress gave a sly smile. "Are you four here because of the dead?"

Jenna paused and glanced at Cabo. Was she referring to the Morgue, or Ritter? Cabo must have had the same question, because he shrugged helplessly.

"Yes?" Jenna tried.

"Why?"

*Dang it!*

"To…learn more about him. Them."

The Mistress stared, her chin lifted so she could literally look down her nose at Jenna. "And what do you wish to learn?"

"Umm…"

*Is this some sort of challenge?*

*Is she trying to find out what we know?*

*Is she trying to figure out if we're here to help solve her boyfriend's murder?*

*And will she appreciate that help…or try to stop us?*

*Are you going to stand here all night with your mouth hanging open?*

"How they died," Jenna blurted. "And...who caused it."

"Everyone dies," the Mistress declared. "Why should the means matter?"

Jenna glanced behind her. The endless groans of the zombie horde could be heard through the heavy plastic flaps.

"Because they seem like they have unfinished business. Like they need closure."

"Closure." The Mistress enjoyed the word, rolling it around in her wide mouth. "Like a coffin lid closing, yes?"

"Exactly." Jenna hesitated, and then went for it: "Especially for those who weren't buried in a coffin."

The Mistress glared at her for hours, days, months. Years came and went and still the Mistress glared, and Jenna knew she had made a terrible mistake.

Then the Mistress spoke: "The Lost Haven Morgue closes for business in ten minutes. I suggest you hurry if you hope to make it out before we bar the doors for the night. Should you emerge intact, I'll be waiting for you. We'll talk about true closure."

The Mistress held her hand out, palm up, and Jenna hesitated before resting her own palm on it. She was ready to be led toward whatever truths Mistress Sara Moanies held secret.

"She wants cash, dummy," Belma said.

"Oh. Right."

While Jenna pulled the money out of her pocket and found the right bills, Cabo cleared his throat.

"Uh, Mistress Moanies?"

She looked at him like she was impressed he could form complete words. Belma and Lawrence also watched completely unaware of what Cabo was going to say, and loving it.

He cleared his throat again. "This is my first time going through the haunted houses in Lost Haven, and you guys have all done an amazing job. I mean, really great. These people here, supposedly my friends, kept saying I was going to wet my pants, and I didn't believe them."

"Have you?" the Mistress asked.

"No ma'am. I took an anti-diuretic with my last smoothie of the night. Shut me off like a kink in a hose until I could get to a toilet."

The Mistress frowned and glanced at the others. Belma and Lawrence looked desperate for a bucket of popcorn to share while they watched this spectacle. Jenna stood with the cash in-hand, eager to get started but equally interested in what else might come out of Cabo's mouth.

"Anyway," Cabo said, "I'd really love to see what you and your actors have put together, but I'll be honest. I've just about had it with fight or flight adrenaline dumps for one night. If you want to tell us something, if there is some way we can help you, let's just find a quiet place and have a conversation.

There's no need for us to go through the entire Morgue, is there?"

The lobby was silent for a moment, making the zombie chatter from outside seem much louder.

"Man," Belma said. "You really are a scaredy-cat."

"I'm just trying to be logical," Cabo said.

"Your mortal logic doesn't apply here," the Mistress said. "But if you must have proper motivation, know that it would be...unseemly for you to leave the Morgue without having seen its horrors."

It was Jenna's turn to frown. "What does that mean?"

"Even empty eyes can see."

"That...doesn't help at all."

"Stop talking, everyone!" Lawrence yelled. "I'm just getting more confused. Let's get this over with and go scream and get chased by fake zombies like normal people."

Jenna looked at Cabo, who shrugged and nodded. She handed the cash to the Mistress, who raised an eyebrow and pursed her red lips as she quickly reviewed the bills, then expertly tucked them into a drawer beneath the counter.

She looked up and gave the same sly smile as she swept an arm toward the open hallway.

"I wish you luck in your search for answers about the dead. I just hope you don't ask the wrong questions. Or the wrong people."

———

Jenna peered down the hallway to the right, but another screen of wide plastic flaps hung about twenty feet in, blocking sight of whatever waited ahead. Thankfully, the hall was wide enough for the four of them to hook arms and walk alongside each other.

Jenna took the left wing, linked to Cabo, then Belma, with Lawrence hunkering inside his hood on the right. He kept shooting furtive glances at the solid, featureless brick wall a few feet away like it was going to open up and swallow him.

Ahead, the wide flaps shivered in a steady breeze pushing through the open doors in the lobby. Music pulsed against the other side of the flaps, thundering, driving drums and howling string instruments that sounded much too close to human.

Just before they got to the barrier, Jenna looked back and saw the lobby was empty. Mistress Sara Moanies had gone.

*Gone where?* Jenna wondered.

*To meet us at the end of the haunt, or to pack up her car and leave town?*

*To warn Kemp or Vance—maybe both?*

*To lock us in the Morgue and handle things the way she had with Ritter?*

Suddenly the meat locker flaps took on a whole

new level of terror. Jenna imagined Dina standing on the other side, a shovel raised above her head, ready to smash down again and again before using that same shovel to dig four more shallow graves.

Jenna stopped. Cabo looked over at her, followed by Belma and Lawrence, to see what the holdup was.

"This doesn't feel good," she said, just loud enough to be heard by her friends. "I have no idea what she meant back there about empty eyes and asking the wrong people, or why she's so adamant that we have to see the entire Morgue. It feels like a trap."

Cabo nodded. "I don't like it either."

"So, what, we chicken out?" Belma said. "We'll never live it down. Just put us up on the wet pants board with Jay Cabo."

"I didn't wet my pants!" Cabo said.

"Yet."

"We aren't chickening out," Jenna said. "We're—"

"You're still here," the Mistress interrupted. "Splendid."

She was in the hallway behind them, appearing from nowhere and possibly close enough to overhear what they'd been saying.

"We, uh," Jenna said.

"I know what you're doing."

"You do?"

"Oh yes. You're our final guests for the night."

That hung in the hallway for a moment, and then Cabo said, "That sounds ominous."

"Oh, crap," Lawrence said, looking over at Belma and Jenna. *We're the last group.*"

"The last group," Belma whispered, her voice carrying something close to reverence.

Jenna shook her head. "I didn't even think about that."

"About what?" Cabo said. "What's the big deal about the last group?"

Jenna said, "The actors. They know we're the last ones through, so they don't have to stay in their spots or rooms once we go through."

"So? What does that mean?"

"It means they're all free to do that."

She pointed toward the Mistress, who was no longer alone. All of the zombies from the Morgue's yard had silently shuffled into the lobby and now stood behind her, waiting.

Waiting to chase.

"Oh, crap," Cabo said. He reached back and pulled his left foot up to his butt, then set it down and did the right, stretching his quads.

The four of them turned away from the horde and faced the meat locker strips, linking arms again.

"I guess we don't go back," Jenna said. "We go forward."

"Yay?" Belma squeaked.

"Cabo?"

"I'm good."

Jenna leaned forward and peered down to the end of the row. "Lawrence?"

"Try to keep up, sweetheart."

Behind them, the Mistress swept her arms forward, releasing her swarm of the undead with their gnashing teeth and clutching claws.

"Go!" Jenna yelled.

They plunged through the old slaughterhouse flaps and ran for their lives.

—

Jenna's suspicions had been right—someone was waiting for them on the other side of the flaps—but it wasn't Mistress Sara Moanies with a shovel. It was a tall, incredibly skinny man in a white lab coat and black rubber apron, his arms covered from fingertip to elbow in more black rubber. He carried a wicked-looking stainless steel saw in one hand and a huge scalpel in the other, and he leered maniacally at them from behind a huge set of protective goggles.

"Hey, you aren't corpses!" he proclaimed, a line he probably recited hundreds of times each night in October. "Well, let's fix that! Yah ha ha!"

Jenna practically stiff-armed him as they blew past, rounding a turn to the left and bowling into a room filled wall-to-wall with hospital gurneys. Lumpy black body bags were strewn atop each one, and the gurneys were arranged in a brilliantly chaotic pattern, creating a path that forced patrons to walk past almost every one on their way to the door in the far right corner

The Main Street crew didn't even slow down. They switched to single-file and flowed along the path, shuffling left and right to maximize speed through the gurneys. At the third turn one of the body bags sat up and fell open, revealing a bloated, moaning corpse inside.

Jenna, Cabo, and Belma were already past by the time it was completely upright, so the corpse was forced to reach for Lawrence, who pointed at it and yelled, "Not right now!"

The corpse turned its head as he sprinted by, and then gave an undead shrug because it had nothing else to do.

Then the skinny mortician and zombie horde erupted into the room, bringing a cacophony of maniacal laughter, groaning, and grunting as they bumped and tussled toward their victims. The body bag corpse fell off the gurney as it scrambled out of its sack to join the riot.

The Main Street crew made a frantic right turn toward the back wall, and after that it would just be a few jogs left and right and another hard turn to get to the room's exit. Then something skittered beneath the gurneys and Jenna looked down in time to see a decomposed hand and arm just ahead, reaching out and grasping for her ankles.

Without planning to, she planted a hand on the gurney to her right and vaulted over it, her shoes slapping onto the linoleum about five feet from the exit—she'd skipped about one-third of the gurney maze. Cabo followed, landing like an agile mountain lion next to her. He reached over the body bag to help Belma just as the zipper started to slide open.

Belma saw the bag opening and hesitated, just for a blink, then dropped sideways onto the gurney and steamrolled over the body inside.

A muffled male voice from inside said, "Oof! What the…I mean, uh, braaains…"

Belma rolled semi-gracefully off the gurney—if 1% grace can be considered semi—and immediately ran for the exit without a word.

Jenna and Cabo exchanged raised eyebrows in her wake, and then reached for Lawrence as the body started to rise. Lawrence stepped back, his eyes bulging at the hissing, blood-splattered zombie emerging from the body bag. The chasing horde closed in behind him, filling the pathway and scrambling over body bags.

"I can't make it!"

"Go around!" Jenna yelled.

He took a step forward and ran smack into the decomposed hand swiping from beneath the gurneys, causing him to leap two steps back.

"No!" Jenna called. "Forward, always forward!"

"Just go! Leave me!" Lawrence bawled.

Belma stuck her head back into the room. "Leave him!"

"Jump over!" Cabo yelled, his arms outstretched. "I'll catch you!"

Lawrence was squared up to the gurney and crouched, ready to make the leap, when the corpse rocketed fully upright and flailed its arms. Strips of bloody flesh dangling from its wrists slapped across Lawrence's face and he gasped, shocked and appalled, then seemed to slip into a catatonic state. He sank to the floor, disappearing behind the gurney as the corpse leaned over him and the decomposed hand twiddled itself closer.

The noise from the pursuers spiked in pitch and volume as they closed in on a kill.

"Lawrence!" Jenna cried. She turned to Cabo. "We have to go get him."

Cabo nodded, his jaw clenched, and managed to take one step before another hand shot from beneath the gurney and wrapped around his ankle. Cabo screamed, a piercing keen that made Jenna wince and even caused some of the zombies to pause and stare.

Cabo reached down to yank the horrid hand loose, but it had already let go to stretch up and clutch his hand.

"Pull!" Lawrence yelled from under the gurney. "Pull like you've never pulled before, Jay Cabo!"

Cabo pulled.

Lawrence came out from beneath the gurney like a fish poured from a bucket of water. He flopped and wriggled, then popped up and shook himself off.

"Whoa! I need about four showers, all at the same time."

Belma was still in the doorway. "Come on you slackers! We got trouble ahead!"

They squeezed through the door into another hallway and assembled into a loose wedge with Belma leading the way. Jenna could see over her chocolate and mint pile of hair, and Belma had been right.

There was serious trouble ahead.

—

The short, wide hallway led to another curtain of meat locker flaps. The plastic was filmed with grime and splatters of blood, but transparent enough to show an erratic blue light on the far side.

In that light, human shapes shuffled and bumped into each other, moaning and hissing.

From behind, the racket from the gurney room rose as the horde grew in numbers and excitement.

"Forward!" Jenna called.

They blasted through the flaps into a macabre autopsy and embalming chamber with a stainless steel table bolted to the middle of the floor and a massive, flickering blue light above it. Saws, spikes, and obscenely large hypodermic needles hung on the walls alongside what appeared to be human scalps and skins.

The semi-dormant zombies perked at their sudden arrival and turned toward them, but the Main Street crew spread out and wove between the shamblers, barely avoiding outstretched fingers and chomping jaws.

The far wall was a grid of square, stainless steel morgue drawers. Jenna was the first to make it that far, bouncing off the steel and looking frantically left and right for the way out.

There was none.

Cabo joined her, then Belma and Lawrence, and the four of them huddled in a tight ball as the zombies closed in. The Mortician and his pack of undead, including the body bag corpses, slashed their way through the bloody flaps and pressed in as well.

"What do we do?" Belma screamed.

Her arms were wrapped around Lawrence's waist, his around her shoulders, and they merged into a single mass of quivering candy maker.

The zombies were reaching for them. The closest had a half-dozen syringes stuck into the back of his hand, which was dripping some foul yellow liquid. The thought of that hand brushing against her made Jenna press further back against the morgue drawers and one of the oversized handles dug into her kidney.

The handles! Of course!

She turned away from the dripping hand and started yanking on the heavy drawer handles, willing one of them to open a hidden exit.

The first didn't budge, neither did the second, but the third moved with a well-oiled ease. Jenna pulled and felt something release, then the drawer directly in front of her face dropped inside the wall and the Mistress lunged forward, screaming with fury.

Jenna launched away from the wall, tumbling into the waiting arms of the zombie horde.

They swallowed her up, and the last thing she saw was a mass of dead hands reaching for her before everything went black.

———

Jenna's eyes fluttered open.

She was on her back, looking up at a strange, flickering blue light.

Something touched her arm, and she let her head fall that way. A woman with half of her face missing and one eyeball dangling from a cord of tissue was staring at her with the good eye. She had Jenna's wrist clamped down, and Jenna realized she was laying flat on the embalming table.

"Whaaa..."

The table was surrounded by more zombies,

their faces glistening with blood and pocked with decay while their deep-set, milky eyes enjoyed her helplessness.

Jenna struggled to sit up, but the one-eyed woman pushed her back down.

"Easy, easy."

Jenna looked frantically for help. The Mistress came into focus, standing just beyond Jenna's feet with that sly smile playing around her lips. Jenna's confusion grew when she saw Cabo standing on one side of her and Belma and Lawrence on the other, all three of them grinning like idiots.

"Oh man," Belma said. "Is fainting worse than wetting your pants?"

Lawrence nodded. "Ten times worse. When you faint, you could cut loose with all sorts of downtown action. I mean, she could have a whole sewage plant going on down there right now."

"I can't believe it," Cabo said.

Jenna blinked. "I fainted?"

"Like a damsel in a corset!" Belma crowed. "When we leave here we're gonna tie you to some train tracks."

"But..." She turned to the zombie clamping her wrist down, and realized the woman was just holding a few fingers against her skin.

"Pulse seems okay," she said. When she saw Jenna's baffled look, she followed up with, "I'm a nurse during the day."

The skinny mortician loomed over her shoulder. "I think she's going to live. Bummer!"

The rest of the zombies laughed. Her supposed friends joined in.

Jenna tried to sit up again, slowly, and a few of the zombies reached out to help her.

"What on earth…?"

"You can relax," the Mistress said. "The scaring is over. I just wanted to get the four of you into this room."

"What…why?"

She pointed to the open morgue drawer. "To show you that."

Lawrence said, "The spot where Jenna fainted and became a legend of Halloween weakness?"

"Oh no," Jenna groaned.

"That," the Mistress said, "is where our Martin used to hide and scare people in his beloved Lost Haven Morgue. He loved seeing their shock and terror change to relief, and eventually laughter. All he wanted was to entertain."

"Did he love the fainting?" Belma asked.

"No one ever fainted before today."

Lawrence could barely contain his joy. "You don't say? Did you hear that, Jenna?"

"I heard."

"You're the first one ever to faint here. Like, in all of history."

"I said I heard!"

The Mistress said, "When we found out the body in Lilac Park was him, we were all devastated. We still can't believe it. Even now, I think he's going to walk through those bloody flaps at any moment, cackling like a lunatic. I know everyone here feels the same."

The zombies nodded and moved closer to one another for consolation. They hugged with bony, maggot-ridden arms and leaned crumpled foreheads onto moldy shoulders.

"I also know he didn't steal the Morgue's money," the Mistress said.

Jenna's head had cleared.

Mostly.

She asked, "Then who did?"

"That's what we need you to find out."

Jenna began to protest, but the Mistress held up a hand.

"Maybe you're just being a snoopy town gossip. Maybe it's for the sake of Lost Haven's history. I don't care. But you're asking good questions, and you solved the Kavanaugh resort murders. I hope you can do the same for our Martin."

The room was quiet for a moment. The zombies looked at Jenna with what she had to assume was an appeal for help, but the exposed molars and bitten-off noses made it hard to tell.

"We'll try," she said.

"Thank you."

"You know," Jenna said, "Cabo was right. You could have just asked us to talk."

The Mistress gave a wicked grin. "Oh, Martin would have been *so* disappointed in us if we'd done that. And we didn't terrorize you all the way to Martin's spot just for sentimental reasons."

She walked over and pulled another drawer handle in the top row, releasing one entire column of drawers. They swung out like a huge door, exposing the hiding spot where the Mistress had waited for them. She pointed inside at a knee-high cube with a cushion on top.

"Martin's seat. Notice anything odd about it?"

The Main Street crew peered in. Jenna half-expected something to pop out and further cement her humiliation, then Cabo pointed.

"There's a dial on the front side there. It's a safe."

The Mistress nodded. "This is where Martin kept our cash. He literally tried to guard it with his life. And someone killed him for it."

"You have no idea who?" Jenna said.

"Oh, I have ideas about who might have done it. Probably the same people the police are considering. They're probably even looking at *me* as a suspect."

The zombies groaned in protest while Jenna and her crew tried to look shocked at the notion.

"We'll do whatever we can to help find the killer," Jenna said.

And none of them knew—not until it was too late, anyway—that the killer was in the room with them.

———

The Mistress left her zombies behind and escorted the Main Street crew back through what little they had seen of the Morgue, gliding among the body bags and gurneys with her hands clasped across her stomach and hidden by the flowing sleeves of her black dress. She pushed through the meat locker flaps without seeming to notice them.

When they reached the lobby, she turned and looked at each of them, finally resting her eyes on Jenna.

"I would appreciate your discretion about what you've seen and heard here tonight. At least until Martin's killer is brought to justice."

"Of course," Jenna said.

"I assume you'll want to document the story for the official town record?"

"Oh boy…" Lawrence said.

Jenna shot him a look. "Yes, I will. Not just for Martin, but for everyone in Lost Haven who loves Halloween and how we celebrate it. I don't want this terrible event to tarnish that, and what you've worked so hard to create here."

"That is kind of you," the Mistress said. "If Martin's death results in any harm to our beloved holiday, he'll actually find a way to rise again and eat our brains out of disappointment. Should you need any information for your historical record when the time comes, do no hesitate to ask."

Jenna couldn't help herself. "Would you be willing to discuss any details about the Morgue's other business, if it's involved?"

"Other business?" the Mistress said.

"Yes. Do you think it had anything to do with the murder?"

"I'm not sure what you're referring to."

"The one that no one knows about, but everyone kinda...does?"

The Mistress gave nothing away.

"She means the brothel," Belma said.

Lawrence nodded. "The prostitutes. Hooker Haven. Hey, that's a good name."

The Mistress eyed them all again, her small smile flashing. "I said do not hesitate to ask, and I can appreciate your willingness to do just that. However, just because you ask, does not mean I will answer. Now good night to you, and Happy Halloween."

# CHAPTER 10

The Morgue's parking lot was empty except for Jenna's Jeep. Preacher Hank's RV had not returned to its perch near the driveway.

The Main Street crew shuffled across the lot and fell into their seats, exhausted after the chaos and emotions of the night. Jenna turned the key and Belma shook her head at the clock.

"What are we doing awake at twelve-thirty on a Sunday night? We have to work tomorrow. Today. Well, some of us do. Cabo's job is to exercise, and that's not a job."

Cabo grunted his objection, too tired to put up any more of a fight.

"I don't know about you guys," Jenna said, "but my head is spinning. Unless you know absolutely one-hundred percent who killed Ritter and stole the money, I say we all go home, get some sleep, and meet up tomorrow sometime."

"Deal," Lawrence said. He dropped his head onto Belma's shoulder and closed his eyes.

Belma opened her mouth to protest, then leaned her head down to use Lawrence's as a pillow.

Mildly surprised that neither one of them burst into flames, Jenna pulled out of the lot and rolled toward town.

———

J enna dropped the other three in the alley behind the Main Street shops with some mumbled good night wishes.

She idled there with the full bank of the Jeep's roof lights on to obliterate any shadows and potential ambush spots while her friends wandered toward their cars. She figured there was a good chance they'd talked to Martin Ritter's murderer at some point during the evening, and may have shaken something loose enough to make the killer think it was a good idea to kill again to protect their identity.

She made a mental note: *Next time, park out front before we go on a mission to irritate murder suspects. And hey, your pad is right there. Make a real note so I don't have to remember this.*

Jenna pulled the yellow legal pad out from next to the driver's seat, unclipped the pen, and scribbled a note about not parking in homicide alley. She ran down the list, trying to make one of the names pop out among the others, and then shook her head to clear it. She was too exhausted to dive into any more hypotheticals and theories.

The other three vehicles started rolling and she followed them to the end of the alley. Everyone was safely tucked into their seatbelts and on their way home.

Jenna turned left and let the Jeep take her the few blocks east to her house, encountering zero traffic before bumping into the driveway so the headlights spilled over her detached garage. She hit the button to raise the door, and something about the harsh Jeep lights and sharp shadows made her stop.

*You already made a note about not parking in homicide alley—what about serial killer garage?*

Well, that seems a bit drastic.

*It's a long walk from the garage to your back door, which you can't even see right now.*

It's like, twenty feet.

*You just came from three haunted houses. How much room did they need to terrify you? And they were just playing.*

Good point.

Jenna closed the garage door, reversed into the street and parked at the curb. She used the flashlight on her phone to spray the darkness away as she hurried to the front door, unlocked it, and ducked inside.

With the lights on and the doors locked—she performed multiple confirmations of the latter—she collapsed onto her bed and closed her eyes, just for a few minutes before enduring the impossible task of undressing, maybe showering, and putting on her fleece Halloween pajamas.

The next time she opened her eyes, it was 7:45 in the morning and she was already running late.

———

Jenna turned the Welcome Shoppe sign from *Closed* to *Open* at 8:04, her hair still dripping from a scalding speed shower. She could see Detective Olson waiting in his car in the spot right outside the door, flipping through sheets of paper inside a folder.

Jenna glanced down to make sure her shoes matched—no time to confirm the socks—and opened the door. Olson looked over, smiled and waved, and held up a finger to tell her he'd be a minute.

That was fine, she could use about sixty.

She hustled up to the mezzanine and got the coffee going. When the machine began to gurgle, wheeze and tick, she finally took a moment to catch her breath, looking out at Lilac Park.

Off to the north the knuckle of the backhoe loader peeked above the tree line, and then disappeared. The Sanctuary Cemetery exhumation crews were working again.

To the south, the bridges of Ghost Ship loomed over everything else in the marina.

And pretty much due west, even though she couldn't see it, was the Lost Haven Grille.

Julian Vance was likely at one or the other, unless he was already on his way over to her shop.

*Slightly awkward*, she mused, *flirting with a murder suspect in front of the state police detective investigating the case.*

But she hadn't gone on a date since she and Garrett had broken up earlier that year—holy Halloween, that *year*—so she'd take awkward, fumbling, even embarrassing if they came with some decent conversation and somebody to watch scary movies with.

Jenna snapped out of the second episode of her *Brunch with Books* fantasy when Olson popped his driver's door open below her. She hijacked the coffee machine's drip and filled two mugs, replaced the pot, and poured a lethal dose of cream into one mug from the carafe she kept in the mini fridge under the coffee counter.

When Olson entered the shop, she called down, "How do you take your coffee?"

"Black as night and bitter as my ex-wife."

Jenna escorted the two mugs down the open stairway and set Olson's on the check-out counter.

"I didn't know you were married."

"Some detective you are." He took a hit of the steaming coffee and smacked his lips. "The fourth cup of the day is always the best one."

"*Fourth?*" Jenna said, incredulous. "It's not even eight-fifteen yet."

"I've been at the medical examiner's, getting the lowdown on Ritter's autopsy. They start early over there, dealing with all of the Sanctuary bodies getting shuffled around."

"Anything you can share?" Jenna noticed he hadn't brought the folder in with him.

"Well, I can tell you Martin Ritter was strangled to death. I'm talking the two-hands-around-the-throat, face-to-face sort of strangling. Old school."

Jenna frowned. "There's a new way to strangle?"

"Ah, kids these days," Olson said, and left it at that. "Problem is, he was wearing that dumb zombie mask of his when he got choked, so the person's hands were wrapped around the latex instead of right against his flesh. Makes it harder to determine hand size, and the potential for any DNA is pretty much zilch."

"No fingerprints either?"

Olson shook his head. "Not on the latex, after being in the ground as long as he was."

"I wonder if any of it would hold up in court anyway," Jenna said.

"Why wouldn't it?"

"Ritter wore that mask pretty much all day and night during October. He shoved it at thousands of people going through the Morgue. I'd bet everyone in town, at some point, has smacked, pushed, or punched that mask. Easy enough for the killer to say that's how their DNA or fingerprints got on it."

"Huh," Olson said. "You shouldn't even be wasting your time with detective stuff. You should go straight to amateur lawyering."

"You put that coffee down and get out of here, buddy."

He grinned. "But the murder method does give us something, even if we can't pull any hard evidence."

"'What?" Jenna said.

"Killing someone like that, looking them in the face while you strangle them—well, in this case it was a zombie mask, so maybe I'm talking out of my butt here—but typically that means it was something personal. The killer knew Ritter well, and they were probably having some sort of heated argument. Things escalated, tempers flared, and boom. Next thing you know one guy's got his hands around the other guy's neck."

"You think it was a man?"

Olson took another drink of coffee. "Boy that's good. What kind is it?"

"I get it from a local guy; this blend is called Hallowed Grounds. He makes it every October. You want a bag?"

"I'd love one. I'll only ruin it with my crappy coffee machine, but still."

Jenna headed for the stairs again, Olson following.

"You said 'guy.' You think a man killed Ritter?"

Olson paused for a few seconds. "Before I answer, do you know anything else? I don't want to lay out all my fancy theories and suppositions based on twenty-plus years of professional police and detective experience, just to have you say, 'Well, so-and-so confessed to me last night, so you can take all of your nonsense and flush it.'"

Jenna laughed. "I have some theories of my own, but nothing solid. So if you tell me a man killed Ritter, then that would take Dina Polk off of the list. She's already on the bubble, but eliminating her for certain would be one less person to worry about."

When they got to the mezzanine Olson looked out the windows and whistled. "Beauty of a view."

Jenna pulled a bag of Hallowed Grounds from the cabinet next to the mini fridge and handed it to him.

He pressed his nose against the outside of the bag and inhaled. "Yeah, this is way too high-quality for me. So, ninety-nine percent the killer was a man. Ritter wasn't a bodybuilder by any stretch, but the guy was active and he worked with his hands a lot, building that Morgue. So he had some muscle to him. Just based on the usual disparity in upper-body strength, it would be very difficult for someone the size of Dina Polk to strangle someone like Ritter to death. Unless he wanted her to, which is a whole different sort of case."

"Yikes," Jenna said, thinking about the brothel

and wondering if Olson was fishing for more information about it.

"Yeah. But with the money involved, the personal grudges going on, my gut says it isn't anything kooky like that."

"You mentioned Dina's size—you've seen her?"

Olson smiled again. "I went through the Morgue last night with the forensics crew, Tina and Gino. As customers, not badge-flashers, but it was still a reconnaissance mission."

Jenna clapped with delight. She loved it when someone got to experience the haunted side of Halloween in Lost Haven for the first time. "What did you think?"

"We had a blast, but the techs couldn't help picking out the flaws in the zombie decomposition. And don't even get them started on what color decaying blood should be. Just…don't. But Dina was the Mistress-lady, right?"

"Yep. We were there too, right at closing time. She made an appeal to us to help find who killed her boyfriend."

"Insinuating it wasn't her."

"Right."

"You believe her?"

"I do," Jenna nodded. "Of course, she's a professional actress, so…"

They both considered that for a moment, and then

Jenna asked, "Was Preacher Hank parked outside when you were there?"

"That guy, whew. You were right to put him on the list. He and Tina got into a whole thing about whether a soul is a physical object, and he just about pulled his hair out when she said she had more faith in maggots than any higher power. I can see Ritter saying the wrong thing to him and Preacher Hank throttling that zombie mask."

"Totally," Jenna said. "We hit Ghost Ship and No Sanctuary last night too, to see Vance and Kemp."

"Whoa, you guys were busy. I didn't make it to those. Find out anything good?"

"Kemp said he has video footage of Ritter defacing one of his rooms the night he was murdered."

Olson blinked. "Seriously?"

"We didn't see it, but that's what he said. Also that he'd operated No Sanctuary all that night, then reviewed security footage, and called the Morgue around three a.m. screaming for Ritter. Who, by that time was already missing and probably dead."

"Maybe," Olson said. "It's impossible to nail the time of death at this point, but I can check phone records to see if he actually made that call, and what time. How did he seem? Freaked out that the body in the park was Ritter?"

"I can't even picture Kemp freaked out. But no, he wasn't. He'd had some time to process it though—he said Vance texted him with the news."

"Vance, as in Julian Vance? From Ghost Ship?"

"One and the same. We broke the news to him, and he seemed genuinely shocked and a little upset."

"Same question I had about Dina: You believe him?"

Jenna shrugged helplessly. "They're all performers, wearing makeup, and Vance had a bunch of barnacles and crabs and stuff on his face when we told him."

"Crabs?"

"He was a drowned navy captain. Or a pirate. We weren't really sure. Anyway, it was hard to read his face, but his voice sounded sincere. You should go through Ghost Ship though—you won't notice the difference because you didn't see it last year, but it has some serious upgrades. Which means serious cash."

"The missing million?" Olson said.

Jenna shrugged. "Vance said he has investors from Chicago. My ring of contacts and gossip sources—and, frankly, my interest—ends the moment you cross the Lost Haven township line, so I have no idea who to verify that."

"I can look into it."

"Perfect." Jenna chewed her lip and picked at a non-existent stain near the coffee maker. "And, uh, full disclosure..."

"Uh oh," Olson said.

Jenna winced. "He asked me out on a date."

"You're kidding me."

"Why is that so hard to believe?"

Olson waved his free hand. "No no, not that part—if this guy killed Ritter, it's a seriously ballsy move to ask you out."

"Because I'm so classy?" Jenna said, touching her damp hair. It crackled, and she wondered if she'd remembered to rinse the shampoo out.

Olson shifted his feet. "Eh, yep. But also, Vance has to know you and this shop are the hub of information in town. All the other business owners coming and going, you collecting history about Sanctuary and Lost Haven—he might be trying to keep *you* close so he can find out how close *we* are to catching him."

"Cynicism is so romantic," Jenna said.

"And now you're picking up on why I'm divorced."

"Well, maybe you can quiz him about it yourself." She pointed out the window at Julian Vance crossing Main Street from the southern corner of Lilac Park. "He's coming here right now."

—

Julian Vance pushed through the glass doors with a large white box in his hands and an even larger smile on his face.

"Warning! Carbs incoming! Evacuate the area if you don't enjoy the smell and taste of warm fresh bread."

Jenna stood behind the counter with her coffee. "You have my full, undivided attention."

Vance set the box on the counter and lifted the lid with reverence. "A selection of fresh breakfast rolls, courtesy of the Lost Haven Grille. We have cinnamon glaze, poppy seed, and some flaky croissant thing that looks like a biscuit to me. Exclusive recipes just for my restaurant from Baker's Cousin. And, of course, enough whipped butter to paint a house."

Jenna's eyes were wide. "No one else has to know about these."

"I'm just the delivery guy. What happens next is your business. I also slipped my card in there in a pathetic attempt to use the bread as bait to give you my number."

"Slightly more pathetic: I'll probably use it as a butter knife, but I'll save your number first. And look, I don't want to stuff my face in front of you, but I got up late and I'm starving, so...you might want to back up."

Vance smiled and took a step back. "Big night after we parted ways?"

"We hit the other haunts," Jenna said around a mouthful of cinnamon glaze.

"Your aunt did what?"

She took a sip of coffee. "Haunts! We went to the other haunted houses after Ghost Ship. No Sanctuary and the Morgue."

"Ah. Well, I guess I shouldn't expect you to be

entirely faithful this early in our relationship. How did we compare?"

"You're the only one with a slide," Jenna said, and took another bite of bread to hide her uncertainty. It was a complete guess, since Ghost Ship was the only haunt they'd gone all the way through.

"Success! But just wait. Next year it'll be like *Chutes and Ladders* around here. They can't help copying the best."

He chose a croissant and took a bite, considered the taste, then nodded at the rest of the roll in approval.

"And speaking of the best, have you thought about where you want to have dinner? My vote is still the Grille—we can just have rolls if you want—but it can be anywhere."

"Oh, don't tempt me with an all-roll dinner date. Those are typically very private, satisfying events. But honestly, I haven't had a spare moment to think about dinner, sorry. We ran into Dave Kemp and Dina Polk at the other haunts, and you know, with the whole Ritter thing happening, it was intense."

She watched Vance's face closely as she mentioned the other haunters. His chewing stopped, then picked up again, slower than before.

"Skull Monger and Mistress Sara Moanies," he said. "How were they taking the news?"

"Dina was upset but keeping it together. Kemp,

who can say? He seemed irritated, but he always seems irritated. Though, he did say something interesting."

Vance's eyebrows went up as he chewed another bite.

"He said you texted him with the news about Ritter."

Vance swallowed, the bread seeming to catch in his throat on the way down.

"Why would he say that?"

"You're asking because it isn't true?"

He paused. "No, it's true. But why would it come up in conversation? That seems...odd."

"We thought we were the ones breaking the news to him, just like with you. But he said you'd already texted him about it."

She closed one eye and pointed at him with the remainder of the cinnamon roll, which was shockingly small.

"But I remembered you saying you didn't allow phones on Ghost Ship, so that seemed odd to *me*."

Vance pointed back at her with his croissant. "Jenna Hooper, you're remembering random things I say. I think you might have a crush on me."

"Don't get too cocky, buster. I'm also remembering random things Dave Kemp says."

"Well, I hope you like waking up next to a skull mask."

Jenna gave a dramatic shudder. "Does the rest of

your crew know you're breaking your own rule by having a phone?"

Vance looked over at the doors, and then glanced toward the back of the store.

Jenna braced herself.

*Is he checking for witnesses?*

*Witnesses to what, exactly?*

Apparently satisfied, Vance shot his arm out toward Jenna. She flinched and put her hands up to block the incoming blow, but it stopped halfway across the counter. Jenna blinked and looked at the arm, the sleeve Vance had pulled up, and the smart watch strapped to his wrist.

The small screen woke up, showing the snippet of a new email, and she could see the text icon as well.

Vance shrugged and gave a lopsided grin. "Don't tell the crew, please. I swear, I usually have it on airplane mode when I'm at the haunt, but I'm still a terrible hypocrite. I'm also an egomaniac, and I've set up my businesses so they can't function without me. I need to be reachable at all times. When I'm here, that means an hour later than usual, since Chicago is an hour behind. I promise I won't wear it on our date. Well, I promise I won't check it constantly. Once every five minutes, tops."

To prove his unwavering commitment, he checked the screen.

"Sorry. Habit."

Jenna relaxed, but kept watching for reactions. "A

hypocrite and egomaniac. Your stock is rising, my friend. I'll make you a deal: You can wear the watch if I can bring a book."

"Wow. Well, that's a first. What book?"

She lifted it from beneath the counter and let its full weight thump next to the cash register.

"*Sanctorum Subter.* It means 'The sanctuary beneath,' more or less. It's from Harrison Kavanaugh's personal library."

"Huh. That's pretty grim. I was hoping it might be fifty shades of something or other, but okay, point taken. I'll ditch the watch; you can leave the doorstop here. I'll just probably lose millions of dollars because someone in Chicago can't figure out how to get more lettuce."

"It's Chicago. Just replace the lettuce with deep dish pizza. No one will notice."

Vance shook his head. "Brilliant. Tonight then? Lost Haven Grille, say, eight-thirty?"

Jenna tried to find the harm in saying yes. She was 99% sure he didn't kill Ritter, but...

*If that 1% comes through, you'll have dated a murderer. One you suspected.*

But if someone else killed Ritter, no harm done. And I'll have had a date.

*With a possible killer.*

And a lot of delicious bread.

*Well, that's undeniable.*

"See you then," she said.

—

Vance left the box of rolls with his card tucked carefully into one of the inner flaps and pushed through the doors, giving a small fist pump on the sidewalk that Jenna probably wasn't supposed to see. He walked in front of Detective Olson's parked car and waited for a few north-bound vehicles to pass— likely headed to the Sanctuary Café for a morning jolt and some pumpkin cookies—then dashed across and turned south toward the corner that would lead him back to his restaurant.

*His restaurant*, Jenna mused.

*A restaurateur.*

*And a haunter.*

*Brunch with Books and Bones...*

Thoroughly enjoying that concept as she tapped his contact information into her phone, she was rudely extracted back to her shop by the clanking of Olson setting his coffee cup down on the mezzanine table. He stood and put his hands in his pockets, watching Vance from the lofty perch for a few moments before strolling to the railing overlooking the shop.

He took his hands out and spread them on the rail, tapping out some tune only he could hear.

Finally, he looked down at Jenna. "Seems like a nice enough guy."

Jenna let out a breath she didn't know she was holding.

"Or," the detective said, "he's an extremely high-functioning psychopath drawing you into his twisted little game so he can use you as an accomplice and possibly murder you next."

Jenna cursed, startling Olson, and took another roll.

—

Olson left to, as he put it, "Drive around and bother people," leaving Jenna even more confused about Julian Vance's true intentions and threat level. In between ringing up customers, answering questions, and refilling the coffee pot, she busied herself with the Welcome Shoppe's Halloween display to keep from storming across Lilac Park and asking him flat-out if he was planning to murder her.

She called her display a Halloween tree—much like a Christmas tree—but the similarities between the two ended once you got past the general shape. First she cleared the stained glass kites and driftwood wind chimes out of the front display window and put down a thick brown blanket with autumn-colored leaves sewn onto it.

Then came the slowly rotating base, which was

actually for a Christmas tree, but nobody had to know that. Things were going to be offensive enough.

She affixed a life-size, startlingly realistic skeleton to the base, and it stood there with its arms raised above its head thanks to the thick wires and construction adhesive she'd spent hours working into the joints and sockets.

Next came the piles of skulls, carved from styrofoam and painted to have cracked domes and missing teeth. Those went around the base of the skeleton and formed a rough skirt shape.

She stepped back and checked her work. It looked like the skeleton was bursting up from a pile of skulls with arms raised and mouth open, and when she checked it out of the corner of her eye it truly did have the shape of a Christmas tree.

It was spectacular.

She wrapped it in orange and purple light strings and hung the ornaments—severed fingers, dangly eyeballs, flappy bats, obscenely bristly spiders for Lawrence, and so on—then went behind the counter to get the final touch. The electric chainsaw was heavy enough to make her nervous, because if the wires and adhesive didn't hold, the thing could come down on some poor person's head.

Jenna hefted the chainsaw and looked up at the thin arms and fingers.

*The responsible thing is to leave it behind the counter.*

Responsible? There's a fake electric chair in here that buzzes butts.

*That won't send anyone to the emergency room if it breaks.*

True. But it's Halloween in Lost Haven. People know the risks.

She zip-tied the chainsaw into the skeleton's grasp, ran the cord down through the ribcage to keep it hidden, then plugged it into an electrical strip built into the rotating platform. She ran the platform's thicker cord to the wall outlet, crossed her fingers, and plugged that in.

The chainsaw-wielding skeleton tree began to turn in a slow circle, and the small speaker she'd concealed among the fake leaves cackled with maniacal glee.

Jenna was grinning like a lunatic and staring at the display when her sole employee, Wendy Blake, walked in for her shift and saw the creation. It was somewhere between five and fifteen minutes after Jenna had finished—she couldn't say for sure.

"Wow!" Wendy said. "You said you had something new for this year, but I was expecting maybe a few extra pumpkins or a witch's cauldron."

"What do you think?"

"Well…it's certainly Halloween-y."

"Check out those fingers, see how realistic they are."

"Ew," Wendy said. She eased closer and leaned in

272 · PENNY PLUME

to peer at the severed digits, and that's when Jenna
hit the button on the remote.

The electric chainsaw roared and rocked the skeleton's arms back and forth, but everything held and
Wendy ran backwards across the floor, turned the
corner of the counter, and dove for cover.

"Yes!" Jenna cried.

Then she hurried over to the counter and bent over
it to look down at Wendy, who was huddled beneath
the cash register and rocking with her phone clutched
between her hands.

"Are you okay?"

"No. I'm traumatized."

"Can you still work?"

Wendy swallowed and stopped rocking. "Only if I
can text all my friends to come see the gross fingers,
so we can do the exact same thing to them."

"You just got a raise," Jenna said.

———

Jenna was looking at her phone, checking for any
news from Olson or the Main Street crew—heck,
even anybody on her suspect list who maybe felt
compelled to confess to everything—when Jimbo
Gelderson strolled in with his ancient canvas tool
bag and whistling something jaunty.

Jenna checked the phone's clock, which displayed

a very judgmental 12:14, and was about to say something when she noticed the trail of mud Jimbo's heavy boots left behind.

She gaped at the clumps for a moment, and then said, "Jimbo! What are you doing?"

He turned and blinked at her from behind his lenses. "The toilet. Unless it managed to install itself last night?"

"No, the mud!"

He turned further. "Oh. Oh, cripes. It's from Lilac Park, I was with the exhumation crew this morning. Otherwise I'd have been here bright and early, around ten."

Jenna bit her tongue against all sorts of comments about how the bodies buried in Sanctuary Cemetery had been there for decades and could wait a little bit longer, and while he was out there drinking coffee and collecting mud her shop didn't have a decent public restroom. She suppressed all of that and just focused on the mud.

"Can you go back outside and clean your boots off please? I'll get the mop and take care of what's already here."

"Oh, a mop won't do it. Might have to get out the ol' scrub brush."

"I don't have a scrub brush."

"No? I think I have an extra one at home, I can run over right quick and—"

"No! You're finally here, let's just get as much done as we can today, yeah?"

Jimbo shrugged and headed for the door. "Something tells me I'll be going to get it sooner or later, but you're the boss."

"Did you notice the Halloween display?"

"The what?"

Jenna nodded toward the front windows and Jimbo turned again.

"Good gravy!"

Jenna hopped up and down. "Is it that scary?"

"Nah, at first glance I thought it was a Christmas tree, and I had a terrible fright I'd slept through turkey day again. But that's for Halloween you say?"

Jenna thought if the display got any more Halloween she'd have to take it trick-or-treating, but she remained silent.

"Say, is that a real chainsaw? The one you were running the other day?"

"It is," Jenna boasted.

"Well, you're gonna need more support than that. Maybe a piece of PVC pipe coming up from the floor, or a wire running up to the mezzanine there. Otherwise it's gonna come crashing down on some poor soul, and a hundred bucks says they'll have a lawyer in the family."

"Do you have a lawyer in your family, Jimbo?"

He snorted. "Me? Heck no."

"Why don't you lean in there and take a good look at the severed fingers?"

She had her thumb on the remote, ready to crush it and let whatever happened, happen.

"Nah, I'll run over to Wedell's and pick up some stuff, we'll string 'er up and make sure you don't get sued and lose this place before I can get the pooper installed."

"Jimbo, you stay right there. Actually, keep going outside and clean off your boots, then come back in and get to work. I'll go to Wedell's and get the pipe."

It would get her away from Jimbo long enough to cool down, and if Unflappable Bob was there, maybe they could have a private conversation...

"Okie dokie," Jimbo said. "You should pick up a scrub brush too. Always good to have one around for times like these."

Jenna shared a look with Wendy, grabbed her phone and keys and got out the door.

And if, by some chance Unflappable Bob did kill and bury Martin Ritter, maybe he could give her some advice on how to get away with it—after Jimbo installed the toilet.

———

Jenna crossed Main Street and walked north on the Lilac Park side. She waved to McTavish, who was serving a full lunchtime patio at the café, and stopped on the corner of Main and First Street for a few minutes to watch the exhumation crew. They were using straps hung from the backhoe's digger arm to hoist a decomposed wooden coffin out of a deep hole, and an idling flatbed truck had backed into the park from First Street, ready to accept the cargo.

Two men in safety goggles and dust masks flanked the coffin with long poles, which they braced against the sides to keep it from spinning out of alignment. Sand drifted down onto them from the cracks in the coffin as the backhoe gently swung it toward the truck, and the two men stoically allowed the grave soil to land on their protective gear.

*Who are you?* Jenna wondered about the coffin's inhabitant.

*What would you say about Sanctuary, if you had the chance?*

*And what would you think of Lost Haven? Not the murders and deceit, just, you know. What we've done with the place.*

Knowing what she did about Sanctuary—which was still just a drop in the bucket of the full history—Jenna imagined whoever was in that box would think the murder and deceit of Lost Haven were a good start for catching up with the buried town and all of its secrets.

More sand fell, in larger clumps this time, and Jenna held her breath, half expecting the bottom of the coffin to fail and spill whatever was left inside all over the sidewalk and crew. But Sanctuary lumber was good lumber, Sanctuary carpenters were expert craftsmen, and the coffin held.

Jenna expelled a slow breath.

*I guess we won't get to meet just yet, which is probably for the best.*

She crossed First while the workers began pulling off the straps and preparing the coffin for transportation to the medical examiner's office. The shop on the northwest corner of Main and First was Bloomers, the florist, and she spotted Hannah putting the final touches on their Halloween display.

It was a lovely arrangement of bright orange pumpkins, crisp cornstalks, and brilliant bouquets of purple beautyberry and twisting witch hazel along with an autumn rainbow of chrysanthemums in orange, yellow, red, and lavender. No doubt it also smelled tremendous, but it was no match for her chainsaw tree.

Hannah smiled, waved and pointed across the street, then down at the display.

Jenna waved back and looked over her shoulder. She verified the coffin hadn't burst open while she wasn't looking, and then turned back to Hannah, unsure what the young woman wanted.

Hannah pointed at the display again, then across the street.

*Wait a second*, Jenna thought.

She stepped back and took in the entire display, and in the front-right corner spotted a toy backhoe she hadn't noticed before. The display was a miniature version of Lilac Park, with pumpkins taking the place of statues, trimmed cornstalks standing in for the oaks, and dazzling flowers filling in for the lilac trees. They even had narrow trails winding through all of it, and the backhoe was parked next to a small hole with a pile of dirt next to it. A small coffin, complete with a tiny skeleton hand poking out from beneath the lid, dangled from straps made of ribbon.

Jenna nodded and gave Hannah two thumbs-up. It was spectacular, and a fine entry into the downtown Lost Haven Halloween display competition. Her chainsaw-wielding maniac skeleton with its skirt of skulls suddenly seemed absurd...but no!

The startle factor had to be considered!

While the autumn model of Lilac Park was beautiful, it wouldn't send anyone scurrying for cover behind a cash register.

Faith in herself restored, she moved along the sidewalk to Baker's Cousin, saw their display, and once again plummeted into despair.

——

The Baker's Cousin display was so brilliant because it struck a deep-seated fear within

Jenna and, most likely, the vast majority of innocent people who strolled by and were accosted by the
nightmare scenario.

It was simple, brutal, and almost too horrendous
to consider.

It was The Creature Who Ate All the Bread.

The master bakers had created a lumpy mon-
strosity out of pretzel bread, a cross between a giant
toad and some sort of pot-bellied pig. It sat back on
its haunches to allow its swollen bread belly to pro-
trude between its longer front legs, but all of those
were dwarfed by the gaping mouth and teeth made
of pita wedges.

Bulging eyeballs made of butter-glazed yeast rolls
stared at the raised platter in front of the creature,
which was heaped with dense loaves of raisin cinnamon, sourdough, oatmeal, apple walnut, pumpkin
and brown sugar, cranberry and cream cheese…

And then the bread was gone, vanished, devoured,
and leaving only a platter with a few lonely crumbs
left behind.

After a few seconds of heartbreak, the bread reap-
peared and all was right in the world.

Jenna knew it was an optical illusion, a trick
of mirrors, angles, and lighting, but the idea of all
that bread vanishing without being able to sample
one bite, one slice, one loaf, seemed to threaten her
very existence.

It was cruel, and she cursed the amazingly talented

husband and wife team that ran Baker's Cousin. Tom Averly was actually the cousin of Mitch Averly, who started the bakery years ago as Knead Bread?, but had to sell because he'd decided it was more profitable to sell a white powder that definitely wasn't flour or baking soda. Tom and his wife Beth bought the business, changed the name, and had been satisfying locals and tourists with their carb creations ever since.

But this…this was too far.

Jenna tried to deny the fact that she was also upset because it—along with the intricate Lilac Park model next door—made her display seem childish and silly.

She told herself, *You do not make light of a lack of bread! There is a line, people, and you have crossed it!*

Then the door opened and Tom Averly stepped out in an apron dusted with flour and presented a large tray of samples.

"Happy Halloween, Jenna. Here"

The bite-sized chunks of bread matched exactly the types of loaves on the display platter, and Jenna felt her furious panic subsiding.

Jenna chose the cranberry and cream cheese. The smoothness, sweetness, tartness…she closed her eyes and shook her head.

"Amazing. The bread, the display, all of it. Well done you two."

"Thanks! Is yours all done?"

"Uh, almost. No need to go look at it now. Or ever. And if you could do me a favor and put all of these loaves in my window, it would really help me out a lot."

"Sure," Tom laughed. "Want another sample?"

"Has anyone ever said no to that question?"

"Not yet."

Jenna took a cube of the raison cinnamon and ate half, wanting to savor this one a bit more. "Do you know if Bob is next door?"

"He is indeed, but I'd avoid him if you can. He's grumpier than usual, which is saying something."

Jenna's eyebrows went up. "Oh? Any idea what has him upset?"

"Nope, and I'm not about to ask him. I find it's better to leave him alone when he's like that. And pretty much every other time I see him."

"Duly noted," Jenna said. "If I do have to talk to him, I might need to come by for a few more samples. You know, cleanse the palette from all the grumpiness."

"Here's a piece of the apple walnut, for emergencies only. I'll be here if you need me."

"Thanks Tom," Jenna said. "And I don't care how grumpy Unflappable Bob is, nothing is more terrifying than the Creature Who Ate All the Bread."

———

The front windows of Wedell's Hardware featured leaf blowers and an outdoor fireplace. Even though the blowers were orange and black and the fireplace had a fake purple flame blowing in its belly, Jenna thought it hardly qualified as Halloween display.

This gave her mixed emotions: sadness because one of Lost Haven's shop owners wasn't fully embracing the tradition and happiness because she was absolutely certain her chainsaw skeleton was better.

But maybe she should get one of those fake flames...

Or a strobe light!

Then she had a vision of tourists collapsed in front of her shop, convulsing from seizures while blinded drivers smashed into each other on Main Street, and decided the spinning skeleton and chainsaw were enough.

She pushed through the heavy aluminum-frame door, the glass covered in decals from various tool and equipment companies. The space just inside was crowded by a rack of red and silver toy and gumball machines that probably hadn't been restocked since lead paint was outlawed.

The small open area near the checkout counter had a selection of snow blowers—perhaps this was Bob's Halloween display, insidious and terrifying—and a stack of oversized bags for leaf disposal. Jenna frowned at those. She was a firm believer that leaves should be in piles, not bags, no matter how much her neighbors disapproved.

The aisles beyond the front area were tall and narrow, filled with everything from two-pronged light socket outlet adapters to tiny drawers filled with tiny screws for fastening tiny things together. And though she had been in the store countless times, she had no idea where the PVC pipe would be.

Near the wrenches?

Next to the electrical wiring?

Somewhere in the vicinity of rope?

It was fine that she didn't know—it saved her from having to fake it in order to ask Unflappable Bob for assistance. Now if she could just find him in the warren of spray paints, glues of varying craziness, and the alarmingly wide selection of spackle...

A muttered curse drifted from somewhere in the back of the store and Jenna wandered that way, finally spotting Bob in the paint aisle, standing on a short ladder trying to wedge a cardboard box onto the overflow shelf above the display racks.

"Get in there, you dog! Swine! You...you turd!"

Jenna felt embarrassed for witnessing this private moment between Bob and the box, so she backed up a few aisles and intentionally kicked a bucket full of driveway reflectors. The box rummaging ceased, and a moment later she heard the ladder creak.

Bob came around the end of the aisle adjusting his handyman's apron with its pouches full of pens, pencils, razor knives, and a bulky tape measure clipped to a sagging pocket flap.

"Oh, it's you."

"Nice to see you too, Bob."

"Ahh," he waved her away. "I don't mean anything by it. I'm expecting a delivery of pumpkin carving kits. I thought you might be it."

"Afraid not. How was No Sanctuary last night?"

"A snooze fest," Bob said. "The elevator was a good idea, but the execution fell way short. And I could see the hinges on the swinging wall when I came out—like I'm supposed to believe the dang thing really moved!"

"What about the spider room?"

Bob shrugged. "I've seen scarier cleaning out my storage room."

Jenna cast a wary eye toward the back of the store while she tried to think of something else to say. This was good. Bob seemed chatty—which for him meant constant complaining and disparaging of others—and she wanted to see how things changed when she switched from talking about No Sanctuary to the Lost Haven Morgue and, by proxy, Martin Ritter.

The problem was, the spider room was the last part of No Sanctuary they'd gone through last night. Everything else was had been observed from behind the walls or via the security feeds...

"Oh!" she said. "How about that giant clown in the water?"

Bob was turning away to adjust an end cap display of smoke detectors, and he whirled back to fix her with a sharp stare.

"What about it?"

"It's, uh, pretty freaky. Rising up and chomping like that."

He glared at her, his eyes searching her face for… something…then relaxed a bit.

"I guess it's scary. If you're a four-year-old."

Jenna almost cut loose into a rant about how you're supposed to let yourself be scared and have fun at haunted houses, not clench your jaw and stomp through like a robot, but she took a breath, collected herself, and kept the conversation going.

"Well, in case you're considering going to the Morgue, they did a great job last night. The actors were all-in and the makeup was top-drawer. I thought I was really being chased by a zombie horde."

Bob snorted. "And what would they do if you didn't run? I'll tell you: they stand there and look depressed because you ain't playing along, screaming your fool head off and running into things. Nothing more pathetic than a depressed zombie. Except maybe the idiots who pay to get chased by them."

Jenna bit her tongue, chewed her lip, and gritted her teeth. "It's better to pay and have zero fun?"

"I pay to test my fortitude. My integrity. And to show the people of Lost Haven that I remain, for this day and all days, Unflappable."

*Unflappable, huh?* Jenna thought.

*We'll see about that…*

She pretended to notice the cans of spray paint for the first time.

"Hey, do you remember if Martin Ritter bought any fluorescent spray paint from you last year, just before Halloween?"

Bob blinked, knocked off guard by the sudden switch and mention of Ritter.

"Spray paint?"

"Yeah, something that would glow in blacklight."

After a moment, Bob said, "Ritter knew better than to come into my store, after the lies he spread about me."

"Do you remember if anyone bought fluorescent spray paint around then? I know it was almost a year ago, but you probably don't sell much of that kind."

Bob put his hands in the pockets of his apron, then took them out again.

"Can't say I recall. Why are you asking?"

"I heard—and I don't know if it's actually true— that Ritter used fluorescent spray paint to deface one of Dave Kemp's rooms in No Sanctuary last year, on Halloween night."

"That's the night he disappeared."

"The night he was *murdered*," Jenna corrected.

"Who'd you hear this from?"

Jenna didn't want to reveal Kemp as the source— not yet, anyway.

"Oh, you know my shop. People come and go, chatting and gossiping all day. But I guess Kemp has video footage of it, from the security cameras."

Bob swallowed. "You've seen it?"

"No, I don't think anyone has but Kemp. But I wonder how he knows it was really Martin Ritter. I mean, anybody could buy one of those zombie masks with the white hair and run around causing trouble, especially if they wanted to make Ritter look bad."

Bob cleared his throat. "He did a fine job making himself look bad, he didn't need any help in that department. And where's the missing money? He stole that, I guarantee you, and it's probably what got him killed. Not some silly graffiti."

"Well, it's probably just a matter of time before Detective Olson gets a warrant to review the footage, or Kemp just lets him. Maybe he'll be able to learn something from it."

"Maybe so." Bob said, his voice distant. He stretched an arm out and braced himself on the smoke detector shelf.

Jenna, satisfied that he seemed thoroughly flapped, perked up.

"Oh! I almost forgot. I need PVC pipe for holding up an electric chainsaw being held by a spinning skeleton."

Unflappable Bob, his voice still distant, nodded. "Of course. Right over here..."

—

The lunch crowd at the Sanctuary Café had mostly headed back to work, but Jenna spotted Belma sitting on the patio by herself and headed that way. Belma saw her coming and gave a small wave, then reached down to slide a large purse—it would be fair to call it luggage—under the table to make room.

Jenna plopped down in the seat next to her and leaned her eight-foot length of white plastic pipe against the table like an idle spear.

Belma frowned at it. "What's that for?"

"My window display. What's in the sack under the table?"

"Uh, more stuff for my window display."

"Really? What else do you need besides a severed Lawrence head?"

"Hmm, I was thinking about making some rats to gnaw on the neck stump. You know, really add depth to the scenario."

The quiet conversation at the table of four directly behind Belma ceased. One woman, frozen with a teacup halfway to her mouth, said, "Did that woman just say 'neck stump'?"

"Nope," Belma called over her shoulder. "Hey, what do you guys think of the cookies?"

"They're fantastic, I can't get enough," the woman

said, and went back to chatting at her table with some nervous glances thrown at Belma's back.

Jenna expected the response about Lawrence's pumpkin cookies to irritate Belma, but she just smirked.

"What's that face for?" Jenna asked.

"What face?"

"The Belma face."

Belma shrugged. "What other face am I supposed to have?"

"You just seem very...smug right now."

Belma shifted in her seat and sat up straighter. "How about now?"

"Still smug."

"Well, I don't know—"

She jumped as McTavish emerged from the café with another basket of cookies, heading for the table of four. Her hand reached for the purse, as if confirming it was still there.

McTavish winked at Jenna. "The usual, m'lady?"

"That would be wonderful, thank you."

He presented the basket to the other table. "My dear friends, it is my great pleasure to—oh, I see you already have some of our delightful autumn treats."

"They're fabulous," the tea drinker said.

The man next to her said, "I can't believe you're giving them away. I'd pay a dollar apiece. Maybe more."

Jenna cringed, knowing this must be stabbing

Belma straight in the heart, but she seemed to be fighting back a grin. Then it clicked.

"You did not," Jenna whispered.

Belma wrinkled her nose and nodded, like she was trying to be ashamed but just couldn't bring herself to feel it.

"Belma!"

"Shush. Let me have this."

McTavish set the new basket down. "I'll pass your compliments along to the confectioner responsible for your delight. And if you're done with these plates, I'll—"

"These aren't the same cookies," the tea drinker said. She had a mouthful of one of the new treats and seemed on the verge of letting it plop onto the table.

McTavish was confused. "I beg your pardon?"

"These cookies you brought, they're different. They're harder. And drier."

Belma closed her eyes, basking in the glory of the moment.

"Do you have any from this batch?" the man said, pointing at the original basket, which held a few meager crumbs.

"Well…" McTavish was at an utter loss. "I'm afraid there's no way to tell which batch they've come from. We get them in a bin from the confectioner, and dole them out from there."

"I can tell," Belma said. She scraped her chair back and hauled the purse out. "Because I'm the confectioner who made that first batch, and I have more just like them right here."

McTavish's mouth fell open. "You what?"

"I swapped my recipe in, bubba, and you heard the reviews. The public can't get enough of them."

McTavish sputtered for a moment. "You can't just bring random food into another establishment and feed it to the patrons."

"Why not?"

"It's a violation of the health code!"

"Really? Why? My shop is four doors away, what's the difference if they eat the cookies here or there?"

"The difference is I approved the Elegant Confections cookies, and yours are imposters! Invaders!"

"Oh, I like that name too," Belma said. "Jenna, write that one down."

"I will not."

Belma addressed the table. "Fine people of the patio. Would you say the cookies from the first basket were vastly superior to the semi-edible briquettes you've just been served, or would you merely say they were much, much better?"

"I like the crispy outside and the soft inside," the woman said.

The man nodded. "You can really taste the butter. That's what did it for me."

The second woman, silent until now, chimed in. "I'm getting a slightly bitter orange aftertaste, and I love it."

Belma turned to McTavish. "I'll sell them to you for ten percent less than what Lawrence gets, and I can have twenty dozen here in the next fifteen minutes."

"I won't do that to him," McTavish said, obviously torn. "But, I will give you a fair chance. Bring your dozens. I'll put baskets of both on the tables, and we'll see whose recipe triumphs."

"Good enough for now," Belma said. She reached into the purse and brought out another basket of her cookies, holding it aloft like a trophy.

The table of four burst into applause.

Jenna shared a helpless look with McTavish, then took two of the cookies and joined the cheering.

———

Jenna's enjoyment of Belma's cookies and the latte McTavish whipped up for her lasted exactly as long as it took her to walk past the Elegant Confections Halloween window display. She slowed as she drew near, and then stopped, staring in complete awe.

Lawrence had carved Lost Haven's Main Street shops entirely out of chocolate, right down to the tables outside of the Sanctuary Café, the slightly crooked awning above Belma's entrance, and the Halloween decorations adorning everything.

That was impressive, but what blew her away

was the carving of Sanctuary's Main Street shops beneath Lost Haven's. He had The Welcome Shoppe, Gallagher's, the Shoreline Gaming House, and the First Bank of Sanctuary, all intricately recreated. The models had to be based on photographs, since the reclamation project was still ongoing, which made them even more astounding.

To top it off, Lawrence had a slow trickle of sugar sifting down from Lost Haven into Sanctuary, no doubt representing the dune sand that had buried the original town.

The amount of effort, beauty, and love poured into the display made Jenna's stomach wrench with guilt over how many of Belma's pumpkin cookies she'd eaten. They felt like a solid lump of betrayal in there.

Crispy, gooey, buttery betrayal.

Movement inside the shop snapped her out of the self-inflicted misery and she darted to her right so she wouldn't have to face Lawrence. She absolutely *had* to tell him how much she adored his display, and she would, but not when she had fresh treachery breath.

Instead, she peered through the front windows of Cabo's Bodyworks studio and saw him at the small front counter with a silver-haired woman in yoga gear. She had a rolled-up mat under one arm and a massive water bottle in the other hand. Probably a woman dedicated to optimum health across all domains.

Jenna wiped the cookie crumbs from her face,

scrubbed her fingers on her jeans, and held the door open as the woman left.

"Whew! What a workout!" she said with an ecstatic grin.

"I know, right?" Jenna had purchased a yoga mat years before, used it once for an unsatisfying nap, and then stashed it out of sight on a closet shelf. She went into the studio, stopped, and listened for human noises beneath the soothing soundtrack of flowing water and random chimes.

Cabo watched from behind the counter, his eyes flicking from Jenna's face to the length of pipe she'd planted against his floor. "Everything okay?"

"Is anyone else here?" Jenna whispered.

"No. What have you done now? And what's with the pipe?"

She walked the rest of the way to the counter and ditched the whispering.

"Don't worry about the pipe. And I haven't done anything. Well, there's a whole cookie thing going on, but you don't need to know about it and I don't need your judgy face right now."

"Uh, okay."

"But, I just came from Wedell's Hardware and a very interesting conversation with Unflappable Bob."

Cabo raised an eyebrow. "Interesting how?"

"He got very nervous when I started talking about the spray paint Kemp told us about."

"The graffiti that Ritter did?"

"Yes. I played the angle like the paint may have come from his hardware store, and maybe it wasn't even Ritter under the mask, and when I mentioned that Kemp had surveillance of the whole thing Bob got really sketchy."

Cabo leaned back. "You think there's something on that footage he's worried about?"

"Maybe. He did not seem pleased to learn that Kemp had recordings. I wonder…do you think Kemp would let us see the footage?"

"Based on our conversation with him last night… no chance. Like he said, he doesn't want Ritter—or whoever it was under that zombie mask—getting any spotlight time from trashing his precious haunted house. My professional opinion—"

"As a yoga instructor?"

Cabo sighed. "As a former bodyguard, security consultant, and excellent reader of people because doing so saved me and my clients from engaging in violent confrontations."

Jenna nodded. "Go on."

"My professional opinion is that he's a proud guy, a control freak, and believes justice doesn't always fall in line with what's legal. I mean, you heard him talking about settling the thing with Ritter between haunters instead of going to the police, right?"

"Yeah…"

"In his mind, showing us the footage will make him look weak, like he doesn't have full control over everything that happens inside No Sanctuary. And that's the main reason he uses animatronics instead of actors, right? Control."

Jenna narrowed her eyes at him. "Have you evaluated me like this?"

"Of course."

"And?"

"And I'm keeping it to myself until I need to unleash the truth bomb upon you, probably to keep you from doing something stupid."

She opened her mouth to protest, but had no valid argument other than being insanely curious.

"Fair enough. But you'd better be ready to spill it, because I have a plan."

"Uh-oh."

"I have a date tonight at eight-thirty with Julian Vance, and—"

"That is a terrible plan."

"That's not the plan. And shut up. And why is it terrible?"

"Just keep going," Cabo said.

After a brief standoff, Jenna said, "I have some questions for him about Ritter, the Morgue, and the money, and based on how that conversation goes, we may need to go back to No Sanctuary tonight."

"To talk to Kemp again?"

"No. To avoid him entirely."

"I'm not following," Cabo said.

"We're going through the haunted house again,

and when we get to the spider room, we're going through the hidden door again. You and I are going to check that security footage."

"Uh, Jenna, that's illegal."

"Why? I didn't see any No Trespassing signs, did you?"

"No…but guaranteed we'll run into Kemp again. And if he figures out we're after the footage, I wouldn't be surprised if he locked it down, stashed it somewhere safe, or deleted it altogether."

"We won't run into Kemp again. He'll be busy."

"Busy doing what?"

"Dealing with Lawrence and Belma."

# CHAPTER 11

Jenna returned to The Welcome Shoppe and discovered that Jimbo had accomplished absolutely nothing noticeable during her absence.

Wendy was restocking a few of the seasonally themed driftwood tombstones on a shelf near the Ghost Ship display, and Jenna sidled next to her.

"What's he been doing this whole time?"

"I think he's been smelling the wood."

"Smelling? The baseboard pieces?"

"I guess," Wendy said. "The long ones stacked against the wall over there."

"Where is he now?"

"Down the stairs, in Sanctuary."

Jenna walked over to the wall and checked the stack of trim. There was nothing about the baseboards that indicated any sort of nasal inhalation was required—at least not that she could see.

"Jimbo!"

"Yah!"

"What are you doing?"

There was a lengthy pause, and then Jimbo's head appeared, rising as it wound around the staircase.

"Checking on the excavation progress to see how much of the old Welcome Shoppe they cleared out."

"And?"

"Jack squat! They must be working on another part of Sanctuary, because I can't see any progress at all."

Jenna waited for the irony to strike him like a bolt of lightning, but after a few seconds accepted that it was never going to happen.

"No progress, huh? Imagine that. What's the story with these baseboards?"

"Story?" Jimbo blinked behind his thick lenses. "Like, the rings and grain?"

"No, why are they still here, in a pile, instead of nailed to the wall? Do they still need to breathe?"

"Oh, no, they've breathed plenty. You can tell by the smell."

"The smell?"

"Sure. Here, sniff this."

He lifted the top piece and held the end under Jenna's nose. She gave it two quick sniffs.

"Okay."

Jimbo set that down and rummaged in his tool bag, emerging with a short chunk of darker wood with rough saw cuts on both ends.

"Now this one."

Jenna looked at him for a moment, wondering if

he was just trying to see how many random pieces of wood he could get her to smell. His smile was harmless and genuine, so she sniffed.

"It smells exactly the same."

"Oh, gosh no. This one smells like a swamp compared to your baseboards."

"If you say so. Why do you have it in your bag?"

Jimbo frowned. "Why?"

"Yes. If it smells like a swamp, why not throw it away?"

Jimbo cradled the piece and shook his head before tucking it back into his bag.

"You don't throw wood away, Jenna. Every piece is the perfect size for something; it's just a matter of finding that something."

Wendy, who was eavesdropping, said, "Awe."

"That is kind of romantic," Jenna admitted, "in a hoarder sort of way."

Jimbo blushed and waved them away. "I see you brought the pipe. She's a beaut."

"Yep, I asked for the most beautiful one. You can make sure the chainsaw won't fall on anybody?"

"I can make sure it doesn't fall on its own. Some doofus jumps up and hangs off it, it's probably coming down on them, and rightfully so."

"I'll make a sign," Jenna said. "*No hanging from the chainsaw.*"

"That'll only encourage them."

—

The next few hours went by quickly, with customers dropping in to sample the various autumn and Halloween samples, visit with each other in the reading nook, and gossip about Martin Ritter's body, the Lilac Park exhumation project, and the Sanctuary excavation.

Jenna didn't learn anything new, but she did get confirmation that the Bloomers and Baker's Cousin window displays were getting a lot of buzz. When she tried to connect the concept of *buzz* to the flies crawling on the edible severed head in Belma's window she was met with horrified silence, so she stopped trying.

At six in the evening, with the setting sun pouring gorgeous colors through the windows, Jenna made sure Wendy was all set to close up, then hurried home to shower again—for real this time, with rinsing and everything—and get ready for her date with Julian Vance.

As she was choosing an outfit, finally deciding on a dark blue wool dress that did a decent job with her curves and would keep her somewhat warm, she was grateful for the distractions provided by the Ritter investigation, window displays, and Belma's pumpkin cookie insurgence. She'd had zero time to be nervous about the date, which would be her first with someone other than Garrett in, what, over five years?

She was curling her hair and muttering along to the Top 40 music thumping out of her Bluetooth speaker, on the verge of dwelling on that span of time between first dates, when she realized she still wasn't nervous.

*Do you have feelings for him?*

No. Not yet, anyway.

*But you like him.*

He's okay. Sort of cocky.

*So was Garrett.*

Garrett was cocky like a middle school athlete. Vance is cocky like a fighter pilot.

*This is good?*

It's different. I'll take that for now.

*Olson doesn't like him.*

Well, Olson isn't going on this date. He'd look terrible in this dress.

*I think you might be overlooking the obvious reason why you aren't nervous.*

No I'm not.

*Do I need to say it?*

Nah.

*Is it because you're going to interrogate Vance rather than flirt with him?*

Interrogations can be flirtatious.

*Don't you ever tell anyone you had that thought.*

Okay. I'm going to have a wonderful time with Julian Vance, Restaurateur and Professional Pirate Captain Haunted House Owner.

*That's the spirit. If you feel the urge to grill him rather than date him, just remember: Books, Brunch, and Bones.*

Shoot, I forgot one title: Murder Suspect.

*This is doomed.*

—

Jenna decided to risk the heavy clouds rolling in from Lake Michigan and walk the three blocks to the Lakeside Grille. She took a moment to turn the corner at Main Street and admire her Halloween display. Wendy had done a great job, closing the shop and keeping the security light dimmed so the orange and purple string would really pop as the skeleton turned. The timer would shut it all off at midnight and turn it back on at six-thirty in the morning.

Thoroughly pleased with the display but disappointed at the lack of a dense crowd clamoring for a closer look at it, she crossed Main and got to the Grille just before eight-thirty. As she reached for the door it opened from inside and Chantel Tully, the Grille's manager, stood holding it open for her.

"Welcome, Miss Hooper."

Jenna hesitated, suddenly suspicious. This was a bit too close to her fantasy.

"Your table is ready," Chantel said. She was about ten years older than Jenna and absolutely lovely in a tight black dress that matched her short, funky black hair.

"Uh, hi Chantel." She stepped into the empty lobby. Sounds of low conversation and silverware against plates came from the dining room.

"Right this way, Miss Hooper."

Jenna stayed put. "What's going on?"

"Please, come along. We're so happy about serving you and Mr. Vance this evening."

"You can still just call me Jenna."

Chantel winked. "Not tonight, hon. Tonight, it's like Cinderella in real life. Except your wicked stepsisters are Belma and Lawrence."

"Does that make Cabo my wicked stepmother?"

Chantel thought about it for a moment. "Him or McTavish. No, Cabo, because he'd make you drink those smoothies while you mopped."

Jenna shuddered. "Please, tell me there are no smoothies on the menu tonight."

"Rest assured. However, Mr. Vance isn't here yet, but he should be arriving momentarily. He just had a few things to take care of at Ghost Ship."

"Oh. Are they open tonight?"

"Not on a Monday. It's one of the things that really bothers Julian—I mean, Mr. Vance—about No Sanctuary. That guy can be open every night in October because he doesn't have to schedule and pay any actors. If we kept Ghost Ship open that much, the actors would have to quit their real jobs or take vacation, and our makeup budget would shoot through the roof."

Jenna had a horrifying thought. "Wait a second. Is Vance going to show up to this date in full dead pirate captain makeup, dangling crabs and all?"

"Oh, no," Chantel said, though she sounded uncertain. "I mean, he's a goofball, but there's no way he'd think that's a good idea. Would he?"

"It would be fine with me, even fun; I just don't want to be distracted by those jiggling crabs all night. Let's make a deal: if he shows up in costume, I'll pull the crabs off and ask you to cook them up for dinner."

"And I'll throw them in the trash."

They shook on it.

"Would you like to be seated at your table?" Chantel asked.

"I'll wait for Vance. I like Vance better than Julian—should I call him Julian?"

"That's between you two. But his last girlfriend called him Sugar Daddy, and that relationship lasted about four minutes longer than a red light."

"Noted, thanks."

"And Jenna," Chantel said, "be patient with him. He's kinda blustery, and he says dumb things sometimes, but it's only because he wants to impress you. Underneath all of that, he's a sweetie."

She broke away to open the door for a group of six and led them to their table, leaving Jenna alone in the lobby. She spent a few minutes strolling around, sitting, and popping back up to peer at the sepia photographs of the Lakeside Grille's grand opening. Brass plates under the photos listed the year as 1846.

Another grainy image taken in 1842 from the Lake Michigan shoreline showed a huge ship wrecked just off the coast, its debris scattered among chunks of ice in the frigid winter waters.

Jenna had examined these photos countless times—she even had copies in her personal library—but the nervousness was starting to creep in now that Vance was approaching ten minutes late.

*He probably stood you up so he could murder somebody.*

Yes, that seems like the most plausible explanation. Or he's just late.

*To his first date with a woman he seemed very intent on wooing?*

He didn't woo me.

*Please. You've been wooed.*

I'd say I'm in the process of being wooed.

*And that process is being derailed because he's nearly fifteen minutes late now.*

Well, woo-hoo.

Chantel emerged from the dining room looking at her phone.

"I texted him right after I sat that group, and I haven't heard back yet. It shows as delivered."

"Is this strange for him?" Jenna asked.

"Very. Either he's really nervous about this date…"

"Or something's wrong?"

"I'm sure everything is fine," Chantel said, then went back to worrying at her phone.

Jenna said, "I'll walk down to Ghost Ship. We'll probably meet somewhere in between."

"I'm sure you will. I'm so sorry; your table will be ready whenever you get here."

Jenna peeked into the dining room. "Is it on the deck?"

"It's the *only* table on the deck. The heaters are burning, the bread will be warm, and the butter will be soft."

Jenna swooned. "Forget Vance, let's you and me go sit down and get to work."

Chantel laughed. "Now you're talking! If he texts or calls, I'll come find you."

"Thanks. I'll text him too; one of us is bound to get through."

Jenna left the restaurant and turned right toward the marina, her smile fading.

*If he's murdering someone, will you come back here and have some of that bread?*

Of course not.

*Really...?*

Maybe. It depends on who he's murdering. Wait, no, he's not murdering anyone!

Even though she believed that, mostly, she walked as quickly as she could toward Ghost Ship, cursing her stupid dress and impractical shoes.

—

The marina boardwalk was three steps away when Jenna heard the engine.

It sounded large and a little rough with a slight wheeze beneath the rumble, and it was familiar enough that she stopped and looked left, up Second Street. Preacher Hank's RV was idling along the southern edge of Lilac Park, coming toward her.

She paused with one foot on the boardwalk. The spotlights and roof-mounted megaphone—which was much louder than the handheld version—were not being used. That was a relief, but also odd; whenever Preacher Hank idled through downtown, he used it as an opportunity to berate everyone for being greedy, materialistic litterbugs, and, if it was late enough, curfew-violating heathens who worshipped the false moon goddess.

Jenna waited for the headlights to wash over her. She would weather the inevitable barrage of curses, damnations, and sudden offers to save her sorry soul in return for a proper donation, then calmly resume the conversation they'd started the night before outside the Lost Haven Morgue. She truly did want to know if Preacher Hank would kill Martin Ritter if his divine honcho told him to do so.

In the current situation, only a "Yes" answer would demand immediate follow-up questions. If he said "No," assuming he was going to answer at all, she'd love to do a deeper dive into why he would refuse that order...but it could wait until she found Julian Vance and got this date officially started.

It may have been her imagination, but the RV seemed to slow right after its headlights caught her. It rolled closer, the tailpipe spewing a dark gray exhaust that thickened in the cool night and gained a yellow halo under the street lamps.

Then Jenna realized she was just a foot stomp and steering wheel twitch away from being a speed bump on Preacher Hank's path to glory. She set her feet and got ready to dive onto the boardwalk, which was wide enough for the RV but had concrete planters at the entrance to prevent accidental—or, in this case, crazed and intentional—vehicle access.

The RV loomed closer and Jenna had to shield her eyes against the headlights. She focused on the sound of the engine. It was still idling at a slow, constant pace, then it roared and the headlights rocked upward as the vehicle leapt forward.

Jenna took one huge step toward the other side of the decorative barricade, her dress and clunky shoes forgotten, but it was a wasted rare example of historian agility. The lights swept to her left, following the sidewalk toward the Lakeside Grille as the RV started to turn right onto Shoreline Drive.

It stopped halfway through the turn and Preacher Hank glared at her from behind his driver's window.

Jenna glared back.

After a few seconds, she said, "Well?"

Preacher Hank continued to stare silently.

"I'm still waiting for an answer to my question from last night."

His left eye twitched and he licked his lips, as though preparing for an epic sermon that would smite her where she stood. Then he broke his gaze away from her and quickly scanned the sidewalks, his mirrors, and gunned the RV the rest of the way around the corner and accelerated up Shoreline. The vehicle tipped and swayed as it took another right turn on First and disappeared behind Lilac Park.

Jenna shook her head and started down the boardwalk, her shoes rapping on the planks. For the second time in two days she'd rendered Preacher Hank silent, but this time there was no one else around to witness it.

———

Jenna hurried the rest of the way to Ghost Ship, constantly expecting Vance to appear beneath one of the arched lamps along the boardwalk. But the remaining pools of light dwindled in number and still there was no Vance, until she stood alone at the bottom of the ship's gangplank. A chain ran across it with a Closed sign hanging from the links.

Aboard Ghost Ship the running lights and a few boxed halogens were on for security, but the bridges and deck were otherwise dark and silent. The vessel was, Jenna thought, scarier this way than with the red lights, fog, and groaning soundtrack.

"Vance?"

The only response was a slap of water against the hull.

She pulled out her phone and went to Contacts, where his information was still up from that morning.

She texted: "Where are you?"

A few seconds later his response came through as an audio message.

She played it: "Ghurk! Hek! Kkkkklll!"

Jenna frowned at the screen. Was this some new mobile fad she didn't know about?

She was tapping out her response of "I'm not fluent in dead pirate" when something heavy crashed aboard Ghost Ship and another recording came from Vance.

"Hep! Hep! Kchh!"

*Is he trying to say "help"?*

Jenna ducked under the chain and ran up the gangplank.

*This could be a trap.*

Or he could be in real trouble.

*Call Olson. Or at least 911.*

Jenna had a brief, awkward vision of Garrett

showing up to her date with Vance on a complete false alarm, but decided that would be better than walking alone into any sort of trouble that might be waiting for her.

She dialed 911 and got the Lost Haven Dispatch Center, currently being monitored by Shirley Timmer.

"Shirley, this is Jenna Hooper, I'm at Ghost Ship, and I think something is wrong."

"Hey hon. What's wrong?"

"I don't know. Maybe nothing. But I'm supposed to meet Julian Vance for dinner, and he's late, and I'm looking for him and I heard some strange noises on the ship. And I got some weird texts from him."

"Ohhh, good for you, he's a catch! Wait, what kind of weird texts? Like…photos?"

"No, just strange sounds."

"Hmm." She lowered her voice. "Well, even if he's an oddball, he's much better than you-know-who, but I can't say who, because they record these calls you know."

"Yeah, can you send someone over? Right now?"

"Bub is somewhere around there, I'll have him swing by. You stay put now, and stay on the line. I want to hear more about this date!"

"Shirley, I—"

Another crash and a thump came from somewhere to her right, in the ship's bow.

"I'll keep the line open, but I have to make sure he's okay."

"Bub's on his way," Shirley said. "What are you wearing for the dinner?"

Jenna ignored her and hit the phone's flashlight so she could pick her way along the deck toward the first passageway leading into Ghost Ship. She entered the hallway, trying to put the phone's beam everywhere at once, and paused just before pushing through the heavy canvas flaps that led to the upside-down ballroom. Weak light seeped from a tiny gap in the fabric.

Shirley said, "Jenna, are you there? Are you okay?"

"I'm fine," Jenna whispered. "But I hear something."

It was a scraping sound, with occasional thumps, coming from the other side of the canvas.

"You stay put, young lady," Shirley said.

Jenna turned the flashlight off. "I'm going to peek. If it's bad, you tell Bub not to shoot me when I come running off this dumb boat."

Shirley hollered for Jenna to behave herself, but she was already poking through the gap in the canvas.

If Vance was there, thumping and scraping a dead body around, or unloading Ritter's stolen cash, there would be a very brief period of mourning for *Brunch, Books, and Bones* before she fled.

Jenna eased the gap wider and peered through.

Vance was there, hanging by his neck from one of the chairs stuck to the ceiling.

—

Jenna burst into the ballroom and ran to Vance, who was desperately trying to keep his toes on the rim of an overturned bucket. The bucket kept rolling away, leaving Vance to dangle by his neck, and then it would creep back under his outstretched toes to give him a momentary reprieve.

A can of red spray paint rolled and rattled along with the bucket. Next to both of them, the words "I'm sorry" were painted on the floor.

Vance's eyes and tongue bulged from his mottled, purple face as he dug at the electrical cord wrapped around his throat.

"Hek! Kchh!"

Jenna grabbed him around the hips and lifted him about an inch, but she couldn't hold him there and get the bucket upright at the same time.

"Hold on! Deep breath!"

It was a ridiculous thing to say and she knew it, but words were falling out of her as she let him go and scrambled to get the bucket.

"Shirley, send an ambulance! Tell Bub to hurry! He's been hanged! Or hung, I'm never sure which one is right!"

She got the bucket upright beneath Vance's shoes. He swung and kicked, rasping and gagging the entire time, and she had to wrap his knees in a bear hug and guide his feet to the bucket. He stood on it, staying on his toes to get as much slack as possible in the cord.

"Ahhh! Guul!"

"I know," Jenna said. "I'll get it off!"

She tried to stand on the bucket with him so she could reach the cord but nearly knocked him back off in the process.

"Can you stay there? Just for a second? I have to go find a ladder!"

Vance shook his head violently.

"Okay, I'm here. I'll stay. Bub should be here—"

"Holy crow!" Bub yelled from the canvas flaps. "What in the name of kinky dates is going on in here?"

"Bub, lift me up!"

"Huh?"

"Lift me up! Do you have a knife?"

"Uh, yeah." He pulled a folding knife from his belt and handed it to her while frowning at Vance, who was still rasping breath against the tight cord. "Are you trying to kill yourself, buddy?"

Jenna said, "Lift me up."

He glanced at her dress and the curves underneath.

"Uh, I'm not sure where it's best to, uh…"

Jenna took a leaping step and planted her stomach against his face. Bub had to wrap her up to keep her from falling.

"Get me to the cord!"

Bub turned and duck-walked closer to Vance. Jenna cut the electrical cord with one slash of the sharp knife, allowing Vance to fall off the bucket and collapse onto the floor. He tugged at the loop around his neck and finally got it loose, then free, and threw it across the ballroom.

"Ambulance is on the way," Bub said. He was panting and sitting on the bucket.

Jenna knelt next to Vance. She didn't want to touch anything that might hurt or make things worse.

"What can I do? How can I help?"

Vance just shook his head. He held up the wrist with the smart watch, showing her the screen with her texts and his audio responses. He tapped the Record button again.

"You saved my life," he whispered to the watch. His voice sounded like it was being dragged over broken glass and gravel.

The message came through on Jenna's phone, appearing on top of the call with Shirley.

"Shirley, Bub is here, the ambulance is on the way, thank you so much. I'm going to hang up now."

"You promise me you'll tell me everything that just happened."

"I promise, unless it might get you killed."

"*What?*"

Jenna hung up and looked at Vance. "You didn't do this to yourself,"

He shook his head again.

"Who did it? Who tried to hang you?"

He shook his head one more time, and then passed out.

—

The ambulance and EMTs arrived five endless minutes later and took over.

Jenna stepped back and watched, her hands balled into fists, while they checked Vance's eyes, pulse, breathing, and a dozen other things she couldn't follow. She didn't realize she was shaking from the adrenaline dump until Bub brought a blanket from his patrol car and draped it over her shoulders.

"Bub, my goodness. I can't thank you enough."

"Hey, it's literally my job. Although...if you have any more of those pumpkin cookies you had the other morning..."

"You can get them at the Sanctuary Café now."

"Seriously? How much?"

"They're free, just like the other ones. It's a competition between Belma and Lawrence to see whose are better."

Bub processed this revelation for a moment, then turned away and squeezed his shoulder mic. "Dispatch, are you aware of a cookie competition happening at the café?"

"Uh, roger that, Bub," Shirley said. "I heard about it this afternoon."

"Dang it Shirley, you're supposed to tell me about vital information like that!"

He pushed back through the canvas flaps to get

more details without disturbing the paramedics. Jenna stayed in the ballroom in case Vance regained consciousness and uttered anything, but she stepped into the corner and kept her voice low when she called Olson and filled him in.

"I'm on my way," he said.

Jenna paced the room, glancing warily at the portrait that had dropped and nearly caused her heart to explode the night before. Those scares seemed completely ridiculous compared to the scenarios her mind was running:

*What if I'd chatted longer with Chantel?*

*What if I hadn't texted Vance?*

*What if Preacher Hank had actually rolled his window down and said something offensive?*

She stopped pacing.

*Preacher Hank?*

Vance coughed, his entire body spasming beneath the EMTs, and Jenna held her breath as his eyes fluttered, rolled around the room, and closed again.

"Is he okay?" Jenna asked.

The EMTs ignored her, which was just fine as long as they kept Vance alive. Jenna turned away to continue pacing as Detective Olson burst through the canvas flaps, slightly out of breath, and gave her a quick hug.

"You okay?"

"Yeah. Maybe. Who knows?"

Olson looked over at Vance. The EMTs were

arranging oxygen and IV tubes, preparing to move him to a gurney.

"He hasn't woken up?"

"Not yet," Jenna said.

Olson asked the EMTs, "What can you tell me?"

The one by Vance's head, a woman who looked about eighteen, said, "He was hung by an electrical cord, that's all we know so far. We need to keep an eye on his throat to make sure the swelling doesn't cut anything off, but from what she and Deputy Thorp told us, how he was talking and coherent before he passed out, he should be fine. That's not a doctor's opinion, of course, so don't quote me. But look at this."

She pointed a gloved finger just below Vance's ear, where the cord had dug into his skin.

"You'll need somebody to take a closer look here. I can't say for sure because of the cord damage, but that looks a lot like a Taser burn to me."

"Somebody shocked him?" Olson said.

The EMT shrugged. "I've seen marks like that before when drunk people take a swing at Bub, but like I said, you'll have to get somebody who knows for sure to take a look."

Olson nodded. "I'll follow you to the hospital. I need to talk to him. And I'm bringing in my forensics crew to process this scene and his wounds, especially that mark there, so don't wipe him down yet. And try not to touch anything on your way out."

"Wipe him down?" the male EMT at Vance's feet said. "Uh, we don't do sponge baths, buddy."

"Whatever. Just be careful with him. And nice find on that Taser mark.'"

The female EMT nodded and they started rolling Vance toward the canvas flaps. They both reached up and flicked on head-mounted flashlights to make sure they could find their way out.

Olson turned to Jenna. "He didn't say anything?"

"Just what I told you on the phone, that somebody did this to him. Well, he didn't say that, exactly. He just shook his head when I asked if he did this to himself. If somebody hit him with a Taser, then staged his suicide…"

"Man oh man. This has to be related to Ritter's death somehow, right? I mean, the haunted house connection, 'I'm sorry' painted on the floor as a suicide note…"

"Someone is trying to frame him for Ritter's murder," Jenna said. She hugged herself under the blanket. "If Vance had died, it probably would have worked. And here's something I didn't tell you on the phone because I didn't think of it until after. I saw Preacher Hank on my way here."

Olson's eyebrow went up. "The RV guy?"

"He was driving around Lilac Park, very slowly, and didn't stop to talk to me. After all of this with Vance, I mean…he could have been trying to get away from here."

"Did you see anybody else?"

"No. And there was no one else there when I saw him. So it would be his word against mine, if it came to that."

Olson puffed his cheeks out. "Well, let's hope it doesn't. We'll see what Vance says when he wakes up. Hopefully he just says a name, I kick a door in, and we call it a night."

"What should I do?"

"It may sound crass, but whatever you were planning to do tonight."

"Um, I was planning on having dinner with Vance."

Olson winced. "Oh, yeah, sorry. I guess you could come to the hospital and have some pudding with him, but he'll be pretty whipped tonight, possibly even sedated. Maybe just head home? I'll call you if I learn anything."

"Okay," Jenna said, wondering if it would be rude to wind down from Vance's near-murder by eating bread at their table on the Grille's deck.

Probably.

She walked with Olson off of Ghost Ship, and when he found out she didn't have the Jeep he dropped her in front of Bodyworks, were Cabo was finishing up his last class of the night.

"Stick with friends tonight, and lay low," Olson said through the open passenger door. "Whoever tried to kill Vance is going to be desperate, and who knows what they might try to get out of this. Like, murdering potential witnesses who foiled their plans."

"Lucky for me, I'm very skilled at hunkering inside my house and not leaving for days at a time."

"There you go," he said. "Being antisocial is a very effective way to not get murdered."

Jenna shut the door and watched him roll away.

She would certainly stick with friends, but laying low wasn't on the agenda.

She pulled out her phone and opened the group chat with Belma, Lawrence, and Cabo and sent three words:

"My shop. Now."

# CHAPTER 12

The Main Street crew kept a brisk pace along Shoreline Drive, retracing their steps from the night before but with a completely different mindset. And a plan.

"You know what to do?" Jenna asked for about the twelfth time.

"Yes," Lawrence said. "Climb up the outside of the mansion, set the roof on fire, and jump into the harbor."

"I'm serious."

"We know what to do," Belma said.

Cabo used a small but powerful flashlight to check the shrubs, shadows, and spaces between parked cars for any potential lurkers.

Jenna said, "If you see Preacher Hank or Unflappable Bob, run the other way. Just run, even if they try to talk to you. We don't know for sure which one of them killed Ritter and tried to murder Vance, but it's better to be mildly offensive and alive than polite and dead."

"What if we see traitorous cookie bakers?" Lawrence asked. "You know, someone who goes behind your back and fails miserably while trying to outdo your recipe, then illegally takes them to the café and forces them down peoples' throats?"

"Lawrence…" Jenna said.

"What should we do then? Should we never ever talk to that person again?"

He tugged at Belma's oversized purse.

"Are you carrying any more in there, just to taunt me?"

Belma jerked her purse away. "They were forcing them down their own throats, buddy—they couldn't eat them fast enough."

Lawrence suddenly stopped and peered into the canopy of the old-growth oaks along the sidewalk.

"Do you guys hear that?"

Cabo sent the dazzling beam into the trees. "Hear what?"

"I think it's a Selfish Over-Coiffed Backstabber. They're rare, but when you find one, you should have it shipped to Antarctica. They're horribly invasive."

"Guys, save it for later," Jenna said.

Cabo grumbled something about shipping his foot to Lawrence's southern hemisphere, and then scanned their perimeter again. They were only three houses away from No Sanctuary. There were no people waiting out front, which wasn't surprising at close to ten thirty on a Monday night.

Jenna huddled them up. "Okay, remember to act scared."

"I am scared," Lawrence said.

"Yes, of getting caught, not of the haunted house. If we don't act like normal, terrified patrons, Kemp might think we're up to something. So giggle, squeal, scream, grab each other. All the usual stuff."

Belma nudged Lawrence. "You're the squealer."

"Better that than a traitor."

"Knock it off!" Jenna said.

Lawrence shrugged. "What? We're acting natural, like we can't stand the sight of each other."

"Oh," Jenna said. "I guess you're right. Carry on."

They fought the urge to hurry the rest of the way to the mansion, clinging to each other and hopping up and down with nervous energy that they hoped looked like giddy anticipation on any security feeds they might be on. They turned the corner and started up the walkway, pointing at the graves and corpses in the front yard, then took the steps up to the front porch and walls of clown dolls.

"Psst."

"Not this time, clown!" Belma yelled. She turned away from the mocking pacifier and said through unmoving lips, "This feels weird. I know the cameras are on us. I don't like being watched."

"Why would the cameras watch you when they can look at me instead?" Lawrence said, also without moving his mouth.

"Shut up!" Jenna blurted through a smile. "Ready?"
Cabo nodded.

"Ready," Belma said.

Lawrence saluted. "My cookies are better."

Jenna scanned another buy-one-get-one free ticket, hit the 2 button, swiped her card, and stepped through the turnstile.

Because hey, you can risk your lives to catch a murderer and be cost-conscious at the same time.

—

The hulking figure waited for them again in the elevator at the end of the long, dark hallway.

They piled in and Jenna had to force herself not to look straight into the camera lens she knew was buried inside the hood. She glanced in the general vicinity of the face, as she hoped any normal patron would, and then buried her head in Cabo's arm as the elevator and operator ran through their show.

Lawrence belted out a shockingly realistic scream when the elevator shook and seemed to drop a few feet, then screeched and whined to a halt. The doors slid open and they were back in the foggy, subterranean passageway with glistening rock walls spotted with fungus and moss.

"Are the spiders here yet?" Lawrence groaned.

Jenna blinked. "No, those are like, three rooms away. Three big rooms."

"But they're coming."

"No, Lawrence, they're still in the spider room. They can't move. Well, other than across the walls and into their spider nests."

He shuddered and forced down a retch.

Jenna hooked an arm around him. "Come on. We'll get you through it."

Cabo led the way through the thick fog, feeling along the twisted passageway until they reached the threshold for the room of judgment. Red light burned into the mist around them.

"Remember, none of these guys are real," Cabo said, raising his voice over the throbbing bass.

"They weren't last time," Belma said. "Who knows about now?"

Jenna touched her arm and leaned in so she'd be heard. "What do you mean?"

"Maybe I'm just being paranoid, but you said Preacher Hank was creeping around downtown. What if he was watching and saw us leave your shop? Or what if Unflappable Bob did? If they knew we were coming here and got in first, they could be waiting anywhere in here to ambush us."

"You decide to bring that up now?" Cabo said.

"I didn't really think of it until we were in the elevator. Which, by then, you know. Too late."

The four of them exchanged worried looks, then

turned to the next room with its fifty sets of fake eyes—and one extra set of real ones, potentially— waiting to stare at them.

"Okay," Jenna said, "we just need to get through this room, then it's the spiders."

Lawrence hurped in his throat.

"From there, we should be okay."

"Okay?" Lawrence said. "Who's going to be okay? I didn't want to go through here again in the first place, especially with this cookie monster here, and now that we're about to dive back into my worst nightmare you say we'll be okay?"

"Lawrence," Jenna said.

"No! I can't take it! I gotta get out of here!"

He bolted into the room of judges, careening off the props and spinning wildly through the red robes.

"Come back!" Cabo yelled. "We need to stick together!"

"Did he call me a cookie monster?" Belma said. "Get back here and admit mine are better!"

She took off after Lawrence, swinging her purse like a morning star and leaving Jenna and Cabo standing with their mouths open.

"You guys, stop!" Jenna followed them and promptly tripped over a strip of red robe that Lawrence had dragged into the path.

Cabo stumbled over her and caught himself on two of the judges, who leaned toward him accusingly.

Neither of them were Preacher Hank or Unflappable Bob, but Cabo still recoiled.

"Yaa!"

He pushed them away and helped Jenna up.

"You good?"

She brushed her hands and did a quick check for anything more than a bump. "I'm good. Look at this mess…"

They shoved and kicked the judges and their robes somewhat back into place, keeping an eye on the other staring masks in case any of them decided to come closer. By the time they were ready to move forward, Lawrence and Belma were long gone, lost in the throbbing bass, red light, and fog.

Cabo leaned close. "What do you think?"

"So far so good," Jenna said. "As long as some murderer doesn't mess it all up."

———

Jenna and Cabo hustled through the rest of the judges, sometimes moving back-to-back so they could watch all directions. Halfway through the room Jenna was certain one of the hooded faces was turning to follow them, but it was just a trick of the lighting and fog.

She hoped.

They reached the final judge in his white robe and

red mask, his right arm blocking the exit. A clear shoe print was stamped in the center of his chest, and Jenna would have bet her shop that the pattern matched Lawrence's shoe.

The red mask and black eyes glared at them accusingly, as if blaming them for their companion's foul behavior.

"Sorry buddy, no time," Jenna said. She ducked under the arm and pushed through the curtains, followed by Cabo, fully expecting the spider room to be engulfed in flames with Lawrence dancing in triumph.

She stood up and took a few uncertain steps in the blacklight strobe, managing to plant her face directly into a curtain of spider web. She fought her way free and saw that no flames licked the walls, and no Preacher Hank or Unflappable Bob lunged from the massive spider nests.

Also, no Lawrence and Belma.

"Watch for vomit," Cabo yelled, scanning the floor. "Lawrence was looking pretty shaky back there."

They fumbled around in the strobe and webs, leaning away from the smaller, dashing spiders and diving away from the lumbering dog-sized creatures. The exit was somewhere ahead, Jenna knew, but they couldn't seem to find which way *ahead* was.

Then her phone buzzed against her hip.

She slipped it out and checked the screen.

It was a message from Belma in their group chat: "Go"

Jenna turned and took a line straight to the wall with the hidden door. She pulled the quilt away, eased the door open, and ran up the stairs with Cabo two steps behind.

In their wake, the door closed, the quilt fell back into place, and the spiders continued their endless skittering in the blacklight strobe.

———

They were alone in the red light of the control room.

The laptops showed no alarms or flashing screens, and the bank of monitors along the right wall displayed the security camera feeds in stark black and white.

Jenna and Cabo rushed over.

"Find the footage," Jenna said. "I'll keep an eye on the real-time. Where are they…"

Cabo sat in the chair in front of the monitors and worked the mouse and keyboard. One of the screens switched from four camera feeds to Windows.

"Wait!" Jenna said, "I haven't found them yet. Go back to the cameras."

"That's the feed for the cameras outside the exit. If they made it that far already, we're in big trouble."

"Oh man, I hope—there!"

She spotted them in the room with Chuckles. Lawrence fell into the frame, reeling from something off-screen, and toppled into the pool around the animatronic clown. Belma stumbled after him, dropped her purse in the corner and reached to pull him out, but he slipped and pulled her in with him. Water sloshed and sprayed as they flailed around Chuckles, who grinned and shook with horrific delight.

"Come on," Jenna murmured. "Where are you?"

Kemp rushed onto the screen in full Skull Monger gear and wedged himself between his precious clown and Lawrence and Belma, who were rolling like two hyper alligators in the shallow water. Kemp tried to pull them out, got his black robes caught in the spin cycle, and went down with them.

"We owe them so big," Jenna said. She scanned the rest of the feeds ahead of where Lawrence and Belma were, gauging how much of No Sanctuary they had left to rampage through to keep Kemp busy.

She saw no sign of Preacher Hank or Unflappable Bob hiding among the props, but something about one of the feeds made her stop and look closer. She remembered it from the night before, when she was looking for the elevator feed—it showed an embalming chamber with a wall of cold storage drawers.

"Hey, look at this one."

"Hold on," Cabo said. "Here, check this out.

These are video files inside a folder from October thirty-first of last year."

He double-clicked one of the files. It was the Chuckles feed, showing the clown coiled and waiting in his pool.

"Man, we can't get away from that thing," Jenna said.

A man came onto the screen from the right, looking back over his shoulder. His face was hidden. When he turned, Jenna recognized him immediately.

"That's Unflappable Bob! Is he carrying any spray paint? Do you see a zombie mask?"

Cabo leaned closer. "Not yet. But he is carrying something."

Unflappable Bob hurried to get around the first corner of Chuckles' pool, and then stopped directly in front of the clown.

"That's an envelope," Jenna said, pointing at the screen. "Hold on. Wasn't he carrying an envelope last night?"

They watched the footage of Unflappable Bob standing completely still as the creature rose from the water, shaking and chomping, it's gaping maw coming closer to Bob's face.

"Huh," Cabo said. "He really is unflappable."

Then Unflappable Bob reached up and shoved the envelope into the clown's mouth, pulled out an empty hand, and left the room.

Jenna blinked. "What did we just see?"

"I have no idea," Cabo said, "but there are more video files here. Maybe they can explain."

"I hope so, because that was insane. But first, look here."

She pointed at the current feed of the Chuckles room, where Kemp was unsuccessfully trying to drag Belma out of the water.

"Up here in the corner, it says 'Loc 1.' What does that mean, location one?"

"Yeah."

She pointed to the feed with the cold storage drawers.

"But this one says 'Loc 2'. Location two. Is that a feed from a separate location? Because that looks a lot like the embalming room at the Lost Haven Morgue."

———

Cabo peered at the feed. "That *is* the Lost Haven Morgue. Hold on."

He dragged the mouse to the quarter screen next to the embalming room and switched the feed from "Loc 1" to "Loc 2".

The screen changed from the No Sanctuary room with the glowing neon masks to the gurney room at the Morgue.

"What the…" Cabo said. "Why would Kemp have cameras in the Morgue?"

Jenna stepped back from the monitors and put her hands on her head.

"Oh, no."

"What?" Cabo said.

"I think...um...oh, man. Try the other files from last year. I hope it isn't what I think it is."

Cabo double-clicked the next file. It showed a new feed of Chuckles, and again a man walked in from the right. He wore a zombie mask with long white hair and lugged a bulging duffel bag.

"That's Martin Ritter," Jenna said. "Or someone trying to look like him."

Cabo nodded. "And I bet that's the missing money."

They watched as the masked man stood in front of Chuckles and tried to stuff the duffel into the clown's mouth. It didn't come close to fitting. The man dropped the bag and kicked it in frustration, then hauled it back up and stormed out of the room.

The file ended.

Cabo opened the next one in the folder.

It showed the No Sanctuary blacklight room with the neon masks. The man in the zombie mask came into view from the left and dropped the duffel bag in the middle of the room. He bent down and rummaged in the bag, emerging with a can of spray paint.

Staring straight into the camera from behind his zombie mask, he shook the can, then turned and began spraying on the wall.

When he was finished, he threw the can back into the bag and walked off the right edge of the screen.

Cabo paused the video and read the graffiti. "'Mariners'? That's the name for the Lost Haven sports teams, right?"

"It's not 'Mariners,'" Jenna said. "It's 'Marinus'."

Cabo frowned.

"The statue in the park," Jenna said. "Where Ritter's body was buried. That's where he wanted Kemp to meet him. So he could give him the money."

"Money for what?" Cabo said. "First we see Unflappable Bob drop an envelope, then Ritter tries to shove what we have to assume is close to a million dollars into Kemp's clown. Why?"

Jenna felt queasy. "Go to one of the last feeds and change it to location two."

Cabo dragged the mouse onto the screen just above his Windows console and made the switch. The screen went from a shot of the entrance to No Sanctuary's spinning vortex tunnel to a Victorian bedroom with a four-post canopy bed and an elegant claw-footed bathtub in the corner.

Dina Polk was filling the tub, checking the temperature and sprinkling bath salts from a small basket.

"Is that..." Cabo said.

Jenna nodded. "The brothel. Kemp got cameras into it, and he was blackmailing them. All of them. Oh, my gosh. Remember what Dina said to us before we went into the Morgue? What was it...'Even empty eyes can see.' She knew Kemp was watching us on the cameras. That's why she wanted us to go through the haunt! If we just showed up, asked a few questions, and left, Kemp would have caught on to us!"

"Yeah, but then she showed us the hiding spot with Ritter's safe," Cabo said. "Wouldn't that tip him off?"

"Not the way Dina played it. She was asking us to help solve the mystery of Ritter's death, but she never said anything that pointed us at Kemp. Remember, she thought Ritter had been missing this whole time, just like everyone else. When we found his body, she had to suspect Kemp, but she couldn't just come out and say so—he was holding the blackmail footage over her head. She couldn't tell us, but she *did* want us to figure out that it was him.

They looked at each other for a moment.

"Kemp killed Ritter," Jenna said. "And right now he's alone with Lawrence and Belma."

She turned to the live feed of the Chuckles room, where her two friends were draped over the pool wall, coughing and dripping. An exhausted Kemp was sprawled in the corner next to Belma's purse, which had tipped and spilled some of its contents across the floor.

Kemp looked down at Belma's phone, the screen open to her texting app. He picked the phone up and held it within inches of his empty skull eyes, then turned and stared into the camera.

"Uh oh," Jenna said.

—

O n the monitor, Kemp lurched to his feet and ran out of the Chuckles room, leaving Belma and Lawrence soaked and confused.

"He's coming," Jenna said.

Cabo began clicking and typing furiously. "I'm uploading these videos to my cloud account. We need to get out of here."

Jenna was already at the door Kemp had led them through the night before. It was a coin toss which way he'd be coming for them, but she knew this door had a semi-direct passage to the emergency exit.

"How much longer?" she asked.

"Couple minutes."

"We don't have that."

Cabo turned the monitor off and unplugged it, the mouse, and the keyboard from the security PC.

"The files will keep uploading. He could come in and unplug the PC, I guess, but by the time he quits fiddling with the equipment and realizes it's all unplugged, the videos will be done."

"Great. Let's go."

"We should call Olson," Cabo said. "Or Garrett."

"On the way, we just need to move."

Jenna turned back to the door just in time to hear a metallic thump from somewhere within its frame.

"What was that?"

She turned the knob and pushed. The door didn't move.

"Electronic locks," Cabo said. "He's locking the place down from somewhere."

"Can we unlock it from here?"

Cabo ran to the laptops. "I...I don't know. I think these are all animatronic controls. I might be able to figure it out, but by that time he'll be here."

"Well, I feel some serious fight or flight kicking in. Can we fight if we have to?"

"Uh, we can, theoretically," Cabo said "But if he comes in with a shotgun or chainsaw, we're screwed."

Jenna pulled her phone out to call Olson.

"Shoot! No signal."

Cabo tried his phone but had the same result.

"Maybe he has this room shielded because of all the equipment. Or he may have activated a jammer."

"A cell phone jammer? Kemp?"

"Hey, he was running a pretty sophisticated operation out of here, a jammer would be simple."

"I do *not* want to go down those stairs into the haunt. You know Kemp will be waiting for us."

Cabo spread his hands. "Where else can we go?"

Jenna cursed. "I almost hope that door is locked too."

They hurried down the stairs. Cabo tested the hidden door, and it moved easily.

Jenna cursed again.

"Okay, Jay Cabo. Remember the first rule?"

"Always go forward."

"Ready?"

Cabo nodded.

"Go!"

—

They burst into the spider room, half-crouching and searching frantically for Kemp as they cut left and rushed for the room's exit.

Jenna tried to check her phone while running, scanning for Kemp, and trying to avoid the spiders and webs in a strobing blacklight. Something had to give, and she ignored the phone for the time being so she wouldn't run headlong into Kemp's skull face.

They fought through the last of the webs and emerged in a black hallway. The only illumination came from dozens of glowing eyes along the walls, and Jenna's vision threatened to boycott as it tried to adjust from the chaos of the strobe light to this.

She blinked and stretched her arms out, flailing against any Skull Mongers lurking in the darkness, then had to squint when Cabo clicked his powerful flashlight on.

"Oh yeah," Jenna said.

She activated the flashlight on her phone, which looked like a squirt gun of illumination compared to Cabo's fire hose. He seemed unimpressed.

"Oh! I have signal!"

She dialed 911 for the second time that night, a new personal record.

"Shirley, it's Jenna again. We're at the No Sanctuary haunted house, and Dave Kemp is after us. He's trying to kill us."

Shirley laughed. "Jenna, sweetie, it's all in good fun. It's Halloween!"

"No! Shirley! This isn't part of the haunt, it's for real! Kemp killed—"

Jenna sprang into the air as Kemp, in full Skull Monger mode, crashed into the hallway behind them and yanked the cord on the chainsaw he carried. Just before it started, Jenna caught the glint of steel teeth along the 18-inch bar. This chainsaw was not like the one in her window display, with the chain removed—this one would cut, fast and deep. It roared to life, terrifying and deafening Jenna and she drove forward into Cabo, shoving him along the hallway.

She forgot Shirley.

She forgot her phone.

She could only think of one thing:

"Run!"

—

They ran.

They ran through a torture chamber with an animatronic dummy writhing on a rack while another thrashed and smoked on a crackling electric chair similar to the one in the Welcome Shoppe. Jenna and Cabo grabbed everything within reach and yanked it down behind them, trying to slow Kemp.

They stampeded up a winding, uneven ramp that took them back up to the second floor and into the notorious lair of Chuckles the clown. Belma and Lawrence were long gone, and Jenna hoped they'd found an exit before Kemp put the haunt on lockdown.

Cabo cut left and pulled Jenna in front of him, and then they both ran around the giant clown's mouth as it dove forward. Cabo grabbed the prop by the hair and pulled, breaking something in the structure so the torso and wobbling head collapsed into the pathway.

They turned the last corner just as Kemp and his roaring chainsaw burst into the room. He saw what had been done to his beloved blackmail repository and bellowed loud enough to be heard over the chainsaw's engine, then jumped into the pool to get at them and tripped over the submerged clown mechanism.

The chain bit into wood around the edge of the

pool and chewed down a few inches before the engine sputtered in the water and died.

Jenna and Cabo didn't stick around to see what Kemp thought about that. They ran out of the room, through another twisting black hallway, and emerged into the room with the colored neon masks glowing in blacklight.

Some of the masks turned to watch them, but the pair was already cutting right and exiting the room before the props had moved an inch. They dashed through the short passageway with the hidden panels that led between the walls and to the fire exit, and Cabo thumped each of them to see if they'd open.

Neither budged.

They kept going and made another hard right into the sand room. Jenna dodged the grasping hands like an Olympic-level hopscotch athlete and glanced back to make sure Cabo was still with her. He was, but he wasn't bothering to jump over any-thing—he just kicked through everything that dared get close enough.

They left that room and stumbled into another strobe light, this one blinding white, stabbing at their eyes in a room cluttered with corpses hanging from the ceiling. There had to be at least two dozen of them, wrapped in cloudy, blood-smeared plastic that distorted the decomposing human features within. They were bound in duct tape and rope, swinging from crossbeams like a roomful of nightmarish heavy bags.

Heavy metal music with more throbbing bass made conversation nearly impossible.

"Where's the door?" Cabo yelled.

Jenna just shook her head and dove in, shoving and battering the swinging bodies away.

"Stick together!" Cabo said from somewhere in the chaos.

"Where are you?" Jenna called.

"This way!"

She turned, guessing at the direction, and pushed between two swaying bodies.

Kemp was there, dripping, chest heaving, with his chainsaw.

The skull mask leered at Jenna, and then jerked as he tried to start the saw.

It coughed and sputtered on the first try. Kemp barely let the cord retract before he yanked it again, this time earning a full-throated roar from the machine.

Jenna shoved the bodies at him and ran the other way, knowing the teeth were going to bite into her spine at any moment. She dodged left, right, trying to weave between the swaying bodies, then a swinging corpse slammed into her left shoulder as she was going right and the impact sent her reeling.

She barely caught herself against the wall, her nose an inch from slamming into the rough, black particle board, and she had to make an instant decision to go left or right. Kemp's chainsaw roared from her left and she dove right, certain she could feel the wind from its blade in her hair.

Jenna clung to the wall in desperate search of a door, a Cabo, or something to bludgeon Kemp with.

She found a corner instead.

She cut right and skidded to a halt as the chainsaw ground into one of the dangling corpses in front of her, sending scraps of plastic, latex, and yellow foam into the air.

She turned back toward the corner and had to duck as the spinning teeth swiped across the wall just above her head.

Kemp had her trapped, and he knew it.

Jenna backed into the corner, wracking her brain for any self-defense videos she may have watched regarding chainsaw-wielding maniacs. It was an unexplored niche.

Kemp let the chainsaw idle and shouted over the music.

"Where do you want to be buried? I'm thinking under the elevator. Or maybe wrapped in spider webs."

"Just calm down, Skull Monger! Hey, I'll pay you! Just like Bob and Ritter, and whoever else you're blackmailing."

She was stalling, but for what, she had no idea.

The skull mask stared at her. "You saw the footage, huh?"

"We did. I have to say, it was pretty brilliant to use the evidence as your alibi. And I'm sure there are other people in town who don't want that footage to go public."

Kemp laughed. "You have no idea."

"But I'll make you a deal. Let me go, and your secret is safe with me."

"And you'll pay?"

"I can't afford much. Do you take books?"

Kemp shook his head. "I don't think so. People just can't be trusted."

He gunned the chainsaw and let it drop back to idle.

"First you. Then I'll find your friends, wherever they got off to. A terrible accident in No Sanctuary, but it was your own fault, of course. Human error."

He stepped forward and lifted the chainsaw, then faltered as something bounced off the side of his mask.

He turned to his left as another small object flew through the staccato light and splashed against one of his eye socket lenses. Kemp let go of the chainsaw with one hand to wipe it away but only managed to smear it across the plastic.

Another smacked into his forehead and stuck there.

It was a pumpkin cookie.

Jay Cabo kicked through two of the swinging corpses and fired his flashlight beam into Kemp's face from four feet away. Even with the black skull lenses it had to be blinding, and Kemp flailed back from the assault.

Belma and Lawrence appeared on Cabo's flanks. They hurled pumpkin cookies at Kemp's head, splattering buttery crumbs across the eyes and filling the breathing holes.

"Weaponized cookies!" Belma shouted. "Finally!"

Lawrence chucked them as fast as he could. "These are almost too soft and moist to throw, and it's making me furious!"

Kemp fell back against one of the corpses, bounced forward and grazed his own leg with the chainsaw. The blade was spinning at a slow idle, but it still chewed into his robes and bit into his skin before stopping.

He screamed and stumbled, then crashed facefirst into the floor when Jenna yanked his robes over his head like a hockey sweater and leaped onto the back of his head.

Cabo piled on next, kicking the chainsaw away and putting his full weight across Kemp's shoulder blades and pinning his arms with his knees. Belma sat on his lower back and Lawrence sprawled across Kemp's legs. The only thing that could move on the terrifying, murderous Skull Monger was his feet, and they drummed pathetically on the floor.

The Main Street crew exchanged wide-eyed

looks of shock and pure, utter relief that they were all unharmed, more or less.

"Everybody okay?" Jenna yelled against the crashing music.

"I'm deaf!" Cabo said.

Jenna patted his shoulder and pulled out her phone. She was amazed and thrilled to see the call to 911 was still going, and she pressed the phone against her ear.

"Shirley? Can you hear me?"

"Jenna, my goodness, what are you up to over there? Bub and Garrett are at the scene, they tried to get in but the place is sealed up. They had to break down a door!"

"Good! Tell them we're in the, uh, hanging corpse room."

"The what?"

"The—"

Suddenly the music cut off and emergency lights popped on, filling the room with a bright, eerie quiet interrupted only by the rustling corpse bags and Kemp's labored breathing and groaning.

"Garrett!" Jenna shouted. "Bub! We're in here!"

She heard a muffled yell from somewhere in the haunt, running steps, and a few moments later Garrett bowled through the swinging bodies and found them.

He stared in astonishment at the scene.

"What are you guys doing?"

Jenna shrugged. "You know. Getting chased by chainsaws. Almost dying. Solving murders. Just another Halloween in Lost Haven."

# CHAPTER 13

I t was the first of November in Lost Haven, a damp, chilly morning.

If you listened closely, you could hear the rustling of children who had been ninjas, vampires, werewolves, robots, pirates, and skeletons the night before; creatures that gorged on endless candy without fear of cavities or waistlines. Now they stirred, sifting through their harvest for any choice pieces they may have missed beneath the Halloween moon.

Jenna sat huddled in a sweater, winter coat, and fuzzy hat with Belma, Lawrence, and Cabo at their patio table outside the Sanctuary Café. McTavish had threatened to put the tables and chairs away for the winter, but he wouldn't risk upsetting his pumpkin cookie suppliers before Thanksgiving was over.

At which point, of course, the Christmas cookie battle would begin.

They were gathered around what remained of the severed Lawrence head from Belma's refrigerated window display and the scraps of Lawrence's chocolate Sanctuary/Lost Haven masterpiece. They all agreed it was okay to eat that much sugar for breakfast the morning after Halloween, since it was not socially acceptable for them to go trick-or-treating.

"I talked to Vance last night," Jenna said.

"On a *date*?" Belma asked, leaning closer.

"On a *phone*. He's back in Chicago. He wanted to see his personal doctor and a plastic surgeon about the throat scar."

"Which one?" Cabo asked. "The Taser or the cord?"

"Both, I guess. He's fine, but his vanity is traumatized. I tried telling him throat scars are in right now, but he wasn't having it."

"Is the date ever going to happen?" Lawrence asked.

Jenna shrugged. "He sounded pretty fed-up with Lost Haven. Once Ghost Ship sails back to Chicago, he won't have much reason to be here unless the Grille needs him for something. We left it as, hey, let's hang out sometime. We'll see."

Lawrence shook his head. "And the date drought continues. I...I think I might faint from the shock of it. Jenna, how do I do it right?"

Cabo and Belma laughed while Jenna scowled at all three of them.

"No, no, the drought is over. He and I had a date

scheduled for that night, and we saw each other. That counts."

"Judges?" Lawrence said, looking around the table.

"'Sad and tragic," Belma declared.

Cabo took a hit from smoothie recipe 8.6 and made a face of complete disapproval.

Lawrence scooted his chair back a few inches. "Is that a vote on Jenna's date, or do you need to evacuate something?"

"Neither, it's my thinking face. I'd say what Jenna did, goes beyond a mere date. She saved his life. That's worth, like, ten dates."

Jenna grinned in triumph. "Eat that, suckers. I'm good for another year at least."

"Congratulations?" Belma said.

"I'll take it. And there's enough going on right now, who has time for dates?"

"I second the sad and tragic vote," Lawrence said.

But it was true, there was a lot happening. Kemp's arrest was still sending shockwaves through the town, Jimbo was stuck in an endless loop of wood glue and finish nails, and rumors were spreading about why the Sanctuary reclamation crew had to halt work altogether. They had even installed a steel cage door at the base of the staircase in Jenna's Welcome Shoppe, blocking access to anyone without a key.

Whatever they'd found, they didn't want anyone else knowing about it.

Jenna and the others turned and watched as Detective Olson's car eased into a parking spot on Main Street. He got out in a dark overcoat and leaned on the decorative metal fence that surrounded the patio, holding an aluminum travel mug of coffee and staring at the crime scene in the middle of the table.

"What are you people doing?"

"Celebrating," Jenna said.

"Oh, did one of you win the window display thing?"

"Good lord, no," Belma said. "That went to the florist and their weak, harmless arrangement. We're celebrating another Halloween season in Lost Haven come and gone. We do it every year."

"And a murderer caught," Lawrence said. "That, we only just started doing."

"Well, you did good work," Olson said. "Kemp ended up confessing when we watched the video footage with him. He met Martin Ritter in Lilac Park about..." Olson checked his watch. "...one year and eight hours ago to collect the cash in return for keeping various, uh, activities at the Lost Haven Morgue secret. Ritter said some things that didn't sit well with Kemp—I'm guessing it had nothing to do with haunted houses, believe it or not—and Kemp ended up strangling and burying him in a shallow grave."

"And everyone just kept paying him," Jenna said.

"Nobody knew Ritter was dead until you guys

found him. They legitimately thought he'd skipped town with the money, and Kemp let them all think it. He told Dina Polk she had to pay as she went, to make up for it, or else he'd expose her and all of her clients."

"What a scumbag," Belma said.

"Once she found out her boyfriend had actually been murdered, she started to care less about her side business and more about justice. But she was still being discreet, which is why she talked to you all instead of me."

"Her clients," Jenna said. "Like Preacher Hank and Unflappable Bob..."

Olson nodded. "They were both paying Kemp too. I'm sure you can figure out why, after you saw the camera setup he had going. And Jenna, you were right—it was sorta genius of Kemp to use the Ritter footage as an alibi. The timestamps on the graffiti video would have worked in his favor, and he really did log a call to the Morgue when he said he did. Even with the Marinus thing, the footage basically would have been circumstantial evidence at best if you hadn't uncovered the blackmail."

"Yay for us," Jenna said.

"And if Kemp hadn't tried to kill all of you."

"Well, yeah, there's that too. What are you going to do about the blackmail?"

Olson shrugged. "As of now, nobody is pressing

charges. I think they all want it to go away so they can keep doing whatever they're doing, and just not have to pay Kemp."

"And what is it they're doing, Detective Olson?" Lawrence asked with a sly smile.

Olson blushed. "That is officially none of my business. If it becomes my official business, I might just use it as a good reason to retire early."

"So what did Kemp do with the cash?" Cabo said.

"Great question. We're still going through his financials and taxes, but so far there aren't any large deposits or expenses out of the ordinary. Well, ordinary for a haunted house owner."

Jenna looked around the table. "So…the cash is still out there, somewhere?"

Olson shrugged. "Kemp won't tell us a thing about it. He's going away for life, so we can't really offer him anything. My guess is he'll brag to someone about where he stashed it eventually, and word will get back to us. If not…maybe somebody gets very lucky."

"I bet it's somewhere in that mansion," Lawrence said. "Stuffed in those red robes, or tucked away in the—*hurrrrp*—spider nests. Oh man…"

"Oh yeah," Jenna said. "What happens to No Sanctuary now?"

"It'll go up for auction as-is, but I don't think

they'll factor a possible million-dollar stash in the walls into the starting price."

"I wonder who'll buy it," Belma mused. "We should pool our money. We'd be awesome at running a haunted house."

"Lord knows you can't bake cookies to save your life," Lawrence said.

Jenna raised her hand. "Ahem. I beg to differ. Belma's cookies *literally* saved my life."

Lawrence turned to Belma. "Congratulations. You have the perfect recipe for blinding murderers in skull masks."

Belma gasped. "Pumpkin Mongers! That's the name!"

Everyone raised a mug to the Pumpkin Mongers—even Lawrence—and they toasted each other in celebration of another Halloween in Lost Haven, a beloved holiday full of festive decorations, terrifying haunted houses, and frightful competitions that would all live on, thanks to Jenna and the Main Street crew.

# THANK YOU FOR READING

## BOOK TWO
## OF
## THE LOST HAVEN COZY MYSTERIES

To learn more about Lost Haven, Sanctuary, and the next book, please join the Penny Plume Exclusive Readers Club at:

## PENNYPLUME.COM

# ABOUT THE AUTHOR

Penny Plume is a lifelong reader, historian, and storyteller. She loves nothing more than getting lost in a great story, ideally with a creamy cup of coffee and sunshine. If the sun isn't out, a fleece blanket will suffice.

For more information and to contact Penny, please visit www.pennyplume.com and Like her Facebook page: www.facebook.com/pennyplumebooks.

www.ingramcontent.com/pod-product-compliance
Lightning Source LLC
Chambersburg PA
CBHW050913250626
47155CB00001B/214